Me & Emma

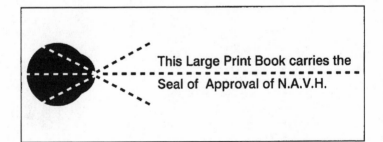

This Large Print Book carries the
Seal of Approval of N.A.V.H.

Me & Emma

Elizabeth Flock

Thorndike Press • Waterville, Maine

BRUTON MEMORIAL LIBRARY
302 McLENDON STREET
PLANT CITY, FLORIDA 33563

Copyright © 2004 by Elizabeth Flock.

All rights reserved.

All characters in this book have no existence outside the imagination of the author and have no relation whatsoever to anyone bearing the same name or names. They are not even distantly inspired by any individual known or unknown to the author, and all incidents are pure invention.

Published in 2005 by arrangement with Harlequin Books S.A.

Thorndike Press® Large Print Basic.

The tree indicium is a trademark of Thorndike Press.

The text of this Large Print edition is unabridged.
Other aspects of the book may vary from the original edition.

Set in 16 pt. Plantin by Carleen Stearns.

Printed in the United States on permanent paper.

Library of Congress Cataloging-in-Publication Data

Flock, Elizabeth.
    Me & Emma / by Elizabeth Flock.
        p. cm.
    ISBN 0-7862-7714-9 (lg. print : hc : alk. paper)
    1. Family violence — Fiction.   2. Child abuse —
Fiction.   3. Sisters — Fiction.   4. Large type books.
5. North Carolina — Fiction.   6. Domestic fiction.
I. Title: Me and Emma.   II. Title.
PS3606.L58M4 2005
813'.6—dc22   2005008014

For my parents — Barbara and Reg Brack

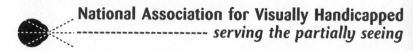

National Association for Visually Handicapped
serving the partially seeing

As the Founder/CEO of NAVH, the only national health agency solely devoted to those who, although not totally blind, have an eye disease which could lead to serious visual impairment, I am pleased to recognize Thorndike Press* as one of the leading publishers in the large print field.

Founded in 1954 in San Francisco to prepare large print textbooks for partially seeing children, NAVH became the pioneer and standard setting agency in the preparation of large type.

Today, those publishers who meet our standards carry the prestigious "Seal of Approval" indicating high quality large print. We are delighted that Thorndike Press is one of the publishers whose titles meet these standards. We are also pleased to recognize the significant contribution Thorndike Press is making in this important and growing field.

Lorraine H. Marchi, L.H.D.
Founder/CEO
NAVH

* Thorndike Press encompasses the following imprints: Thorndike, Wheeler, Walker and Large Print Press.

"Nothing is sinful to us outside of
  ourselves,
Whatever appears, whatever does not
  appear, we are beautiful or sinful in
  ourselves only.
(O Mother — O Sisters dear!
If we are lost, no victor else has
  destroy'd us,
It is by ourselves we go down to eternal
night.)"

— Walt Whitman,
Leaves of Grass, 1900

One

The first time Richard hit me I saw stars in front of my eyes just like they do in cartoons. It was just a backhand, though — not like when I saw Tommy Bucksmith's dad wallop him so hard that when he hit the pavement his head actually bounced. I s'pose Richard didn't know about the flips I used to do with Daddy where you face each other and while you're holding on to your daddy's hands you climb up his legs to right above the knees and then push off, through the triangle that your arms make with his. It's super fun. I was just trying to show Richard how it works. Anyway, I learned then and there to stay clear of Richard. I try to stay away from home as much as I possibly can.

It's impossible to get lost in a town called Toast. That's where I live: Toast, North Carolina. I don't know how it is anywhere else but here all the streets are named for what's on them. There's Post Office Road and Front Street, which takes you past the front of the stores, and Back

Street, which is one street over — in back of them. There's New Church Road, even though the church that sits at the end of it isn't new anymore. There's Brown's Farm Road, which is where Hollis Brown lives with his family, and before him came other Browns who Momma knew and didn't like all that much, and Hilltop Road and even Riverbend Road. So wherever you set out for, the street signs will lead the way. I live on Murray Mill Road, and I s'pose if you didn't know any better you'd think my last name's Murray, but it's Parker — Mr. Murray passed on way before we got here. We didn't change a thing about the Murray house: the way in from Route 74 is just grass growing up between two straight lines so your tires'll know exactly where to go. The first thing you see after you've been driving till the count of sixty is the mill barn that's being held up over the pond by old stilts. We still have the board with peeling painted letters that says No Fishing on Sunday nailed up to the tree on the edge of the pond. Just to the side of that, taking up a whole outside wall of the mill, is Mr. Murray's old sign that shows a cartoon rooster cock-a-doodle-doing the words Feed Nutrena . . . Be Sure, Be Safe, Be Thrifty. It's getting hard to read the words of the poster now that a fine red dust from the dirt outside the mill has settled over it top to bottom. But you can see the rooster clear as day. Tacked up to the door of the old mill is this: "WARNING: It is unlawful for any person to sell, deliver, or hold or offer for sale any adulterated or misbranded grain. Maximum penalty $100 fine or 60 days imprisonment or both." I copied that down in my notebook from school.

"Whoa!" The notebook goes flying out of my hands into the dirt.

"Betcha didn't see *that* coming!" Richard laughs at me as I scramble to pick it up before he gets ahold of it. "Must be something pretty important, you grabbing at it like that. Lemme see there," and he pulls it out of my hands before I can make a squeak about it.

"Give it back."

" 'Collie McGrath isn't talking to me on account of the frog incident' . . . what's the frog incident?" He looks up from my diary.

"Give it *back!*" But when I go to try to get it back he shoves me away, flipping through the pages, scanning each one with his dirty finger. "Where am I? I can't *wait* to see what all you write about *me*. Hmm," more flipping, "Momma this, Momma that. Jesus H. Christ, nothing about your dear ole *dad?*"

He throws it back down to the ground and I'm mad I didn't listen to my own self when I thought I shouldn't reach down to pick it up until he leaves, 'cause when I do bend down again he shoves me into the dirt with his boot.

"There! Gave ya something to write about!"

I live here with my stepfather, Richard, my momma, and my sister, Emma. Emma and I are like Snow White and Rose Red. That's probably why it's our favorite bedtime story. It's about two sisters: one has really white skin and yellow hair (just like Momma) and the other one has darker skin and hair that's the color of the center of your eye (that's just like me). My hair changes colors depending on where you're standing and when. From the side in the daytime, my hair looks purple-black, but from the back at night it's like burned wood in the fireplace. When it's clean, Emma's hair is the color of a cotton ball: white, white, white. But usually it's so dirty it looks like the dusty old letters Momma keeps in a shoe box on her closet shelf.

Richard. Now *there's* a guy who isn't like anyone we've read about at bedtime.

Momma says he's as different from Daddy as a cow from a crow, and I believe her. I mean, wouldn't you have to be likable to make everyone line up to buy carpet from you like Momma says they did for Daddy? Richard's not half as likable. I told Momma once that I thought Richard was hateable, but she didn't think it was funny so she sent me to my room. A few days later, when Richard was back picking on Momma she yelled out that no one liked him and that his own stepdaughter called him "hateable." When she said it I just stood there listening to the tick-tick-tick of the plastic daisy clock we have hanging in the kitchen, knowing it was too late to run.

Momma says our daddy was the best carpet salesman in the state of North Carolina. He must've sold a ton of carpet because there wasn't any left for us. We have hard linoleum. After he died Momma let me keep the leaf-green sample of shag that she found in the back seat of his car when she was cleaning it out before Mr. Dingle took it away. The sample must've fallen off the big piece of cardboard that had lots of other squares on it in different colors so folks could match it to their lives better. I keep it in the drawer of the white wicker night table by my bed in an old cigar box that has lots of colorful stickers of old-fashioned suitcases, stamps and airplanes (only on the cigar box they're spelled *aeroplanes*) slapped on every which way. Sometimes if I sniff into that shag square real hard I can still pick up that new carpet smell that followed Daddy around like a shadow.

Back to me and Emma. Our hair is different colors but our skin is where you see the biggest difference. Chocolate and vanilla difference. Emma looks like someone got bored painting her and just left her blank for someone else to fill in. Me? Well, Miss Mary at White's Drugstore always tilts her head to the side and says, "You look tired, chile," when she sees me, but I'm not — it's just the shadows under my eyes.

I'm eight — two years older than Emma, but because I'm small people probably think we're mismatched twins. And that's the way we think of each other. But I wish I could be more like Emma. I scream when I see a cicada, but Emma doesn't mind them. She scoops them up and puts them outside. I tell her she should just step on them but she doesn't listen to me. And she never gets picked on by the other kids. Once, Tommy Bucksmith twisted her arm around her back and held it there for a long time ("until you say I'm the best in the universe" he told her at the time, laughing while he winched her arm backward higher and higher) and she didn't make a peep. Emma's not scared of anything. Except for when Richard turns on Momma. Then we both go straight to behind-the-couch. Behind-the-couch is like another room for me and Emma. It's our fort. Anyway, we usually head there when we've counted ten squeaks from the foot pedal of the metal trash can in the kitchen. The bottles clank so loud I think my head'll split in two.

Richard starts bugging Momma after about the tenth squeak. I don't know why Momma doesn't stay out of his way from squeak eight on but she doesn't. Me and Emma, we've started a thing we call the floor shimmy where, when we hear squeak eight we start to scoot our behinds real slow from the floor in front of the TV toward behind-the-couch. With the volume up you can't hear us, and Richard's concentrating real hard on Momma so he doesn't notice that we're inching toward behind-the-couch. By squeak nine, we're about two Barbie-doll lengths from the front of the couch, and just before squeak ten we're sliding between the cool paint on the wall and the nubby brown plaid back of the couch. We used to think it was stinky behind-the-couch, but we don't even notice it anymore. I brought some of Momma's perfume there once and squirted it twice right into the fabric so now it smells just like Momma on Sunday.

We live in an old white house with chipping yellow shutters. It's three floors high, if you count the attic where me and Emma sleep. We used to have our own room across the hall from Momma and Daddy's room, but after he died and Richard moved in we had to go up another floor. But here's the worst part: Richard's making us move. I cain't even think about that right now. When I don't want to think about something I just pretend there's a little man in my head who takes the part of my brain that's thinking the bad thing and pushes on it real hard so it goes to the back of all the other things I could be thinking about.

Momma says it's trashy to have stuff out front of our house like we do so she goes and plants flowers in some of it so it'll look like we've got it there on purpose. Here's what we've got: three tires — one of them has grass already growing from the pile of dirt that's in the middle of it; a cat statue that's gray like a sidewalk; Richard's old car that he says will come back to life one of these days, but when it does I think it'll be confused since it doesn't have any tires on it; Momma's old tin washtub with flowers planted in it; a hammock Emma and me liked to swing in when we were really young, but now one side's all frayed because we never took it inside in the winter; a bale of hay that smells bad on account of rain rot; a metal rooster that points in the direction of a storm if one's coming; and Richard's old work boots. Momma up and planted flowers in them, too. I've never seen flowers in boots before, but she did it and sure enough there're daisies pushing up out of them right this minute. Oh, I almost forgot, Momma's clothesline is out there, too.

We don't have a front walk to get to the door to the house. I wish we did. Snow White and Rose Red have a front walk that takes you through an archway of roses. We just have grass that's been walked on so much it's dirt. But then you get to the front porch and that's the part I like best. It makes a lot of noise when you walk on it but I like being able to look out over everything.

"What're you doing?" Emma asks. Where she came from I don't know. I didn't even hear her.

I'm standing here on the front porch, surveying our yard and all the things we've got. Sometimes I pretend I'm a princess and that instead of things they're people, my subjects waving up to me on the balcony of my castle.

"What do you mean what am I doing?"

"Who're you waving at?"

"I wasn't waving."

"Were, too. You're pretending you're a princess again, aren't you?" Emma sits in Momma's old rocker that's missing most of the seat. She's smiling 'cause she knows she nailed me.

"Was not."

"Was to. What color dress you wearing?" I can tell by the tone in her voice because she isn't making fun of me anymore, she just wants to hear me talk my dream out loud so she can dream it, too. She's all serious now.

"It's pink, of course," I say, "and it's got sparkly beads sewn all over it so it looks like the dress is made of pink diamonds. And I have a big ole lace collar that's made by hand. It's not scratchy at all. In fact it's so soft it tickles me sometimes. The sleeves are velvet, white velvet. They're even softer than the lace. But the best part is my shoes. My shoes are made of glass, just like Cinderella's, and they have diamonds on the tips so they can match my dress."

Emma's eyes are closed but she's nodding.

"And here are my loyal subjects." I sweep my arm across the railing toward the yard. "They all love me because I'm a good princess, not a mean one like my stepsister. I give them food and money — and I talk to them like they're in my family. My loyal subjects . . ." I say this last part to all the stuff in the yard. Oh, yeah, we also have an old iron bed out there. It's rusted now but it used to be bright metal. It's right up front so I pretend it's the river of water that runs in a circle around my castle and that the front steps are a drawbridge. I wish the drawbridge could stay up and keep Richard from coming into the castle.

Uh-oh. Richard's noisy truck is pulling into its parking space to the side of the house. I cain't tell for sure but it looks like he might not be in too bad a mood right now. I'm keeping my fingers crossed on that one.

"Whatchoo up to on this fine North Carolina day?" He's walking toward us,

19

but I can tell by his speed that he isn't interested in our answer.

"Nothing," Emma and I say at the same time, both of us backing up to put more space between us and him. Just in case.

"Nothing," Richard mimics us with his chin sticking out extra far. But he keeps on walking past us into the house. "Libby? Where you at?" I hear him call to Momma once the porch door slams behind him. "It's payday and I'm in need of in-ee-bree-ation!" A second later I hear vacuumed air pop from a bottle and then the sound of a tin cap pinging onto the counter in the kitchen. Momma's voice is murmuring something I can't make out.

"Hey, Pea Pop, how'd you like a nice cold orangeade?" Daddy rustled my hair like I was a pet dog. "Lib? It's payday! Getchur bag, we're going shopping."

Payday was always the best day of the month when Daddy was alive. I'd hear orangeade and it was all I could do to fit the tiny metal fork into the hole in the strap on my sandals, I'd be so excited.

"Can I get a large, Daddy?" I called out from the back seat, loud enough to be heard over the wind blowing in through all the open windows in our car.

"You can get a *jumbo,* pea." He smiled, and caught my eye in the rearview mirror.

Our first stop was the grocery store. Momma pulled a cart from the stack all folded into one another by the glass entrance. The cold air gave me gooseflesh at first but by aisle two I was used to it.

"Stop swinging your feet, Caroline," Momma tsked at me, "you're kicking me in the stomach." So I tried to keep my legs still while Momma threw food into the cart over my head.

"Momma? Can I pull from the shelves?"

"I guess," she answered, checking her list, which was long since we hadn't been to the store in a while. Maybe even since Daddy's last payday.

"Whole oats. No, not that one. The red label. That's it," she said, moving the cart before I could even drop the tin into the cart. "Flour. The big sack. Yes, that's the one."

Daddy popped up from behind Momma, startling the both of us. "I'm going over to the meat counter. What you want me to order up for supper?" he asked her. "How 'bout some liver?" He winked at me since he knew I hated liver.

"No!" I whined to Momma.

She was still studying her list. "Be sure

to get the ground chuck. Four pounds."

"Now, what do we need four pounds' worth of meat for?" he asked her over his shoulder.

"I'm freezing it for later," she said, pulling a box of cereal from the shelf that was high up over my head.

Seven aisles later, the cart was filled to the brim and Momma wheeled us over to the checkout stand. Daddy was already there, talking with Mr. Gifford, the store manager he played cards with from time to time.

"Time to settle up," Daddy said to him, slapping him on the back.

" 'Preciate it," Mr. Gifford said. "You'd be surprised how many people — now, I'm not naming names — I got to turn away, they so overdue on the bill. Your credit's always good here, Henry. 'Sides, might as well take your money here than at the card table!" Mr. Gifford laughed, shaking Daddy's hand. "You got yourself a fine family here, Culver." And he tipped an invisible hat on his head to Momma and me and went over to talk to Mrs. Fox, an old lady who dressed in her Sunday best every time she left the house.

"C'mon, Pea Pop." Daddy lifted me out of my seat in the cart while Momma unloaded the groceries onto the moving belt. "Let's you and me pack up these sacks."

After we got everything on our side of the belt, and then after the cash register, Daddy squeezed behind me to count out bills for the cashier, Delmer Posey.

"What'd we owe you from last time?" he asked Delmer.

Delmer Posey went to my school when he was little, but he stopped going right after the seventh grade. No one knew why until he showed up at the grocery store asking for work. Momma said the Poseys were strapped worse than us, so every time I'd see Delmer I pictured him with a saddle tied to his back.

Delmer ran his finger down a long list of names on a page in a thumbed-up ledger that was kept behind the register. "Thirty-four fifty-seven, Mr. Culver," he said.

Daddy let out a slow whistle and added that to the amount we just spent. "Here's an extra five for the books," he said, smiling his smile at Delmer, who looked confused. "Just put it down as credit so Mrs. Culver can come grab whatever it is I'm sure we forgot today."

Whenever you'd say anything to Delmer Posey, it'd take a minute or two before he could understand it, like he spoke foreign and was waiting for someone to tell him what it meant in English. But soon he got what Daddy said and we wheeled the cart to a spot alongside other carts by the glass door with the bright red Exit sign above it.

"You keep an eye on this for us," Daddy winked back at him. "We've got some business over at White's."

Momma and Daddy held hands down the sidewalk to White's Drugstore. They never used to mind when I ran ahead to put in my order at the counter.

"Hey, Miss Caroline," Miss Mary called out after the bell over the door jingled to let her know someone's inside.

"Hey, Miss Mary," I said. "May I have a *large* orangeade, please?"

Miss Mary put her paperback book down so the pages were splayed out on either side of the middle. "I don't see why not." She waddled over to the countertop. Miss Mary was always fat. Fatter than fat. Daddy used to say there's more of her to love.

The jingle up front told me Momma and Daddy had come into the store.

"Miss Mary, how are you?" Daddy said from the stool alongside me. Momma was picking out a few things from the shampoo shelf. "Isn't that a pretty dress."

24

But it didn't sound like a question.

"Thank you, sir," Miss Mary said shy-like, smiling down at herself so hard her cheeks almost folded over the corners of her mouth. "Mrs. Culver here, too?"

"Oh, don't mind her," Daddy said, "let's you and me run away together. Let's really do it."

"I'm over here, Mary," Momma called from behind the only aisle in the place. "Just picking up a few things we been needing for a while. I'll be right over." Momma was used to Daddy asking Miss Mary to run away with him. He did it every time he went into White's. I reckon she smiled so hard and blushed 'cause no one'd ever asked her that before. She's about a million years old and lives alone with two tomcats and a rooster named Joe.

"What about me, Daddy?" I asked him. "You gonna run away without me?"

"I'm gonna put you in my pocket and take you with me," he said. Then he leaned over from his stool and kissed me on the head like he always did.

"Orangeade for you, too?" Miss Mary asked Daddy, still smiling.

"You bet."

Miss Mary cut each orange down the middle until there were ten halves. I counted each one. Then — and this was the best part — she put each one in the big metal press and leaned all her weight onto each orange rind until nothing more dripped into the glass jar underneath it. Then she poured sugar into the jar, added some soda water, screwed a lid on and shook it good and hard until it was fizzy and frothy. The glasses were kept in the icebox so there'd be a nice cool film of cold all over them. I wrote my name in the frost on the side of my glass. White's had bendy straws so I never lifted the glass off the counter, and that was how Daddy and I'd drink them: without hands.

Ping. Another tin beer bottle cap hits the kitchen counter.

"What do you want to do now?" Emma asks me. She's been leaning against the porch railing, counting the *pings* of the bottle caps just like I have — both of us wondering how many it'll take to turn Richard into Enemy Number One.

"I don't know."

"How about we walk down to the fence out back and do the balance thing?"

The balance thing is something Emma and I like to do when we're superbored. Actually it's kind of fun. The top logs on the fence that used to separate our land from the neighbors, back when we all cared about that sort of thing, are all missing. So Emma and I walk on the lower logs between the fence posts and see who can stay up the longest without falling off. The loser has to do whatever the winner makes her do.

"I'll start, you count." Emma is already on top of the first log. It's the easiest since it's so old it's split long ways in the middle so it's wider than all the rest. The tricky one is the newer one that's next.

"Go," I say, and I start counting out loud. Emma can do this without even extending her arms and that makes me mad for some reason so I count slow.

"You're counting too slow!" Emma says. She's concentrating real hard on the next step she's going to take.

I don't speed up, though. Not much she can do about it while she's trying to stay on the log. Instead of saying the word *Mississippi* in between numbers like Momma did when she used to play hide-and-seek with us, I spell it all out and it takes twice as long to get to the next number.

She's on to the next log and I can tell she's not going to make it to twelve. For once I may even beat her.

27

Yep, there she goes. She's off the log.

"Eleven!" I say as I pass her, and hop up onto log number one.

"Cheater. You counted so slow I felt my hair grow," she grumbled. And before I could even prove I'm the Queen of the Log Fence she added, "Let's go over to Forsyth's."

Forsyth Phillips is a friend of ours who lives in the house that's as close as we're going to get to having a neighbor. Forsyth's a cure for boredom if I've ever seen one. If the Phillips's house were a flower it'd be a sunflower, all smiley and warm with lots of clean windows and white tablecloths for fancy occasions.

Before I can even balance my way along the log to the post, Emma's lit out for Forsyth's.

"Wait up," I call out to her, but it's no use. I'll have to hurry to catch up to her.

"Well, hello there, Miss Parker." Mrs. Phillips talks that way to kids: like we're the same age as her. "Forsyth's upstairs. Y'all can go on up." Once again, it's Emma who's gotten to the door first, so I have to let myself on in.

"Hey, Forsyth," I say, all breathless from taking the stairs two by two.

"Hey, Carrie," she says. Emma's already

called the spot across from Forsyth, who's playing with her Old Maid cards on her single bed that has its own legs, like it's on a throne. Her room has matching fabric all around, daisies on a sky-blue field hang from either side of her window, on a cushion just underneath it, and stretched neatly across her proud bed. I cain't imagine what it'd be like to fall asleep every dag-gum night with my head on soft daisies. I guess I'd never have nightmares at the Phillipses'.

"Y'all hungry for some cookies?" Mrs. Phillips pokes her head in the room, smiling above her apron that must just be there for show since it's never been smudged not once since we started coming over. "Come on down when you feel ready, they're just coming out of the oven."

Momma hasn't baked us cookies in, well, forever. Mrs. Phillips bakes so much that Forsyth doesn't even look up from her cards, doesn't even seem to be in a hurry to get 'em while they're good and hot, the chocolate chips melting on your fingers, making it two desserts in one when you lick it off once the cookie's gone.

"Aren'tcha gonna go on down for a snack?" I ask her. Please, Forsyth, say yes.

"I reckon," she says, but she still doesn't budge.

"What're you playing?"

"Old Maid, silly. You blind?"

She must've woken up on the wrong side of her daisies.

"Can we play?"

"We?"

"Me and Emma."

"I'm tired of playing with Emma," she sighs. She always does this . . . refusing to play with my baby sister like she's got the plague. Emma doesn't seem to mind, but I think it's mean to say it right in front of her like that.

"Come on," I whine.

"Aw-right," she says, scooting over on the bed to make room for me, too. "Y'all better take your shoes off, though, or my momma's gonna tan your hide."

I don't think Mrs. Phillips has ever tanned a hide, though.

It's a hot day, maybe that's why Forsyth just ends up being as bored as the two of us. This kind of hot sucks out all your life blood and then expects you to be able to breathe and not suffocate. In the middle of Forsyth's ceiling she's got her very own ceiling fan that beats the hot air back out the window and brushes our skin with a nice breeze instead. Seems like every room in this house has one of those fans.

"Didja do your homework yet?" I ask her, hoping she'll lose interest in her game and notice she's hungry.

"Mmm-hmm. Momma makes me do it the minute I come in the door from school," she says. "Did you?"

"Mmm-hmm," I lie. I don't do my homework till it gets dark and then I hurry through it like it tastes bad. Emma's still too young to have homework.

"Let's get some of your momma's cookies," Emma says, and I glare at her 'cause it's rude. Momma would tan *her* hide if she heard her ask outright for food from someone else.

Momma and Mrs. Phillips have talked on the phone, but I don't think they like each other much. Momma always says she ruins Emma and me for anyone else. I guess she's talking about all the food we eat when we come over — we're never hungry for dinner when we finally drag ourselves home.

Forsyth is my best friend outside of Emma. We been going to school together since we were smaller than beans. We sit together at lunchtime and then we play on the jungle gym at recess when I'm not get-

31

ting hit by a dodgeball. Usually she's in a better mood than this.

"What's the matter?" I ask her, trying to ignore Emma.

She shrugs just like Emma always does.

"Tell me."

She shakes her head. She has curly red hair with freckles to match.

"Is it your momma?"

She shakes her head again.

"Your daddy?"

Again, no.

"It's gotta be school, then," Emma says.

"It's Sonny, isn't it," I say.

Sonny's the school bully. If someone falls down the stairs, Sonny's usually up at the top, laughing. If something's gone missing, it's usually in Sonny's backyard. And if somewhere in the recess yard a fire breaks out, Sonny's usually the one holding the lighter.

For the first time since we came into her room, Forsyth looks up from her Old Maid cards. She nods and the mop on her head shakes like Momma's Christmas Jell-O mold.

"What'd he do?"

Tears spill past her rims onto her freckled cheeks. "He's meaner than spit, is all," she cries, the way you would if you were choking.

"Tell me something I *don't* know. He's our second cousin, don't forget." Sonny's the one who short-sheeted our bed last summer. Sonny's the one who made me put my tongue to the bottom of an ice tray and then led me around his house laughing. Sonny truly is meaner than spit.

"When God gave out brains, Sonny thought he said trains and he ran for it," Emma says, flipping through the cards, trying to shuffle.

"What'd he do *this* time?" I ask Forsyth.

"He pulled down my pants at band," she cries, "and *everyone saw*."

This is worse than I thought.

"What?" I ask her, but I'm glaring at Emma, who's trying real hard not to crack up. I think Emma secretly likes Sonny but I couldn't tell you why.

Forsyth is nodding her head, assuring me that I have indeed heard correctly. "I stood up to play." Forsyth plays the recorder. "And just like that he reached from the row behind and pulled on my pants and the next thing I know everyone was *laughing* at me," she cries even harder. "And I didn't even have my good panties on." See, there's another difference between Forsyth and us. There're no such things as "good panties" in our family.

"You want me to talk to him?" I ask her. Please, Forsyth, say no.

"No," she practically screams at me. "Carrie, promise! Promise you won't talk to him about it. Promise." She's clutching at my arm like I'm a log in the river she's drowning in.

"I won't," I say. And that's the God's honest truth.

"Honor bright?"

"Honor bright."

I get to thinking and it hits me. "You know what?" I pause to make sure they're listening real good. "Sonny needs to taste his own medicine."

"Huh?" Emma says. Even *Emma* looks interested in what I'm going to say.

"Seriously, we've got to get Sonny back for everything he does to us all the time," I say. Forsyth isn't looking away so I keep going.

"What can we do to get him back?" I think. Emma thinks. Forsyth thinks. "There's got to be some way to get him"

"We should sic Richard on him, is what we should do," Emma mumbles. Forsyth pays no attention.

"We could pull *his* pants down," Forsyth

says, all excited-like.

I shake my head. I don't know what these two would do without me sometimes, I'll tell you what. "It's got to be something no one's done before. Something he won't expect. But it's got to be *good*."

"What're you thinking?" Forsyth asks. She's leaning forward, waiting to catch my idea as it leaves my mouth.

"We could take his G.I. Joe and get one of Jimmy Hammersmith's firecrackers, take G.I. Joe's head off, put the firecracker in his body and watch him explode!" Emma shouts out.

Forsyth looks like this might be the way to go but I have my doubts, and once she sees the look on my face she starts acting like she doesn't like the idea, either. She's sort of a copycat, if you want to know the truth.

"It's got to be even better than that," I say. "But that's good, though." I sound just like our teacher when he doesn't want to make us feel stupid.

"Well, what, then?" they both ask at the same time.

"Cookies are ready!" Mrs. Phillips calls up from downstairs and I cain't take it any longer. I stand up and I know they'll follow me since I'm Miss Idea.

"Thank you, ma'am," I say, making sure I don't grab, like Momma always warns us.

"Help yourself, sweetie." Mrs. Phillips smiles while she shovels two more from her pancake turner onto the plate in the middle of the kitchen table, just like a television commercial. This kitchen is already tidied up — wet measuring cups and mixing bowls lie next to the sink air-drying in the V-shaped rack made just for that purpose.

We carefully wait for her to leave the room so we can plot our revenge.

"I've got it!" I say, with my mouth full.

Forsyth practically jumps out of her chair, which, by the way, has its very own cushion on it so you never get uncomfortable sitting on hard wood. "What? *What?*"

"How about," I say real slow-like, drawing it out 'cause it's fun to be the center of attention every once in a while. "How about we go into the boys' washroom before he goes in to use it and we grease the toilet seat so he slips in when he goes to the bathroom!"

Two sets of huge eyes blink back at me.

"My mom has Crisco," "I can scout it out and give a signal when he asks permission to go," "I'll guard the bathroom door so we know it's him who's going in and not anyone else," "I'll spread the word that something really funny's about to happen in the bathroom so everyone can go in and see him all dripping wet!" We talk all at once and *whammo!* We've got ourselves a plan.

After we eat so many cookies I can feel the dough rising in my stomach, we go back upstairs to Forsyth's room and work it all out so we're sure it's foolproof. You've got to be foolproof with a boy like Sonny.

"He's in room 301 second period," Forsyth says. "I know 'cause that's across the hall from me. After second period he's *bound* to have to go to the washroom."

"Yeah, they have snack period after first, right?" Emma asks. She looks like she loves this plan as much as Forsyth does, which is funny considering she's the only one Sonny hasn't picked on. Truth to tell I think Sonny's a little afraid of Emma since he knows she has no fear whatsoever.

"Yup," I say. "Okay. So, Emma will scout him out and make sure he heads to the bathroom down the hall next to the gym. Forsyth, you have to come get me when Emma gives you the signal."

Forsyth looks confused.

"Oh, yeah," I say, "we've got to come up with a signal."

"How 'bout I call out 'My favorite color is blue!' " Forsyth says.

"You can't yell that down the hall," Emma sneers at her. "He'll know something's up our sleeves."

Forsyth nods.

"I know," I say, "the signal will be that Emma will scratch her chin when she sees Sonny ask Mr. Stanley for the key. Then I'll run down ahead of him with a pat of the Crisco in a bag under my shirt and, Forsyth, you watch the washroom door and make sure no one's in there when I go in."

"Wait! How're you going to get into the boys' washroom without a key?" Emma asks. And she has a point.

I think on this for a minute.

"Well," I say out loud, but in my head I have no idea how I'll finish this sentence. Then it comes to me. "I know! I'll go to the bathroom right when I get to school 'cause that's when the janitor cleans them and leaves the doors open for them to air out! I'll click that thingy in the middle of the doorknob that keeps it from locking when it closes and that way I'll be able to slip in when you tell me he's coming!"

Now, that's a darn good plan, if you ask me. Foolproof. Emma and Forsyth look like they're thinking the same thing. They're both smiling like cats that ate canaries.

"Okay, then how're we going to get everyone in there so they can see him after he falls in?"

I'm thinking again. How come I've got to come up with the whole dang thing?

"How 'bout we count to ten so we're sure he's falling in and we tell anyone who's around us in the hall that there's a bag of free candy in the boys' washroom." Emma shouts this out she's so excited. "Everyone loves candy. Especially when it's free!"

That's my little sister for you. She always comes through in the clutch.

"That's it, then," I say as Forsyth falls back on her bed of daisies. "Don't forget to bring the Crisco in tomorrow morning," I remind her.

"I won't." She smiles up at the ceiling. "This time tomorrow Sonny Parker'll be the laughingstock of the whole entire school."

Emma stands up and stretches her arms up over her head — after leaning back on them for so long I expect they're stiff. "We better go on home before Richard gets to five."

"You asleep, yet?" Emma whispers, knowing full well there's no way I'm sleeping.

"No."

"You reckon it'll work for real?"

"It cain't not," I say, but inside my head I've been thinking it over and now I'm not so sure.

"What if he doesn't have to go to the bathroom?" she asks.

"He's got to go sometime," I say. "Besides, say he doesn't go after second period. We just scoot the plan up and do it after fourth."

"You think?"

"It's foolproof."

"You're right," she yawns. "It's foolproof."

I don't remember sleeping, but I must have because the next thing I know Momma's calling up to us from the landing. "Rise and shine!" She sounds like she's in a good mood, but we won't know for sure till we get downstairs and see what's waiting for us in the kitchen. When the cereal bowls are already out on the counter we're home free. Sometimes, though, she says, "You got arms to reach up, don'tcha?" And other times she's not there at all . . . still sleeping. Sure enough it's a breakfast-bowl-on-the-counter morning. Phee-you. One less thing to think about today.

We ride the bus to school and there isn't much to say about that except that Patty Lettigo (who everyone calls Patty Let-Me-Go and then runs away like she's holding on to them too tight for real) glares at us when we walk up the aisle to the back of the bus where there's an open two-seater. Patty Lettigo always glares. It's her job or something.

My stomach's in knots. Emma's clutching her books close to her chest even after she sits down so I'm betting she's as nervous as I am.

"Remember," I whisper to her with my hand up to her ear just in case anyone can hear over the loud bus engine, "get the bag of Crisco from Forsyth the minute you see her at your locker and then pass it to me when I come by after homeroom."

"Okay, okay, stop reminding me," she hisses at me.

"I'm just saying."

"I got it."

But after we pass three farms and the second flashing stoplight she leans over and whispers in my ear. "Where're we meeting up again after?"

"Jeez! We've been over this a million times! At the end of the hall that leads to the gym. You're going to be the signal girl."

"Right," she nods, remembering. "Got it."

"You sure?"

"Yes. Sure as manure."

I smile, thinking about how I told her that Daddy always used to say that to me. He'd rhyme the words and it made me laugh every time.

The bus lurches to the curb right in front of our school, squeaky brakes and smelly fumes. Emma hits my arm and I look to where she's looking and sure enough it's Sonny at the bike stand, pulling his books out of the trap that's fixed over his back wheel.

"Here we go," I say to no one in particular, and we head in through the front doors just in time for the first bell.

"Bye," she calls to me, which is weird 'cause we never say goodbye to each other at school — we just sort of walk away. But in a nice way. Yep. She's nervous all right.

Homeroom drags by so slowly now it's me who can feel her hair grow. Miss Fullman calls attendance and everyone's got to add their funny little thing they say back instead of "here" like boring old me. Mary Sellers: "Is the best!" (everyone laughs — she changes this every day). Liam Naughton: "Yell-oh!" (laughs). Darryl Becksdale: "Who?" (not so many laughs, but still better than "here"). The list goes slowly while Miss Fullman gives everyone the evil eye and says, "People. That's enough now, people," and waits for the laughter to die down before she calls the next one on the list.

The second bell rings almost as loud as my heart is beating. It just occurred to me that this whole thing is riding on *me*. I cain't chicken out now. I just cain't. Forsyth would never speak to me again.

First period goes by even slower than homeroom did, but the good thing is we're right on track. Forsyth passed a slab of Crisco wrapped in plastic to Emma, who gave it to me just like we planned. Now I'm sitting here in second period with Crisco grease in the space between the snap and zipper of my pants and my stomach. I wore a looser shirt than I normally wear for this exact reason. Planning ahead works every time.

Bzzzzzzz. Second period is over and as we file out of the room I bump into two desks because I'm concentrating on my heart, which is beating in my chest like a bird flapping its wings against a cage, trying to get free. Oh, Lord, please help me carry this out.

Out in the hallway in front of the gym Forsyth is standing in front of the boys' washroom like she should be but I cain't see Emma over the heads of the other kids in the hallway. I didn't think about how tough it'd be to see her in the crowd! Oh, God. Oh, God. Emma? Where are you?

And then she appears — standing in between Betsy Rutledge and Collie McGrath, talking to Perry Gibson and . . . there it is . . . she scratches her chin! That means Sonny's asked for the key and is about to head to the washroom. I whip around to see Forsyth shaking her head to someone who's trying to go in but then turns away after she whispers to him. Just like we planned, Forsyth is telling anyone who wants to use the washroom — who isn't Sonny, of course — it's "out of order." We practiced it dozens of times before we left the Phillipses' last night.

There's no time to waste. I push past

people I barely recognize because I'm so nervous and feel up under my shirt for the packet of Crisco. In front of the boys' washroom I look over my shoulder quickly just to make sure Sonny's not right behind me. The coast is clear so I rush past Forsyth, who's mouthing something to me and waving her arms around, but I push through the door to the boys' washroom so I can carry out our plan.

Oh. My. Lord.

I hear the door shut behind me and rest my eyes on not one, not two, not three, even, but about twenty — twenty — boys! Boys from every grade. Boys standing with their backs to the door. Boys facing the wall. Boys with their pants practically down to their ankles. Boys combing their hair. Boys leaning against the tiled wall. *Boys in every nook and cranny of this washroom!*

"Lookee-lou, it's Scary Carrie," a hollow voice bounces off the tiled walls and mixes into all the laughing that breaks out like firecrackers on the Fourth of July.

Everything happens so fast I cain't even tell you what I said or how I got out of there. I just know that as I fly out the door I see Sonny, smiling and sauntering up to the door without a care in the world.

The girls' washroom is right next door but I want to get as far away from here as I possibly can. So I run. I run down the hall, past Emma, who's looking at me weird, past Mr. Stanley, past a million laughing kids I never want to see ever again, and out the double metal doors that lead to freedom. They can arrest me if they want, but I'm not going back into that school. I hear the door slam behind me and soon Emma's beside me on the second step of the rickety old bleachers by the baseball diamond.

"What happened?" she asks.

"Forsyth," I sob, "Forsyth . . ." It's all I can manage to say. I'm crying too hard. *I'm* the laughingstock of the school.

"Forsyth *what?* What happened?"

Then it comes back to me . . . oh, Lord! Forsyth's lips moving. Her arms swishing back and forth like windshield wipers. She was trying to warn me. She was trying to *warn me.*

I wish I could disappear.

"It'll be okay," Emma says. "Don't cry. It'll be okay. You'll see. It'll all be okay." Her hand rubs circles in the middle of my back.

"How?" I sniffle. "How will it be okay *now?*"

But she's quiet so I know she was just trying to make me feel better.

"If anyone makes fun of you I'll beat 'em up, that's how."

"You cain't beat up the whole school. And that's who's going to make fun of me." I wipe my runny nose on my sleeve.

"We'll think of something," she says, "but we better go on back. Mr. Streng's going to be after us if we cut out altogether. Come on."

The halls are empty when we go back through the double doors — everyone's in third period, I reckon. After my eyes adjust, I head toward my locker and Emma pads alongside me. Even in echoey halls she doesn't make any noise.

"Here's what you do when third period's over." She hurries up to in front of me so she can face me. "You pretend you're deaf so when anyone says anything — or even laughs at you — it doesn't make a lick of difference. Just pretend you can't hear a thing."

What she doesn't realize is I've been trying this all my life. It never works.

"Caroline, you knew this stuff backward and forward yesterday." Mr. Stanley's mouth is all twisted up, like it's fed up with talking to me altogether. "What I wonder

47

is how on earth you could completely forget multiplication."

Am I supposed to answer him?

"Young lady? Young lady, I'm talking to you."

"Yes, sir?"

"If you forgot to do your homework, say so. But don't give me this little act like you think I don't know what you're up to. I'll see you after school."

When on earth did we learn multiplication? I swear I have no idea how an x between two numbers is supposed to change what they're worth. Mr. Stanley keeps looking over here like I'm going to make a run for it and I suppose I could, but where would I go? Home to Richard? Here's the thing Mr. Stanley doesn't get about me: I don't mind school. Mary Sellers, Tommy Bucksmith, Luanne Kibley and all them can pretend to love it all they want in front of the teachers, but I hear them in the lunchroom talkin' trash about it. I like everything about school — except for the other kids, a'course. I like getting out of the house all day long. It's like a field trip every single day.

"Caroline!"

Mr. Stanley's voice is louder than I've ever heard it.

"Yes, sir?"

"The bell rang five minutes ago. Don't you have somewhere you need to be?"

"Yes, sir." I swear I didn't even hear the bell ring. I'm the only one left in the classroom. Just before I get through the door his gravelly voice throws words at me: "Remember, after school."

"Yes, sir."

Emma's going to have to wait for me. I bet Momma won't even notice we're not home on time. She don't care. To tell you the truth, I bet she's glad to have us out of the house as we are to be gone. She's got to manage her piles and I reckon she can do it a whole lot better with some peace and quiet. All day she sits there folding letters into three sections, stacking them in tall towers until the envelopes all have the address stickers on them and then she stuffs those with the letters. We're not allowed to read what the letters say; Momma's sure we'll crinkle the paper and she'll get fired. I don't care what they say, anyway, since Momma looks so bored doing all this it cain't be interesting. Momma's so smart she didn't even have to go interview for the job. She answered an ad in the newspaper about working from home, making you a ton of money. They liked her so much on the phone the job was hers, they said. Emma and me try to figure out why it is we haven't seen the ton of money they promised Momma, but I think it's babyish to think a truck is going to pull up to the back of your house and unload bagfuls of cash like a bread truck delivering to the grocery store. Emma's still waiting for the truck.

"You're late, Caroline." Miss Hall looks about as happy with me as Mr. Stanley did. "That's the third time this week." She made a little mark next to my name in the book on her desk.

I don't ever set out to be late but my mind sometimes takes a detour. Like when I write with another kind of handwriting. I know which way the letter *k* is supposed to face but then, whammo! — there it is backward. And usually when there's a backward *k*, it's in the other handwriting I surprise myself with; it almost looks like I could be in Emma's class with this handwriting. It's really shaky and big and, like I said, the letters are sometimes mixed up. But most of the time I keep my brain focused on what I have right in front of me. Not today, I guess. Momma won't even know to look at the line on my report card that says I been tardy for classes. If she did see it she probably wouldn't care.

"What's the matter, Scary? You forget how to tie your shoelaces, you little *baby?*" Mary Sellers started this nickname, Scary Carrie. They all point at my hair, which is funny since it's not half as tangled up as Emma's, but they point anyway. My shoes have been bothering me all day. I hate it when you tie one side kind of tight and the other side doesn't match it. These are saddle shoes that look like my Momma could've worn them back when she was my age. That's how come I have them, she saw them at the store last year and practically started crying right there in front of Mr. Franks, who insists on sliding our feet into shoes with that metal shoehorn instead of letting us wriggle our heels into them, the way we do the rest of the time. What does he think anyway? That we use shoehorns every single day? The shoes are mostly white with a saddle of black across the middle and down the sides. That's how come they're called saddle shoes. The toes are rounded so you have plenty of room to grow, which is a good thing since Momma said she spent so much on these shoes that we wouldn't be able to get me new ones for a while. No one at my school wears saddle shoes. They're just another weapon

Mary Sellers can use in her war against Scary Carrie. She calls them "domino shoes." I tell myself I don't care. And I don't. Really. I don't.

Two

We're moving and I'm not speaking to Momma on account of it. I don't want to leave but she says we have to. And Emma's on her side. She doesn't like it here, either. Last night Momma got fed up and said she'd just take Emma with her and I could stay here and live on my own, but when I said "fine" she sent me to my room, so I don't think I'm going to get to stay here by myself. Eight-year-old kids shouldn't be living in big old houses by themselves, anyway, but still . . . I don't want to go. Richard says he's moving on and moving up. He's been saying that a lot lately. He got a new job across the state so we have to go with him, I guess, even though some of us don't want to move on or up, thank you very much. Momma says it'll be a fresh start. But starts are only fresh for grown-ups. Third grade was never fresh for me, and even after a whole school year I'm waiting for it to stop being a start altogether.

Thanks to the stupid Washroom Plan I've been getting picked on more than ever in school. My teacher, Miss Hall, says I talk out of turn and that's just been an open invitation to Patty Lettigo. On the playground at recess she hollers at me, calling me a space cadet. The other kids laugh because to them that's what it looks like, I suppose. What's really happening is that I'm thinking of things I have to re-member to tell Emma after school lets out and the next thing I know I'm saying them out loud. I don't set out to talk out loud, it just ends up that way.

"And that's why we use long division," Mr. Stanley is saying, "so we can figure out how many little numbers make up what-ever big number is under the line here. Who can tell me how many times nine goes into eighteen?"

Outside, the buds on the tree branches look like tiny knobs on a television. I wonder what kind of show a tree would want to watch. Nothing involving a saw, I bet.

"Miss Parker?" Mr. Stanley's voice reaches out to my head and turns it toward the front of the room but I'm still thinking about Tree TV. "Can you tell us?"

"What, Daddy?"

Oh, my dear Lord — what did I just say? What did I just *say?* Maybe I thought it but didn't say it out loud.

"Class, quiet down," Mr. Stanley is saying to all the kids around me who're laughing and pointing at me like I've just climbed off of a spaceship. "Class, please," he's saying, but no one's quieting down one bit.

This ringing in my ears makes it sound like the classroom is one big glass jar — the voices echoing from side to side in my brain.

Mary Sellers snorts her little snorty laugh that always sounds like it's going to turn into hiccups. My face is on fire.

"All right, class, that's enough," Mr. Stanley finally says, but I cain't see his face because I'm just looking down at my desktop, tracing the carved "EMB was here" that's in the corner. Who was EMB? I wonder about this every single day. EMB could have been a boy, but I like to think she was a girl, brave enough to dig lines in her desk when no one was looking. EMB. Maybe she died and this is the only evidence that she lived, but her parents don't know it and every night they cry themselves to sleep wishing they had just one thing with her initials on it and here it is, right under my fingernail, which, I now notice, is packed with dirt so it looks brown. If I knew who EMB was I could let them know it's here, this last piece of her. Then they could sleep at night.

"Caroline, please see me after class," Mr. Stanley sighs. "Tommy, what is eighteen divided by nine?" And the class is back to normal for everyone else but me. By recess, I'll once again be the laughingstock of the school.

Emma is the only one who understands me talking out of turn since she does it, too, sometimes, but when she does it no one picks on her because they know she'll beat them up after school if they do. Plus she's pretty, and pretty girls never get into trouble with the other kids. The boys all like them and the girls want to be their friend. So Emma's got it made. Me, on the other, well I guess I'll be getting a whole new life out in western North Carolina.

"Would you like to tell me what's goin' on, young lady?" Mr. Stanley says to me after everyone's filed out of the room.

"I'm sorry, sir," I say. My face still feels hot and I can't look him in the eye even though Momma's drilled it into us since we were weensy.

"Now, Caroline," he says in a voice that sounds like warm doughnuts, "you've got a lot of potential. You're a smart young lady.

56

But you've got to apply yourself . . ."

Apply myself. Apply myself. If one more teacher tells me that, I'll scream.

". . . and then you can write your own ticket . . ." He's saying something about college. Apparently he thinks that's the key to the universe.

". . . so you can go now, but remember what we talked about, you hear?"

"Yes, sir," I say to him over my shoulder, bolting out of the room to my locker so I won't be late for the next period and I won't have to have another teacher lecture me.

"Shh, here she comes" is what I hear when I come through the door of Miss Hall's room. Nothing like hearing that when you're about to go somewhere you don't want to be in the first place.

"You better sit quick, Carrie Parker," Luanne Kibley says, "or *Mommy*'ll send you to your room without supper." The class erupts like a volcano; they've been waiting for me.

"Did you and *Daddy* have a nice talk?" Mary Sellers sings to me from over the din.

"Who's your uncle?" Tommy Bucksmith shouts. *"Mr. Streng?"* Mr. Streng is our principal. Everyone hates Mr. Streng except maybe Daisy, his one-eyed dachshund who sleeps on a checkered cushion in the corner of his office.

Where is Miss Hall?

The skies have turned black outside — the clouds are ready to break open with water, I can just feel it. I hope it waits till after we've gotten home. I know I'm just trying to come up with things to think about other than where I am right now, but can you blame me? When I'm a teacher I'll show up to class on time, that's for sure.

"All right, people," Miss Hall says before she even shuts the door. "Everyone please get out your social studies workbooks and turn to page nineteen. I hope y'all remembered to read this over last night. . . ."

I didn't. I don't even remember her telling us to. What else is new?

Three

Right now I'm in our room with the ceiling that leans in like it's protecting our beds from the sky. Our room is the best part of the house, but Richard thinks it's the worst. I suppose I can see his point, because even though it's only May, it's hotter than Hades in July and the only window up here has a fan in it that only sucks the air out of the room. When Richard moved in, he stomped up through the house with the boxes from the back of his truck and told us we'd better get on up the stairs with the string that pulls them down from the ceiling. No one's gonna build our nest for us anymore, he said, so we better start getting used to it. Ever since he called our room the nest, that's what we call it, too. I didn't know what was up his sleeve but I went up the stairs first, which is surprising considering how Emma's normally the brave one. Once we were at the top he pushed the stairs back up — something he still does to this day. Because it's summer, the hot air in the Nest hits you in the face like the cloud of smelly smoke that shoots out from behind Richard's truck every time he pulls out from the side of the house. There's only that one side that you cain't stand up straight in and that's where our bed is. Our quilt on the bed we share is patchwork and reminds me of *Little House on the Prairie.*

The ceiling has a lot of cobwebs and all I can think of is Charlotte and Wilbur in one of my all-time favorite stories about the pig and the spider who get to be friends. I wonder if spiders can really spell like that in their webs. And since these webs are on the high side of the ceiling that's not where the bed is, I let them stay . . . until I see a spider dropping down. Emma loves it up here. She knows now that you can't jump up and down on the bed and it only took her three bruises to figure it out. She likes to put the window fan on and talk into it really slowly, and to tell you the truth I like that, too. At first she wouldn't go near it because she thought her hair would get pulled off her head, but now she knows to put it in a ponytail and then there's no risk. She says things like "I hate you, Richard" and "You will die" and "Leave us alone" right into the fan, knowing he cain't hear a thing because the fan blades chop the air into little pieces and carry her words out and away from the house. I don't think she cares if he does hear her, anyway, since sometimes, when he lays into Momma real bad, she shouts right into it before it gets itself up to speed.

I can hear Richard right now out in the second-floor hallway and I know it's only a matter of time before he pushes the stairs up again and locks us in here. Momma hates it when he does this but I don't mind it anymore. When he pushes the stairs up I know he won't be bugging me and Emma. He used to do that all the time, but since we're gonna be moving on and up I think he's got other things to bug.

Uh-oh. Momma's calling us. Here's the problem — if we call out and let her know we're up here, then she'll see that the stairs are up. If she sees the stairs are up, then she'll know Richard was being mean to us. If she sees that Richard's been mean to us then she'll lay into him about it and then he'll start laying into her and it won't end up like *Little House on the Prairie*, let me tell you.

"We better not answer her," Emma says, and I'm thinking that's a fine idea.

"But then we'll be stuck up here all day," I say, and Emma just squinches her shoulders up and then lets them fall back down again and I know it's settled, whether I like it or not.

I'm tiptoeing over to the stack of books near the fan, which we cain't turn on since the noise will alert Momma and then it's all downhill from there, and I'm leafing through this battered old book of stamps from around the world. Someone who lived here before us left it behind, but I don't think they missed it since they died and that's how we came to live here. Anyway, I love to look at the different stamps and picture living somewhere really beautiful. Even though I'm old enough to know better, I think the countries are the colors on their stamps. It's weird in geography class hearing how Finland is such a dark place since its stamp is so bright and colorful.

Uh-oh. Momma's under the pull-string staircase. I can hear her calling out. I look over at Emma but she's fallen asleep reading again. Richard must've been at her last night. When she sleeps that way during the day I know what's happened the night before.

There's that creaking sound the springs make when the stairs are pulled down and I know the day's not going to end up well for Momma.

"Caroline? You up there with Emma?"

I hurry to the top step so she won't wake Emma.

"Emma's asleep," I hiss to her. "You need something?" I ask real nicely so she'll forget that Richard's locked us in again. Maybe then she won't go near him.

I can tell by the way she eyes the fold-out stairs and by the way she sighs that she doesn't have the energy to take up for us today, and I'm glad. Well, sort of glad.

"I need you in the kitchen," she says. "I've got to go out for a little while and you need to get everything ready for dinner."

"Where're you going?" I ask. "Can I come?"

"It's none of your business where I'm going and no you cannot," she says all in one breath. "Now, come on and get moving."

Usually when Momma calls to me and Emma both that means she's in a good mood, but I guess that's not true today. Here's the reason why she only calls on me most times — she likes me better than Emma. We both know it and so does Momma. She's even said it out loud. "I don't care what Emma wants to do, I'm telling you I only want you to go," she says when we go to someplace fun. Or she'll ask me for favors, not Emma. This really hurts Emma, even though she doesn't admit it, because when I do the favor for Momma she's really nice to me in return. Emma wants to be able to have Momma be that grateful to her, but I don't think that's going to happen any time soon.

I think Momma doesn't like Emma because she looks just like Daddy and Momma says some things are best forgotten.

Like the first time Richard called to me from his room. You cain't make an angry voice into a pretty one, but that's what Richard is trying to do, I thought to myself at that very moment. Why is he calling me like I'm a little kitten. "Here kitty, kitty," he calls. Come on up here, he says, like his room's a fun place to be. "Come here, sweet girl," he calls.

"Don't go up there," Emma says to me with those eyes of hers that know it all even though she's two years younger than me.

"I'll be right back," I say, trying not to look scared, turning the day's events over and over in my head. I didn't do anything wrong, I think. Breakfast was my turn and I made the eggs just like he said to, I tell

64

myself at the bottom of the stairs. I know from the sound in his voice it's a trap. It's the way you call to one of the chickens when it's dinner. You don't chase it, you let it come to you. You call it by trying to sound pretty. Here chicky, chicky.

"Coming," I answer him.

The stairs feel steep so I hold on to the banister even though I go up and down them a million times a day without even thinking twice about it.

"What's taking you so long, girl," he hollers, the try for sweetness turning the word *girl* into a curl in the air. I picture him reaching out with chicken feed in the palm of his hand, waiting for me to peck it so he can grab me with the other when I'm not looking.

"No," Emma says from the bottom of the stairs. "Carrie," she calls to me. "No."

The sound in her voice makes me want to throw up.

Momma's not here, I think to myself. I've got to do as he says.

At the top of the stairs I look around for a safe place to run, but in our house there are none. Except behind-the-couch, but right now I'm too far away from there.

I look into Richard and Momma's room and inhale. Even from the top of the stairs

I can smell it. Momma's perfume cain't cover the smell of Richard and his sweaty clothes. Richard is sitting on the edge of the bed that used to belong to my grandmother. The bed is covered with a graying fabric that has a pretty flower pattern sewn on it in the same material. I love to trace that pattern when Momma's still soft from sleep and me and Emma crawl up onto the bed 'cause Richard's not home.

"Come here," he says. He's hunched over and is resting his elbows on his knees. When I tiptoe into the room he straightens, and I can see that his pants are unzipped. Now I really want to vomit.

"I said get over here," he says to me, but I cain't move my legs. They're like dandelion roots that won't let go of the soil. Just as he's about to say it again, Emma comes in from behind me, pushes me out of the room and closes the door. Just like that. I waited there a few seconds and then I ran behind-the-couch. That's how much of a coward I am. I let my little sister take the heat for me. I don't know why Richard would have forgotten to do up his pants before the beating but I try not to think about that. There are no sounds coming from up there but I know it's bad. Emma never cries when it's bad. Only when she thinks she can change something does she cry. She couldn't change this. I put my forehead down onto the tops of my knees and wait for her to come back down but she never does. I am wedged behind-the-couch picking at the yellow line in the plaid pattern, hoping she's okay. Why hasn't she come back down yet? I wait. Then I wait some more. Then I think maybe she thinks I went back upstairs to our room so maybe I should go there and look for her to see what that was all about. So I start out from behind-the-couch by digging my heels into the linoleum and pulling my rear end along an inch or two and then repeating the process.

But Emma doesn't come out of the room for a long time and when she does she doesn't come looking for me like I come looking for her after it's my turn for a whipping. I hear her tiny footsteps heading up to the Nest so I scoot out from behind-the-couch and go up after her. Richard's door is closed so the coast is clear and I take the stairs two at a time. She's sitting on the edge of the bed and it doesn't look like she got a beating. It looks more like she got stuck in a rainstorm. Her hair isn't silky anymore, it's matted in the back and the bangs in front are damp. Her face is all puffy like she's been crying, but I listened real hard for that so I'm not sure if that's what happened.

But her mouth is clamped up like the meat grinder that's fixed to the edge of the counter in the kitchen, so I don't think I'll be finding out any time soon what Richard was so mad about.

I go over to the fan and turn it on, thinking maybe she'll talk into it like she always does and then I can find out what went wrong, but she just sits there on the bed, so I give up and go for the stamp book, flipping past Romania and getting right to my favorite — Bermuda. I touch it and pretend I'm touching the white sand under the palm tree that leans into the sun. If I could live anywhere in the world, it would be in Bermuda. It's too pretty there for anything to be wrong, and I bet they even have a law that would keep people like Richard out altogether. 'Sides, his thin brown hair wouldn't keep the top of his head from getting burned and his arms with all the veins popping out up and down them would turn beet red.

I look back at the bed and I see that Emma's curled up like a little baby wanting to get back into her mother's stomach. She's trying to be really small, hugging her

68

legs up to her chest like she is.

I hate Richard.

When Richard first met me he patted me on the head and walked on by. I didn't pay him any mind because I had no idea he'd be here to stay. Momma had dropped some hints — "You better be real nice to my new friend," "Why don't y'all go on up and put on those sundresses I bought you last spring" — but I didn't notice until it was too late.

Emma and I were playing jacks on the front porch when he came by carrying a tin can full of nails, which Momma made such a big deal over — like he was the one who said "This loaf of bread is great but what if we made lines across it and cut it up." He told Momma the nails were to fix the floorboards that bent up and stubbed our toes when we walked barefoot. Big deal. *I* could've done *that*. Besides, no one had stubbed their toes since Daddy died so I don't understand what the fuss was all about. But Richard winked at me and said it's so my baby sister doesn't hurt herself. Momma gave us this look so we had to say "Thank you, sir" to him even though his wink looked as fake as the left hand on Mr. Brown, who plays the harmonica outside

White's Drugstore every day.

One day I went with Richard to White's 'cause Momma asked us to. It was still early on, when Richard did favors for Momma. "Caroline, why don't you go along so Richard has some company," Momma said. But I guess I wasn't the kind of company Richard must've wanted: once we pulled away from the house and Momma was out of sight, the smile went away from his face and he stopped talking altogether.

"Hey there, chile," says Miss Mary from behind the counter. Then she tilts her head to the side and mumbles to herself loud enough for me to hear. "I don' know what they be givin' so much work to them kids at school fo'. Y'all look so *tired* all the time." Then her head snaps back upright and she looks over my head altogether. "I'll be right with you," she says to Richard.

"I'll be right with you . . ." Richard says it like she did but he drags out the end so it's clear she left something off of the end of her sentence.

"I'll be right with you, sir," she says, looking down at her work. Richard likes everyone to call him sir, even people who're old enough to be his grandma.

Miss Mary's nails are long and make a

tapping sound when she pushes the numbers on the calculator to figure out how much you owe. Sometimes she uses the eraser end of the pencil that usually sits behind her left ear, but that day was a fingernail day. I watch her total up Mr. Sugner from the library that's also the Toast Historical Society — if you need to know anything about Toast, Mr. Sugner's the man to talk to. *Tap-tappity-tap.*

Richard looks as happy to be here as if you'd driven a railroad tie into his foot. He scowls at Miss Mary and shifts from one leg to another, huffing, like it was Mr. Sugner's fault he was here and not the fact that Momma needs Band-Aids, toothpaste and a cup measure. I got a funny feeling in my stomach when I saw the way he looked at Miss Mary, all mean like she smelled bad, so I went over to the rack that holds dusty postcards that no one's ever bought even though they're only ten cents each. They're not postcards of our town, they're North Carolina state postcards with pictures of the capitol and a town called Mount Airy.

When I turn around Richard's nowhere to be seen. I even check the aisle that has diapers and other soft-like things but no luck.

"He ain't here." Miss Mary aims a fingernail at a spot to the left of her chin and gently scratches. "Mmm, mmm, mmm." Her mouth was turned down and she was shaking her head like she thought of him the same way he thought of her.

"Where is he?" I ask. I only turned around for a second.

"Check out by the Dumpster," and I think I heard her say — she was mumbling, though, so I couldn't be sure — "That's where trash ends up."

"Miss Mary?" Mr. White's voice slices the air like a paper cut. "Is there a problem here?" It's weird how he can smile at me but keep that teacher tone with Miss Mary.

"Miss Caroline, how would you like to choose a piece of penny candy?" He was holding out the big glass jar with fingerprints all over from where all us kids point at the exact piece we want. It had been refilled and was brimming full of Mary Janes, Tootsie Rolls, little-bitty Necco wafer rolls and Hershey's. It was so packed that Mr. White's thumb knocked a piece onto the floor when he gripped it from the top. The Mary Jane was lying on the floor between us like it was saying "Pick me, pick me!"

"I'm sorry, sir." I stare at it while I say

this, hoping it would magically unwrap itself and hop into my watering mouth. "I don't have any money with me right now."

"Oh, don't be silly —" he smiles even nicer "— this is a gift. Take your pick." He says this last part in Miss Mary's direction, even though I think he was talking to me. Before he has time to change his mind, my arm, like it had a mind of its own, shoots down to the floor, past the old glass jar, and scoops up that Mary Jane.

Miss Mary was busying herself with the zipper on her gray cover-up that has White's Drugstore sewn over her heart and looks just like Mr. White's, but is gray instead of, well, white.

"Am I to understand you got separated from your escort?" he asks me. This always happens: people ask questions right when I've got my mouth full and I can't answer. Mr. White's so polite, though, and he keeps talking till he sees my jaw stop moving up and down on the peanut toffee. "This must be my lucky day, if this is true. I was just thinking how nice it would be to have a helper in the back room, someone to alphabetize bottles, you know, get things in order. Would you be so kind as to help me out for a bit, young lady?"

He timed this question perfectly: I had

just finished scooping the Mary Jane that was stuck in my back teeth out with my tongue. "Yes, sir, but I don't know if I'm allowed."

"What if I call your momma for you and we can ask her permission," he says.

"Yes, sir," I say. I don't know where I'd have gone, anyway, since Richard had up and left me there. Mr. White went over to the phone near Miss Mary's cash register and dialed our number without even looking it up — that's a small town for you, I guess.

"Libby? Dan White." He pauses waiting for Momma to greet him. Then he clears his throat, "A-hem, well, don't mean to bother you, but Miss Caroline and I were wondering if I might be able to retain her services for the day, here at the store. It seems her companion had some, ahem, pressing matters to tend to, so if you could spare her I'd be much obliged."

Pause again. No telling what Momma is saying from the look on Mr. White's face. He must be tired, his eyes are halfway closed and he looks like he was studying for a test, memorizing her voice or something.

"I don't quite know," he says, shifting his eyes over to me for some reason. "We had a bit of a wait, so I'm sure he'll stop back in when he sees we're not so busy after all." Then he winks at me and his voice rises back up to a normal level.

"Well, it's settled then," he says, clearing his throat again. "I'll keep Miss Caroline here with me until five and then I'll bring her on home —" Pause. "Oh, it's no trouble 'tall. I have to go out that way, anyway, to pay a call on the Godseys." Pause. "See y'all then. Bye."

It takes my eyes a few seconds to get used to the back room, which was night compared to the day outside. Mr. White was right: it was a mess back there. Momma would say it's a viper's nest. There's barely enough room for me to walk to the other end of the room; the boxes are piled one on top of another in every spare space on the floor.

"Here's what I was thinking," Mr. White says from behind me, surveying the packed crowd of cardboard. "A lot of these boxes are pretty much empty. If you could go through and find the ones that only have one or two bottles in them, take those bottles out and put 'em all here on this lower shelf, and then go back and break down the boxes, that'd make a lot more room."

"Where do I put the empty boxes?"

"Come on out back and I'll show you where we stack for the garbageman." I turn and follow Mr. White back into the store and then out the door that leads to a tiny parking lot out back. A huge Dumpster sat in one of the spaces.

"Just stack the flat pieces here, next to the Dumpster."

"Okay."

"You sure you're up to this?" he asks me.

"Yes, sir."

"All right, then," he says, patting me on the head. "The apple doesn't fall far from the tree. You're just like your momma. Once she sets her mind to something, she never lets it go." He walks back into the store, smiling.

I liked the idea of straightening up the storeroom. Plus, this way when Richard comes back, he cain't call me lazy.

One by one I empty out most of the boxes that sit about eye level to me. Mr. White was right; a couple of boxes only have one bitty bottle in them. They were just waiting for someone to remember them. I have no idea how much time has gone by, but I do know that I've flattened fifteen boxes flat and it's time to start taking them out to the Dumpster.

When I cut through the store with my

first armload, Miss Mary is tapping into the calculator, figuring out how much to put on Mr. Blackman's tab. Back and forth I go and pretty soon I've taken out all the pieces I'd worked on.

"Oh, my dear Lord," Mr. White says when he comes in to check on me later on. Uh-oh. I hope I haven't messed up, but I look over at him and his open mouth is turning into a smile. A real smile, eyes and all. "Well, I'll be darned. Miss Caroline Parker . . . you're hired!"

I'm *hired?*

"Sir?"

"The job's yours if you want it," he says, running his eyes over the spaces I'd made on the floor. Now two people can stand side by side in there. "I guess I didn't realize how much we needed you. You think your momma could spare you once or twice a week?"

"B-but, I'm only eight," I say, my face getting all red for some reason. "Are eight-year-olds allowed to have jobs?"

Mr. White looks at me the way I think my own daddy used to look at me and I don't feel embarrassed anymore. I feel relieved. "Honey, with what all you've been through," he says real soft-like, "seems to me you could use a little break now and then. Place to get away. You know."

And right then I guessed I did know what he was talking about. I nod. He pats me on the hand, shakes his head and turns to go back out to the store.

"Little Caroline Parker," he says more to himself than to me. "Little Miss Caroline Parker."

I wonder what Emma is going to think when I tell her. Maybe Mr. White would let her come with me to work. She's scrappy but she's strong, that's for sure. No telling *how* many boxes we'd get through, working together. She sure could use a break now and then, too.

A little while later Mr. White comes back.

"I reckon that's about all the work we can force out of you today," he says, smiling again. It's hot back here in the storeroom and he wipes his shiny forehead with his handkerchief. I don't know why anyone would want to keep a used handkerchief in their pocket, but that's exactly where the kerchief headed after he was through with it.

"I promised your momma I'd take you on home, so let's get this show on the road."

"Yes, sir," I say, stepping on top of the

box I'd emptied and untaped so it just fell flat like a pancake when my foot said hello. I s'pose Richard'll find his own way home sooner or later. Unfortunately.

Mr. White's car is hotter than the store-room and the Nest put together since it'd been baking in the parking lot all day. The car seat scorches my rear end so I tilt up, pushing my weight into my shoulders until the air cools the seat off. Mr. White doesn't seem to notice and I'm glad.

Pulling out of the parking lot, he starts talking. "Your momma was the belle of the ball back when she was just a hair older than you," Mr. White says. "Now, you know we went to school together, don'tcha?"

"Yes, sir," I say. I'm testing the seat but it's still hotter than a butcher's knife. Back when I was little, I used to study Momma's high school yearbook — she looked like a movie star in it and Mr. White still had all his hair and looked funny, all dressed in black, the mean look he was trying to give the camera turned out to be just plain goofy. There was a haze around Momma's head that made her look like she belonged up in heaven. Her hair was shiny, not quite brown and not quite yellow, and it was in a poufy hairdo that made her look older than she was. Her smile was perfect and it was from looking at that picture that I realized she has dimples. You'd never know it now. Her eyes were wide and sparkling with no trace of the lines that carve up her face now. She was wearing pearls that I know for a fact she borrowed from her grandmother just for that picture. The famous pearl necklace. I'd heard so much about the pearl necklace that I felt like I was actually there, later on that same picture day, when Momma and my daddy slipped in back of the school to kiss. Daddy was holding her head between his hands when the school principal came out, caught them in the act, startling Daddy so his hands slipped. They caught the necklace and sent the pearls scattering across the asphalt to their ultimate doom down the town drain. Momma was beaten within an inch of her life when she went home, shamed.

"Did she mention she went to school with me?" Mr. White looks over at me, and when he does I can see, just for a second, how he looked back then.

"I don't remember. I guess I just knew it, is all." No need to tell him about the yearbook. I bet he'd be embarrassed about his picture, anyway.

"Oh," he sighs. "Well, all the boys were in love with her. 'Cluding me, I reckon. But back then I didn't have sense enough to come in outta the rain, so I surely wasn't going to ask your momma out on a date. No, sirree," he whistles. "Your daddy did, though, and truth to tell, I don't know if I ever forgave him for taking my Libby away from me." He winks at me, which is a relief because I don't know if I could stand hearing Mr. White say anything bad about Daddy.

"We were all real jealous of your daddy," he says, nodding. "I s'pose I thought they'd light out of this town once they got married, but your momma wouldn't have it. No, sirree . . ."

While he's talking, I ease my rear down onto the seat real slow. Phee-you, it feels good to sit normal.

". . . she dug her heels in and I reckon they grew roots so they stayed on."

I don't quite know why, but all of a sudden a cloud comes over Mr. White's face when he says this. So I keep my mouth shut. Nothing different from what I've been doing, really, but now it feels like I should be coming up with something to say.

"How's school going?" Mr. White asks

after we turn onto Route 5. We're only about two minutes from my house, so luckily this won't be a long part of the conversation.

"Fine, thank you."

"Yeah? Well, that's good. That's real good," he says as he turns his big boat of a car onto our dirt road. His car looks so out of place driving where Richard's truck does.

"Here we are," he says, trying to sound cheerful, but the look on his face doesn't match his voice. So I hop out of the car fast.

"Thanks again, Mr. White," I call out to him.

"You betcha," he calls back. "Now, you talk to your momma and have her call me once y'all work out when you want to come in again. You can come anytime you like, Caroline. Anytime at all." He winks again and I shut the door and run up the front porch stairs to find Momma and Emma to tell them about my day at White's.

Mr. White is just like everybody else here in Toast, North Carolina — it's never occurred to him to leave. Imagine that. I mean, I can understand it when you're my age, but when you're old enough to get out of town, why wouldn't you?

"Momma?" I holler before the porch door even slams shut. "Guess what?"

Momma's in the kitchen smoking with one hand, stirring something in a pot on the stove with the other.

"Momma, Mr. White gave me a job! I cleared out all the boxes from the storeroom and he said he never saw it so neat and clean and he hired me right there on the spot. I can eat penny candy anytime I want. Momma, please say I can do it, please."

"Slow down, Jesus H. Christmas, slow down," Momma says, turning to the icebox and staring at what's inside. "Go on and get me that molasses out of the pantry, will you?"

"Momma, can I work there after school? Can I?"

"Just get me that molasses can first of all," she snaps at me. "We'll have to talk about it."

"Why cain't I? It'd be great. I'd earn my own money and I get to have candy anytime I want. Please, Momma."

Momma's back stirring again, the wooden spoon turning slowly on account of whatever's in there being too high up next to spilling over. I creep up closer to her 'cause I can hear her mumbling something, but I know by now you cain't push Momma too hard or she'll turn around and do just the opposite of what you're hoping for.

"Storeroom clerk . . ." she's saying. I think. "Moving . . ."

See, all I get are snippets of words or phrases, so I know she's working something in her head.

"Momma?"

"Goddamn son of a bitch." The spoon picks up speed so it's only a matter of time till something slops over the edge.

It's like she's reciting a grocery list in her sleep; her words don't make any sense.

"Momma? Can I? Please?"

"What?" She whirls around like I startled her out of the conversation she was carrying on in her brain, still holding the spoon but forgetting, I guess, that it was no longer over the pot so the red sauce dripped onto the kitchen floor like blood. Splat. I watch each drop spread into neat circles on impact. Splat.

"Can I work at White's?" Splat.

She's sizing me up like she just now realized I'd grown out of my jeans a month ago.

"Just until we move? Please?"

"Oh, why the hell not," she sighs, and turns back to the bubbling blood on the stove.

I forget for a second and hug her from behind, I'm so happy. When she stiffens up like a board I remember I shouldn't touch her.

"Go on and get," she says woodenly into the pot.

I run up to the Nest to find Emma to tell her my news.

"Emma? Emma!" I take the stairs two at a time. "Where you at?"

"Up here," she hollers back to me.

"Guess what I've got a job at White's Drugstore and I can have penny candy anytime I want," I say all at once since I'm out of breath from coming up the stairs so fast.

Emma's on the bed with Mutsie, her favorite stuffed animal. "What?"

I straighten up after letting my breath catch up with my body. "Mr. White? He offered me a job after Richard up and left me behind at the drugstore to go I-don't-know-where."

I fill her in on everything and, just like I figured, she got to the number one obvious question: "Can I work there, too?"

I'd like to think it was 'cause she wanted

to be with me and not here alone in the Nest while I'm gone, but I betcha it's the penny candy. I don't mind. Me and Emma, we're slaves to candy.

"I bet Mr. White'd let you come on and help," I tell her. And I honestly believe it's so. "He even said he needs all the help he can get. That back room's messier than a flower bed in February."

And that's how we came to work at White's Drugstore nearly every day of the week after school.

Four

"I don't s'pose y'all ever seen the Box?" Miss Mary looks over at Emma and me from her spot behind the cash register. She's folding her book back up and takes off her reading glasses. Miss Mary's been real nice to us all week, but I guess that's nothing new. She's always patting our hair like we're her pets or something. The other day she even put some of the bright pink barrettes from the dime basket next to the register in Emma's hair, one on either side of her face so she could see without strings of hair blocking the way. Miss Mary doesn't have kids herself so I guess we'll do.

"What's the Box?" Emma asks.

"Ooooeee, the Box is sumthin' you got to see to believe," Miss Mary says with a smile that spreads out across her wrinkled face. "It's real scary. You have to be old enough even to ask about it."

"Are we old enough?" I ask her, but Emma talks at the same time.

"Where is it?" she asks. Not one single

breathing soul's come into the store yet and it's already four in the afternoon. I bet it's on account of the heat that looks like it's melting the tar right off the road.

"I thought ev'rybody knowed 'bout the Box." Miss Mary pats her lap and Emma crawls up in it like I've never seen her do with anyone else. "It's over at Ike's place and the kids go in one by one — if they brave enough to go into the room it's in."

"Yeah? Yeah?" We both want her to keep talking about it. I rub my arms so the gooseflesh will settle down.

"How big is it?" Emma.

"A little bigger than a shoe box," she says.

"What's inside it?" Me.

"No one knows for sure."

"I bet it's boogers," Emma says from Miss Mary's lap. She's leaning her back into Miss Mary's front and her legs are dangling on either side of Miss Mary's, which are pressed together to make a nice spot for Em.

Miss Mary shakes her head. "Whatever's in the Box has them kids runnin' scared for years," she says. "I ain't never heard of no one who be able to stay in the room long 'nough after the lid comes up to know for sure what all's so creepy."

"We've *got* to see the Box," I say. Emma nods.

"I don't know," Miss Mary says, smiling her smile that makes her skin look even more crinkly. "I don' know if y'all're up to it."

"Yes we are!" Emma pushes away from Miss Mary so she can swivel around to face her. "We most certainly are."

"We?" Miss Mary says to her like she was only meaning me in the first place. She knows that just cements it in Emma's mind that she's going to be on board no matter what it is we're doing.

"Miss Mary, if I go, my little sister is sure to follow." Which is straight up true. "Everyone knows that."

"I'm not scared of anything." Emma's nodding. Which, of course, is true. If only Miss Mary knew that I'm the scaredy-cat of the both of us. I mean, if I'm scared of spiders I can't even *think* of what I'll do when I'm in the room with the Box. But I've just got to see it. I've got to.

"Where's Ike's? Jinx!" We ask about Ike's at the same exact time but I call jinx first so I'm the winner.

"Way over in Lowgap, by the Knob," says Miss Mary. Lowgap is this little-bitty place on the edge of a forest near the

Cumberland Knob, which is called that for a reason I don't know. Momma says it's on account of the shape of the mountain right above the town, but I just don't see what she's talking about — the mountain looks just like every other mountain in the world to me, not some ole knob. Lowgap's a creepy place on account of all the trees shading it from the sun. When we were little and went there I thought the sun forgot to shine over the whole place, that's how shady it is. On a day like today, though, it might kindly be the place to be. The sun in Toast is making up for no sun in Lowgap.

"Carrie, we got to get to Lowgap." Emma's jumped down from Miss Mary, who's smoothing out the place on her lap where a little girl used to be. "How're we gonna do it?"

"Let me think on it a minute," I say, annoyed-like since that's what I am. I know we got to get to Lowgap, I just cain't imagine how we can pull it off.

"We-ell," Miss Mary says all long and dragged out, "I got a friend outside Lowgap at a place so small it ain't on the map. They been at me for a visit for's long as I can remember . . . I s'pose I could —"

"*Please* take us with you, Miss Mary!"

90

We both jump on her at the same time. "Please! We won't be any bother." Emma tugs on her skirt and I grab her arm and yank it up and down for a reason I don't know. "Please. Pretty please with sugar on top and whipped cream and a cherry and nuts even!" I throw that last part in since I bet for a grown-up the nuts are the big draw, from the way Momma hoards her Mr. Peanuts.

Miss Mary's laughing, and when she does her belly folds into and back out of itself like it's a whole other set of lips. Then Emma seals the deal. She climbs up onto Miss Mary's lap and gives her a big ole hug.

"Don't you be gittin' me all messed up now while I in my work clothes," Miss Mary says into the side of Emma's hair in the middle of the hug. "Go on and git an' let me think on it awhile."

But we know it's settled. We're going to see the Box tomorrow after school lets out and we show up for work. Tomorrow's Miss Mary's day off so she says she'll pick us up in back of the store after we ask Mr. White for time off "on the HH." That's Miss Mary's code for "hush-hush."

"Look out, here comes Scary Carrie!"

Tommy Bucksmith yells out across the map of the country that's painted on the tar in the middle of the recess yard. "How's your *boyfriend,* Charley?" I'm trying to pretend I don't hear him.

Charley Narley is a guy in town who everyone makes fun of. His body grew up but his brain forgot to. Momma says he lost his marbles. She says every town's got a Charley Narley but I can't imagine that. He's big like a bear and all anyone knows is his first name's Charley. Someone somewhere long ago started calling him Charley Narley 'cause of the rhyme, I suppose. He doesn't comb or cut his hair and it's all matted up underneath and most likely dirty to boot. When you go down the street he follows along like a puppy saying out loud what all you're doing. It goes like this: You walk to Alamo Shoes and look in the window and from behind you, out loud, you hear, "Now she's stopping at the window. She's looking inside at the white shoes. No, it's the pink shoes she's looking at." Then you keep going and you hear, "She's going on down the street. She's getting something out of her pocket. It's a piece of gum! She's unwrapping the gum. She's putting it in her mouth. She's chewing." Like that. He wouldn't hurt a fly, Charley Narley. What the boys will do is walk along and get Charley to follow and talk and then one will drop back behind Charley and imitate him talking about them. Like this: "Now Charley's watching Tommy. He's slowing down. He's looking at Tommy. He's talking." Charley gets all confused and wants to get behind whoever's talking about him and gets more confused and then he starts yelling even louder and then the boys run and Charley gets in trouble with the sheriff. Once they packed sand into an old stocking like the kind the ladies wear at church and hid it in the bushes so that just the tip was peeking out. When Charley Narley came by and saw it they wriggled it to look like a snake and Charley screamed all high like a girl, thinking it was real or something. Just last week they threw stuff at him like he was a target ("ten points if the Coke can hits his right arm!") and me and Emma went out to try to get Charley to go in the opposite direction. Mr. White came out after us and told the boys to scat but ever since then they call Charley Narley my boyfriend.

"Oh, hush up," I say under my breath, thinking Darryl Becksdale's a good distance away and can't hear me.

"What's that?" Uh-oh. He heard. "You sticking up for your *true love?*"

"No."

"Then what?"

"You think you're so smart," I say without even thinking first about what I'm going to say, "but you don't know *anything.*"

"Yeah?" he says, trotting alongside me while I walk toward the doors to the inside of the school. "Ask me anything — I bet I know the answer to it. See? You can't think of anything!" He starts fake laughing. I know it's fake 'cause it's louder than his real laugh, plus he's looking around for an audience.

"Okay," I say, just before I go inside where it's just as hot but I don't have to be in the sun that burns the part line in my hair, "you know about the Box?"

For a second I think he's stumped 'cause he's not saying anything, but then he says, "The Box isn't real, moron."

"It is, too," I say.

"*You've* seen it?"

"Not yet," I say, smiling for real, knowing I'll be seeing it in five hours and twenty-two minutes.

"You lie," he says, and then he backs away from me and goes over to his friends, who're showing off how they can form a bridge with shuffling cards.

"Mr. White?" My hands are sweaty and it's not on account of the heat.

"Yes, Caroline," he says, putting down the pad of order forms. "What can I do for you?"

"Um . . ." I clear my throat. Maybe that'll make some room for the words to come out. "I was wondering . . ."

"Yes?" he says.

"Um, if it's okay with you, sir —" I clear my throat again "— could Emma and I please have this afternoon off of work? We worked superhard yesterday lining up all the bottles to the front of the shelves like you said and we got to the *M*s already even though you said *G* was enough, so if you could spare us we'd sure appreciate —"

"That'll be fine," he says before I can even finish. He picks up his order-form pad again like the subject's closed so I hate reopening it to ask him to keep it quiet, and somehow the thought of asking a grown-up to keep a secret embarrasses me but I know I have to do it.

"Um . . ." Ahem.

"Yes?" He looks back up at me all serious over the half-moon glasses holding on to the tip of his nose.

"I was wondering if you might be able to keep this just between us?"

What did I just say? Of course he'd be able to! He's not a baby, for goodness' sake. Stupid, stupid me.

I can tell he's thinking on it and I'm burning red because I'm sure he's insulted I'm treating him like a baby and then he says, "I think I can pull that off." Phee-you.

"Thank you so much, sir," I say, and I'm almost out the door when he calls out.

"Oh, Caroline . . ."

I turn around and catch him smiling just like his high school picture. "Yes, sir?"

"Y'all better be careful," he says, "the Box is the scariest thing you'll ever see."

He knows! Could he have heard us yesterday? I stumble back-first out the door while my mind tries to wrap itself around this question, and then I see the noisy old rusty car Miss Mary borrows to drive herself to town pull up, the windows sealed up tight to keep in the little bit of cool air that trickles out of the one un-broken vent, and I hurry to grab the front seat before Emma can call it and I forget all about Mr. White and how he came to find out about the Box.

"Emma, I'm older, I get it!" We've both grabbed the front door handle and are trying to push each other out of the way. It's one thing to ride in the back in Momma's car — I do that 'cause Emma's so picked on by her. But this is a horse of a different color. Emma gets plenty of attention from Miss Mary so I think I should get it. Plus, I was the one we decided had to do the Mr. White asking.

"Em-ma!" I jimmy my shoulder in between her head and the car door, but she's strong from beating up so many people after school so she isn't about to let go of the handle without a fight. Now Miss Mary has herself halfway standing, halfway sitting out her side of the car, calling out to us, "You better git in 'fore I change my mind and that's that."

We cain't get into the car fast enough. The cool air gives me gooseflesh at first but then I settle into it.

"So? Y'all ready for the Box?" Miss Mary says as she pulls the car out of the parking lot and onto the main road that leads out of Toast.

"Is it alive or dead?" Emma asks.

"Don't be startin' on me with all them questions. This ain't no game show." I can see the top half of Miss Mary's face in the cracked rearview mirror looking back at the both of us, the lines around her eyes crinkled from smiling. I once heard one frown line on an old person's face is caused by one hundred thousand frowns all added up. If the same's true for smiles, then Miss Mary's been a happy person all her life 'cause she has a ton of lines around the corners of each of her eyes.

"Just say," Emma says. "Is it alive or dead?"

"I just do not know," Miss Mary says. She's at the blinking yellow light that keeps you from getting hit by an eighteen-wheeler racing fast as can be through Toast and on to bigger and better places. Not one today, though, so Miss Mary pulls out slow and onto the highway toward Lowgap.

"I bet it's a head cut off of someone's body," Emma says.

"I bet it's a pig's tongue," I say. "You know, Daddy used to eat tongue — did you know that?"

"I bet it's blood," Emma says, not paying any attention to this tidbit of Daddy information I parcel out to her. Too bad for her.

"That's not all that scary," I tell her. "I mean, who hasn't seen blood before? No one'd hightail it out of the room over a box full of blood."

"I'm telling you, it's boogers," Emma says, crossing her arms and sitting up straighter so she can see the road we're driving on. I don't know why she'd care about that, though, since there ain't a thing on it to see.

"What if Ike won't let us see the Box?" This is what I've been most worried about. "What if he says we're not old enough?"

"He let you through," Miss Mary says.

"How big is it again?" Emma asks.

"She already *told* you." I roll my eyes just like Momma says not to. "It's about the size of a shoe box. Jeez."

Miss Mary says, "Y'all start that bickering an' this drive gits longer an' longer so quit it."

This, of course, makes no sense a-tall since bickering cain't make the distance between two places any farther. But I'm not about to point this out to Miss Mary. We're so lucky her friend lives near Lowgap.

Soon we're slowing down in the middle of the main road in Lowgap. "The City on the Rise!" it says on a signpost right before the stores start lining up. It doesn't feel like it's on the rise, though, since not many of the places are open. Some have windows so dusty they look like they've been locked up for a thousand years. Miss Mary pulls up to the curb outside a glass window with a sign: Dot's Kountry Kafaye.

"Reckon you as hungry as I am," she says, fishing in her purse on the seat next to her. She finds her lipstick and shimmies up to the rearview mirror so she can re-apply. She doesn't have those tiny smoker's cracks outlining her mouth, like Momma does, so the lipstick stays where it's sup-posed to. On Sundays Momma's lips look like they're bleeding. Miss Mary pops the cap back on and throws the lipstick back into her bag and turns to face us.

"We better get some food in your stomach 'fore it gets too tied up in knots over this ole Box."

I was hungry up until now, but once Miss Mary says the word *Box* I lose my ap-petite all over again. I couldn't eat dinner last night, even though Momma made bis-cuits and gravy — my favorite.

Dot's Kountry Kafaye looks just like Mickey's Country Kitchen in Toast. There's a counter where you can watch them make your food or there are booths if you want to be surprised. I like the counter and lucky for me that's where we go. The seats at Dot's swivel all the way around! At Mickey's they only make a half a circle.

Miss Mary says we can order one thing and split it on account of the fact that she's paying and we aren't so we decide on a hot dog.

"All the way?" the waitress asks.

"Yes, please," I say. The bell on the top of the glass door jingles as Miss Mary turns to back out through it.

"Y'all going over to Ike's after this?" the waitress asks me and Emma after she clips our order slip onto a metal tree that sits on an island between the kitchen and the restaurant.

"Yes, ma'am," we say at the same time.

"I expected you would." She nods, all serious like Mr. White was. "Good luck," she says, and the way she says it I know I won't be doing any more than picking at my share of the hot dog.

"I'll tell you what," the waitress says, trying to sound cheerful, "I'll bring you a Coke with a side of peanuts, on the house since y'all ain't never seen the Box 'fore."

We both sit up straight and swivel. Peanuts and Coke! It's the best thing in the universe.

"I call I get to drop the first one in," Emma practically shouts.

"Let's shoot for it," I say. And I lose.

The first peanut into the Coke causes the most bubbles, and this time when Emma drops it in is no different. It's like a science experiment, the foam gets high up to the edge of the glass and then, just as quick-like, drops back down. The rest of the peanuts just plop in. But they make the Coke taste even better than when it's on its own.

"Aw-right, here you go." The waitress pushes the sloppy hot dog in front of the both of us. There's a pickle on the side for good measure.

I eat my share but then my stomach lurches and it occurs to me I might throw up so I ask if I can visit the washroom before we go.

"Sure, sugar," the waitress says. "Lemme unlock it for you." She takes a wooden mallet with a little chain and key attached from behind the register and flicks her head to the side, which means I'm to follow her. We go past the kitchen and the smell makes me swallow hard. Uh-oh. She unlocks the door just in time for me to run in and lean over the toilet to throw up hot dog and Coke. I hear the door click closed behind me, and before I can reach for the toilet paper to clean myself up I hear a tap on the door and Miss Mary's voice. "You okay, chile?"

I cain't answer her 'cause I'm still gulping air, but she doesn't wait for my answer, she's through the door and stroking my back and then I feel her cool hands smoothing my forehead and pulling my hair back from my face and up from my neck. It feels so good that I stay leaning over even though I don't have to anymore.

"I went too far'd with the talk of this Box," she says. She's talking soft, like you'd talk to a baby bird. "Don't you worry anymore about it. We go on back home if you like. We just stop by my friend's house to say howdy and then we hit the road —"

"No! Please, no," I say, whipping around to face her. She dabs my chin with tissue from out of her purse that has the same Miss Mary smell of flowers mixed with cleaner fluid. "I feel fine now, for real. Please? I have to see the Box. I just have to."

"But you worried sick 'bout it, chile."

"No I'm not. I swear. I feel fine. Please?"

I cain't breathe until she says, "Okay." She frowns when she says it. "But I don't think it's a good idea no more. We go by for a second and give it the once-over."

I throw my arms around her without

even thinking first, the way I used to with Daddy when he came home from a trip. "Thank you."

I say into her waist. Her clothes smell so good. I feel her hand resting on my head, and for that second I feel like nothing could ever go wrong. Not when there's Miss Mary to hug.

Ike's General Store is a few doors down from Dot's, but it's set back farther from the road. I guess this is so they can have a front porch, where there are rocking chairs and a normal chair that has no seat on it. You'd have to be really big so you won't fall through if you want to sit that bad. There's an old guy in one of the rocking chairs and he's staring straight ahead like he's waiting on a ride somewhere, but when we walk up he turns his head to us and I get the feeling maybe he was sleeping with his eyes open. Inside the screen door there's a little fan that's turning its head from one side to another, but it doesn't stay in any one place long enough for you to cool down any. Right by the cash machine there are candy jars with sugar sticks in all different colors. A whole jar with just red ones (my favorite) and another whole jar with the purple kind (Emma's). There must be ten in all. Behind them are all kinds of bottles like at White's, but the rest of the store has stuff you'd normally find at Feed-n-Plow back in Toast: barrels of grain, rakes, burlap sacks of flour that've leaked a bit so the floor looks like it's dusted with fairy powder. I cain't tell what's toward the back of the store 'cause it gets dark, but I bet it's cooler than here up front where the sun slashes through the door right onto us.

Emma takes hold of my hand and I pretend not to notice since she's real proud and would pull away if I looked at her being scared.

"Now, what can I do for y'all today?" the man behind the counter asks. He looks like he could be a twin of the old man out front in the rocker, only both straps of *his* overalls are snapped up and his shirt looks cleaner. Also, his hair is combed and not quite so gray.

Miss Mary's been looking at the table that has cookbooks on it and starts at the sound of his voice. I see she's been reading the book called *Sweet Tooth Heaven*.

"They here to see the Box." She looks over at me and Emma and says "the Box" in a lower tone, like it's a secret between them and them only.

The man nods his head like the preacher does at church on Sunday when people stand up to confess their sins out loud in front of everybody. It's a nod that says he knew all along they'd been sinning.

"I see," he says. "And how old are you, young lady?" he asks me. He must think Emma's going to hang behind when I go in.

"I'm eight and my sister's six but she's brave and wants to see, too," I say.

The man looks at Miss Mary, who whispers something across to him like she's sticking up for Emma, who does look pretty much younger than six. The man looks us up and down while Miss Mary whispers and then he whispers something back to her and I think they've been able to strike a deal.

"So you want to go in together, that right?" he says after thinking on it a minute and scratching his chin.

"Yes, sir," we say at the same time again, only this time neither of us calls jinx. We're too scared.

"I s'pose that can be allowed. Let me go on back and let them know you're comin'," he says, wiping his hands on the apron he has tied around his thin waist. On the way to the back there's an icebox that I bet has meat in it since the man's apron's streaked with red. Either that or it's blood from the Box!

"I'm so scared," I whisper to Emma. She squeezes my hand tighter. "I don't know if I can move my legs to walk back there."

Miss Mary bends down so she can look us in the eyes. "You change yo minds an' we can leave right now."

I just shake my head and look over hers at the man who's coming toward us and motioning with his arms that we should go on back to him to save him the rest of the steps it would take for him to come fetch us from the front.

"Aw-right, then." Miss Mary straightens up and pats us on the heads. "Good luck, girls. I be right here the whole time, hear?"

I don't remember how I take the first step on the dusty floor but somehow I'm walking toward a wooden door smack in the middle of shelves that line the whole back wall of the store. Our steps are tiny, though, 'cause the door stays far off in the distance even though we're moving toward it.

"Oh, Lord," I whisper my prayer out loud. "Oh, Lord, make us strong."

Emma's grip on my hand tightens and

it's hard to know whether it's her or me sweating.

The man isn't smiling anymore. He's holding the door open for us to go through and he has a real serious look on his face like we've done something wrong. That's fitting, I guess, since we're walking toward him like we have something to answer for.

Once we're at the doorway he says, "Now, girls, you sure you're ready for the Box?"

My mouth is so dry 'cause I've had it hanging open, I now realize, so all I can do is nod to him like I see Emma doing out of the corner of my eye.

I look from his face into the darkened room and I see three figures standing around a table with a red-and-white-checkered tablecloth on it, like the picnic one we used with Daddy. My eyes haven't adjusted to the dark yet but I think one of the men is the old man from the front porch. It's smoky in here and I notice that toward the back there's a card table set up and a cigarette is tilted against the side of an ashtray. One of the other men is wearing glasses, but I notice they only have glass in one side.

And there it is. The Box. Sitting by itself in the middle of the red-and-white tablecloth. It's more a rectangle than a square; dark gunmetal gray with a lid that fits perfectly to the bottom. No one says a word to us. They stand to the side of it, waiting for one of us to reach out to lift the lid.

With a few more baby steps we're up to the edge of the table and I know it'll fall to me to open it. If I hadn't throwed up at Dot's, I would have now, so I s'pose that was good luck I got it over with early. I let go of Emma's hand and wipe the sweat onto my blue jeans. I breathe in and breathe out and move my arm out in front of me so my hand is a dollar away from the edge of the box.

I jump when one of the men says, "Go on, now," and that makes my heart race even faster.

Then, I do it. I reach . . . for the edge . . . of the lid . . . and I carefully lift it . . . just a tiny bit, not even more than a dime, when a 'lectric shock runs through me so fast and hard I scream, drop the lid and run, not waiting for Emma, pushing past the man at the door, escaping from the laughter that echoes out from that smoky room across the general store, and I bolt right to Miss Mary's waist where I cleave on like moss to a tree. Emma's there in a heartbeat, trying to hold on to Miss Mary, too, and I feel her nudging us toward the screen door, her voice over our heads saying, "Thank you, sir," in a way that — can it be true? — sounds like she's smiling. "I guess the Box live up to the hype after all," she's saying from the front porch to the register man, who's opening her car door for her. I can tell because even though I still haven't let go of her waist I can see dusty work boots alongside Miss Mary's shoes that look two sizes too small for her fat feet, plus she isn't talking louder so he can hear her from inside the store. Is she trying not to laugh?

"Y'all be sure to drive safe, now," he says, shutting the door after we slide into the back, gripping on to each other like we were still at Miss Mary's waist.

After all that, I still couldn't tell you what was inside that dreaded box. I just know it's the scariest thing I have ever seen in this whole entire world.

Five

It's moving day and I don't mind saying that Momma's right — I am as bothered as a bee in a jar. Emma's packed up most of our things since I refuse to take part in one bit of this move. She doesn't mind. She's a neat girl for someone as little as she is. She keeps all of her picture books and stickers in a nice low stack by the bed so all she has to do today is lower the stack into the box Momma put together for us to share. I'm the messy one. My things are like cows scattered across the meadow, they're stubborn and hard to round up. And just when Emma thinks she's gotten them all, another one turns up on the stairs. Or at the top of the mattresses where our pillows go.

The stamp book will be the last thing to go into the box because I'm studying it right now, trying to memorize the order the countries are in to keep my mind off of this move.

Lately Momma's been calling it a fool's errand, this move. I don't understand what she means. Fool's errand. The way she says it to Richard it sounds like she's coming over to my side, but when I ask her what it means she just shoos me away. She barely has time for me and Emma these days. She's got her mind all tangled up with the bits and pieces of moving a family of four. She said that when we move we aren't going into a new school and I don't know *what* to make of this news. I think I'm happy about it because then there won't be any more of Sonny's tortures or Mary Sellers's snorting at me, but I don't know where Momma expects us to get our learning. I was making real progress reading. And Emma, she's starting to add and subtract, but without school I bet she'll forget how and I'll have to do all her counting for her. Momma says to quit talking about it, but I'm an eight-year-old — eight-year-olds are supposed to go to school; it's our *job,* for goodness' sake. Plus I was just starting to try on the idea that in a new school I could be popular for once in my life. Nobody'd know I was picked on at my old school. I've been practicing telling the new kids how I was voted the most popular girl in my third-grade class, and once they knew that, I know they'd want to be my friend. Emma doesn't seem to care she's not going back into school. That's because, like I told you, she actually was cool and cool people don't give a d-word what other people think of them. That's what makes them cool.

"Carrie, Emma," Momma calls from downstairs. "Get on down here, we got some errands to do."

"Okay," I call out for both of us. Emma, she's been real quiet lately and I think it has to do with Richard and how he's been closing the door with her on the other side of it with him. It's like they're sharing a secret and I don't get it. He looks pleased as punch he's got this secret, but Emma looks like she doesn't want to be holding it for him. She's one loyal girl, though, because she's not even telling me the secret and I'm the closest person in the universe to her. But she's always been good with secrets. She never tells anyone anything. That's yet another reason why she's got a whole army of friends.

"What's taking you so long?" Momma's starting to sound annoyed.

"Okay, okay," Emma says, and we go down the attic stairs and then down the real stairs to the kitchen, which is Momma's headquarters.

"We got to go get some more boxes so put on your flip-flops," she says.

I can barely remember Momma the way she used to be, before Richard broke her into pieces. One time when I went into the Cash-n-Carry to pick up a carton of cigarettes for her, Mr. Appleton himself told me to say hello to her for him. That alone isn't anything new here in my town but it was the way he said it, all smiley like he and her had an inside joke and just my telling her hello from him would be giving her the punch line, that made me think more than once about it.

In the car I get right into the back seat even though Momma says I'm old enough to sit up front with her. But I don't want Emma to feel left out so I stay in the back with her.

"It's Tuesday and I think Harold's just got through unpacking their delivery," Momma says. Harold's is the stationery store in town and Mondays they always get boxes of fresh papers, so we head there first since their boxes are clean and don't smell bad.

"Jackpot," Momma says, pulling up alongside the pile of flattened cardboard next to the Dumpster in the back. I'm glad about this, too. "Go on," she says.

We get out and lower the back of the station wagon and start loading in the pieces that are always heavier than they look when you first pull up. I count thirteen small ones and get sad, since Momma says thirteen was Daddy's favorite number. His lucky number. Our daddy never walked under ladders and was known to throw salt over his shoulder if the shaker spilled so you'd think he'd shy away from thirteen, it being unlucky and all, but Momma says he was full of contra-something-that-means-opposites so I guess it makes some kind of sense.

"Let's go," she says as we crawl back into the car, and we're off to the market. The all-time worst place for box-getting I can think of. Why would anyone want to put their favorite things into soggy boxes that smell like squash? I asked Momma this once and she called me little miss fancy and then gave *us* the box with eggplant written on the side just for spite. So I'm staying just as quiet as Emma, and I know from the way my sister looks at me that we're both hoping Momma gives us a Harold's box for the rest of our stuff.

At the market Momma parks and heads inside. "I'll be right back."

Me and Emma get out, too, and scan the

mess alongside the Dumpster here. Not a good box day. First of all, a lot of the boxes have tops and bottoms ripped off and the flaps on some of the others don't touch each other so if you put something in them it'd fall right through.

"I hate market boxes," Emma says. I'm a little surprised since it's the first thing she's said to me all day.

"Me, too," I say.

"I wish we could just run away," she says, and I nearly tip over since I'm squatting by the grape boxes when she says this.

"Why cain't we?" I say, all excited now that Emma's back on my team. Finally, a secret with my sister! Just like the good old days.

"They'd find us," she sighs. "*He'd* find us and then it'd just be worse than it already is."

"What if we went somewhere they couldn't find us?" I ask her quickly so we can get the ball rolling before Momma comes back out of the market. "We could go anywhere!" I say. "They wouldn't even know where to *begin* looking."

But Emma's shaking her head. Her hair is matted all the time now. Momma says she must have rats' nests in there but Emma won't let her comb them out and she won't let her cut it so I guess it's going to stay matted for a while.

"Yes, they would," she says. "They'd find us for sure. Grown-ups would tell on us and then they'd come get us."

Just then, before I can try to talk some sense into her, Momma comes out of the back door to the market, the one the delivery guys use, and she's looking right past us.

"Get in," she says, even though we haven't loaded a single rotting box into the back yet. Her voice is hard and low, almost like a man's. She starts the car and revs it up really loud and Emma and I look at each other and scramble in before she turns on us.

Momma hasn't turned on the car radio and that's a bad sign. Momma never drives without the radio on. Even if we're out in the middle of nowhere and all that comes in is staticky foreigners talking, she'll listen to it.

"I don't know how he thinks we're supposed to eat," she mumbles in an angry voice. "I had one nerve left and that man killed it dead."

We pull up to the house and when the car stops, the cloud of dust the tires make keeps billowing forward, like it thinks the car will catch up. By the time we get out and go to the trunk to unload, Momma's already slamming into the house calling, "Richard, Richard? Where are you, you son of a bitch!"

Emma and I take all the boxes out of the back and she makes a neat stack of them just outside the kitchen door but we don't go inside. No way do we go inside.

Emma turns and walks out to the meadow and I follow.

"Hey, wait up," I call out to Emma. When she sets her mind to it she can out-walk me any day of the week. I guess she has her mind set today.

I'm out of breath when I catch up to her. We're on the edge of the meadow where the cattails scratch our legs and the ticks look for ways to jump on board. So we keep moving till we get to the lower grass in the middle.

"We should just do it," I say. "Let's just do it. Before the move. There's a million and one places we can go to hide and they'll have to move without us. Richard's new job starts next Monday and by then they'll have to give up on finding us."

Emma looks at me for a second and then goes back to picking at the grass with her dirty fingers. I can tell she's listening.

"Seriously, it's a good idea and you know it," I say. "We could leave on Friday, they won't notice we're gone until Saturday, they'll look for us on Sunday and then they'll have to go. Richard won't care a whit and Momma will just plan on coming back to look for us later in the week and by then we'll be long gone."

Emma is looking at the tree that stands on the far edge of the meadow from where we're sitting. We climb that tree a lot, we know every branch, every knot. We know just where to put our feet. We can even do it in flip-flops.

"No way," she says.

"Why not?" I say.

"Because," she says.

"Because why?" I say.

"You sure don't think like you're two years older than me," she says. That just plain makes me mad.

"What's that supposed to mean?"

"It means we can't do it. If there's one thing parents don't like it's when kids run away. He'd kill us." She looks over at me. "He'd kill us."

And she looks serious as a heart attack, as Momma always says. But I don't get it. She's the one that started talking about running away. I'm going to talk her into it

119

if it kills me, and the first thing I'm going to do when we're living on our own is get her hair combed. It's so pretty when it's all silky and soft, like petals on a yellow pansy. She used to like it when I combed it so I know she'll like it again someday.

Right as I'm eyeing her she gets up and walks back toward the house.

"Stay out here," I say, but when she keeps on going I get up and follow her. Again.

We listen at the kitchen door and when we don't hear anything we open it slowly so it doesn't creak. We open it just wide enough for us to squeeze through and then we carefully slide out of our flip-flops and walk barefoot across the kitchen floor like it's made of broken glass. I'm holding my arms out to keep really steady but Emma can just walk that way without the arms. Upstairs we hear Momma and Richard yelling at each other. A thump. The sound of Momma hitting the floor. Each step feels like it takes forever to get past the landing outside their door but finally we make it up to the Nest.

"What're you doing?" I ask her.

"What does it look like I'm doing," she says back, like we didn't just have that talk in the meadow.

She's taking some of her stuff out of the box she packed just last night. The neat little piles are on the quilt on our bed and I think I'm getting my wish.

So I go over to my clothes and I pick just the things that I like wearing, not the things Momma gets me in town from the White Elephant, which everyone calls the hospital store 'cause the money they make goes to the hospital like it's some charity and not a mean old place where they stab you with needles. Those clothes are smelly before we even get them home, and when I tell her I don't like buying things from the smelly hospital store she calls me little miss fancy again and then makes me wear them for spite. So I leave those in the box and I fold the ones my grandma sent me from the store in Asheville and put them next to Emma's on the bed.

We don't say anything to each other. We just pick and fold and sort and soon we have enough to live in for a week at least.

"I'm going down to get the big bag," she says, as though this makes all the sense in the world to me and I guess it does since I am pretty sure we're running away after all.

Just then I remember the stamp book

and I get it from over by the fan in the window and I put it on top of our pile. I can't believe we're really going to do it. I thought I'd talk her into it but I thought it'd take a lot more work than this.

Emma comes back and the next thing I know we're loading our things into the big duffel bag. It's not as full as when Momma packs it up, but then again we're not as strong as Momma is so we've got to make it lighter all the way around, if we're going to put some distance between us and this life we're stuck in.

"There," she says, sounding just like Momma does when she clicks her seat belt closed after coming out from inside the bank on payday. Momma's always happiest after visiting the bank on payday, cashing Richard's check like she does.

"When're we going?" I ask my baby sister, figuring she's gotten it all figured out by now, anyway, so there's no use me trying to act all bossy.

"Tonight," she whispers to me. "After they're asleep."

I know I should be happy about this but all of a sudden I feel like I did the time Tommy Bucksmith hit me with the kickball on purpose. I cain't take in enough air. Emma, well, she looks better than she's looked in a long time. I figure I better be brave for her sake, so I am. At least on the outside.

"What's Momma going to do without us?" I ask her.

"What's Momma going to do with us," she says. And, just as simple as that, it's decided for one hundred percent sure. We're running away and nobody's going to stop us.

Six

"Shh," I say to Emma, because she's making way too much noise for a little girl who's supposed to be sleeping. It's two o'clock in the morning and we're already running late because we both fell asleep at midnight and didn't wake up until five minutes ago.

Emma is hopping with one leg in her jeans and the other dangling out, trying to keep the rest of her body from toppling over and making even more noise than she's making right now. Getting dressed in the dark is harder than either of us thought it would be. Good thing we planned ahead and laid out what we're running away in. "Shh," I say again.

When we're both dressed, we tiptoe over to the big bag that's sitting underneath the quilt in a big heap. We knew Momma wasn't going to come up here, she stopped doing that when I was younger than Emma is now, but we wanted to be safe so we put the quilt over it and stashed it behind some boxes that're pushed into the corner of the room.

"You get the end with the handle," I whisper to her. Emma goes to the end that has a tan strap that's made out of the same material my sneakers are and she grips it, squatting down alongside the bag, getting ready for balancing it like I showed her to before we went to bed.

The thing is, it's much heavier than it felt a couple of hours ago. I don't know why this is but I don't like it. We aren't saying anything out loud because Momma can be a light sleeper, but I'm thinking, Please, Lord, do not let us drop this bag. We're toast if we do. Please, Lord.

I look across at Emma and even though it's pretty dark, there's a line of light from the moon that hits her face and I see she's waiting for me to nod like I said I would when I got a good grip on my end. I nod to her and we back up to the top of the stairs and all of a sudden I think they're too steep. We'll never get down with this bag the way we're holding it. Plus my hands are getting sweaty on account of nerves and the bag's slipping so I bend my knees and hope that Emma sees that I'm lowering the bag. Phee-you, she does and we set it down quietly and just stare at it like we're both willing it to be lighter. That'll never happen so I open up my end and start taking stuff out. I cain't see very well but after two whole handfuls of clothes I try to lift it and it's like someone waved a magic wand over it and gave us our wish. I tie up the open end and nod at her again from across the big bag and we start again.

Taking one stair at a time we get down the Nest stairs without making a peep. Now we're in the danger zone — right outside Momma and Richard's room. I listen real hard and I think I hear Richard snoring, so I nod to Emma again and this time she can see me because the window on the landing is big and lets in more of the moon's light. This is going to be the hardest part because the stairs are old wood and sometimes creak when you least expect it — usually when you don't want them to. Sure enough, on the first stair I hear that dreaded *crrrreeeaaak*. It's so loud it might as well be the boat horn Richard once blew right next to my head thinking it would be funny to see me jump. Emma stops right where she is and we both wait to hear if the snoring stops. The door stays closed and even though I cain't hear Richard I'm guessing he's still fast asleep. It was a seven-squeak night at the trash bin so we've got that going for us. The next three steps are fine. But then, on step five, there it is again. *Crrrreeeaaak.* This one is lower and sounds like a cow I saw once that was lying on her side trying to push her calf out of her. We stop again and inside I'm praying, Please, Lord, don't let them wake up.

This time it's Emma that nods at me and so, since she's higher up and can probably see that the bedroom door is still closed, I keep going. After three more quiet steps we've made it to the bottom and we're almost home free. Now it's the front door we've got to worry about since the screen part on the outside can slam shut if you aren't careful. But tonight we're more than careful so I think we'll be in business, like Momma always says. I turn the doorknob of the inside wooden door before I pull it open and now all that's standing between us and freedom is a rusty metal screen. I push the latch in and open it in slow motion. No, slower than slow motion. I'm opening it so slowly you can't even tell it's moving. That's how careful I am and sure enough, it pays off: no creak! Phee-you.

Now it's up to Emma to let it close as slowly as I opened it. She reads my mind and does exactly what I did on the way out. Let me tell you, it's not easy doing all this while you're holding a duffel and I'm thinking to myself that when I grow up I'm never going to have a duffel bag. They are too much trouble to hold, if you ask me.

Emma lets the latch close behind her and we look off down the dirt driveway where Richard's truck sleeps at night and all that's in front of us is the rest of our lives.

It probably doesn't get dark like this in Bermuda. It's taking all my energy to squint into the night to see where we're heading, so I don't even think about how tired I was a few minutes ago. I'm not hungry, either, and that's a good thing since we didn't bring anything along but a half-eaten jar of Jif peanut butter I grabbed at the last minute.

Everything's asleep right now; the leaves aren't even crinkling against one another like they do when it's daytime and I figure that's because they're storing up their energy for tomorrow. Tomorrow. What're we going to do about tomorrow? I haven't said as much to Emma, but to tell you the truth I am a little worried about where we're going to hide when the sun comes up. We're not moving as fast as I thought we would so I don't think we're going to make it to the bus station to catch the 5:55 to Raleigh. I'm going to have to go to plan B. Trouble is I didn't really think of a plan B so I'm thinking real hard right now. Hmm.

"Do you think they'll find us?" Emma asks me.

"No," I say, even though I am not really sure.

"Good," she says, and she keeps walking.

"Hey, Em," I say.

"Yeah?"

"How come you changed your mind?"

I've been dying to ask her this question since yesterday when we came in from the meadow and she started packing up, but I was afraid to talk out loud about running away in case Richard was at the bottom of the stairs.

"I don't know," she says, but I don't believe her.

We walk some more.

After a long time of walking in the quiet, the bag starts to feel real heavy.

"When we get up there to the barn, let's set this down for a minute," I say.

The barn up ahead looks taller than it does in the daytime. The pitched roof is cutting into the black sky and it looks like a witch's den in the picture books we read.

In front of the doors with the crisscrossed white wood we let the bag fall to the ground and it thumps like a dead body's in it. That's exactly what it was feeling like, a dead body.

"It's so heavy," Emma says, rubbing her arms.

Then I get my idea.

"Hey, Em. What if we didn't take the bag," I say.

It's just an idea, I'm thinking to myself. We're going to need all the clothes we have in there so I don't imagine she'll go for it. Plus we only have fourteen dollars and thirty-eight cents to our names, so buying new stuff is out of the question, even if we went to the White Elephant. Which we won't. Believe me.

"We can't just not have clothes," she says. And she's right.

"But it's holding us up," I say in what Momma would call my devil's-argument voice. I think that's what she calls it. Oh, Lord, I'm already starting to forget the things Momma says.

"I know it," she says, and from the tilt of her head I can tell she's looking at it to decide what we can do.

"I got it! What if we take out the clothes we think we'll really need and we put them on over the clothes we're wearing and then we won't have to carry anything," I say.

"Yeah!" she says.

So that's how come we end up wearing all these layers that're making me sweat and making Emma look fat.

Best decision we ever made, though, let me tell you. It feels great not to have to carry anything but the Jif and my stamp book and I know no one really goes in that barn all that much so they won't find the big bag we left behind. At least not for days. By then we'll be long gone.

I sure wish I had thought to bring along a ponytail holder, though, because my long hair is really bothering me. It's hot against the back of my neck so I am trying to think about what I can use to hold it back.

Jackpot. Up ahead I see the long arms of a weeping willow and I know I can use one of the thinnest limbs that play the ground like it's a piano.

"Just a sec," I say to Emma, and I bend a branch back and forth to break it since it's still alive and won't snap off easily for me. But it's good that it won't because then I bend it around my hair in back and sure enough there's my ponytail. I feel cooler already.

"Are you scared?" Emma asks me. And

before I can even answer her I feel her little hand sneak inside mine.

"No," I lie to her. I give her hand a tiny squeeze to let her know it's okay to let me be the brave one for a change. But I don't feel very brave. At least not right now in the dark miles away from the Nest. Oh, Lord, what're we going to do?

While I wait for a sign from God telling us what to do next, we walk. And walk. And walk.

Emma has long since let my hand go and she's trailing behind me so I know she's real tired. About three times as far as I can throw a rock is the Godsey farm and I know that's where we'll hide out. Once, when we were much younger, Momma took us with her when she went to see Mrs. Godsey about something that made her spitting mad and we played outside while the two of them talked inside. We couldn't tell what they were saying to each other but the way Momma warned us about bothering them I figure it was top-secret money business. That stuff's really boring, anyway, so I didn't care a whit about finding out. I was happy because Emma discovered a hole under their front porch that was just big enough for us to squeeze through. I hope no one got around to fixing that hole since that's our ticket to safety once the sun comes up. We could even sleep a little if the coast is clear.

"Hey, Em," I say. "Momma still hates the Godseys, right?"

"I don't know," she says back. "I think so."

"Perfect," I say. Momma won't want to come over here to the Godsey farm to look for us so I figure we've got all day to plan out where to go later.

We're not that far from the front of the house and that's good news since it feels like the sun's about to wake up. Also, I bet the Godsey boys are working the fields today and my guess is they'll be up soon. The Godsey boys have black and sticky hands half the year from all the tobacco they prime. It's like they never wash or something.

We stop, trying to size up the side of the porch where the hole was, trying to see if it's still there.

"Do they still have that dog?" I whisper to Emma.

"How'm I supposed to know?" she hisses back.

"I'm just saying. If they do have that dog still you better get ready to run 'cause his barking'll wake up the whole house."

I can tell Emma's cranky from no sleep. I'm older so I don't get as cranky with little sleep.

No sign of the dog. What was that dog's name, anyway? I can't remember. It was something stupid, something a boy would definitely call a dog: Spot, Buddy or something like that.

I start over to the left side of the porch that looks as rickety now as it did back the last time we were here and sure enough, the hole is still there. Only it looks a heck of a lot smaller than it did when we crawled through it last.

"What happened to the hole?" Emma says quietly.

"Nothing happened to the hole," I say. "We just grew, that's what. We can still get through it, though. You watch. I'll go first."

Now this is a big deal, me going in first and all. There are probably a million different kinds of spiders and caterpillars hiding under this porch, and not the cute doodlebug kind of caterpillar that's fuzzy and soft. I'm talking about the scaly ones that have a hundred legs to make it run superfast right toward you. But I have to go in first because Emma's acting all weird, I can just tell. I'm not used to seeing her like this so I better suck it up, like Richard always tells us to do.

I'm on my knees right in front of the crisscrossed wood that makes an open-air wall with diamond shapes on the side of the porch. I feel like it'll be sunny any second now so I stick my head through the hole first, and sure enough, my shoulders get caught by the jagged pieces of wood. I wish I said cusswords because I'd say one right about now. What a good thing I don't because if I said the d-word like I want to, then someone would hear me, and if someone heard me then someone would find us and if someone found us then we'd have to go back home and if we went back home, Richard'd kill us.

I turn to the side a little and try to move in that way, but it's like the porch is keeping me out on purpose.

"Let me try," Emma whispers. So I pull my head out and crouch over and out of the way so she can try. What's that? Jeez-um. I think it's the dog.

"Hurry up," I tell her. "Come on!"

She hears it, too, and pushes her second shoulder blade past the jagged wood like it's only fingers holding us out. Next thing I know the sound is right above our heads. It's a clicking noise — paws on wood.

"Hurry!" I say.

She pulls her legs through and now it's my turn but it's amazing how fast you can go when you're afraid of getting caught. I stick my arm and shoulder in first, like I'm reaching for something on a shelf, then I fit my head through — but just barely, I feel the wood scratching my cheek — and sure enough, my other shoulder blade pops in with no problem. Good thing because the dog is now barking up a storm above us and footsteps are hurrying to the door to let it out.

Underneath the porch I feel around for rocks, the bigger the better. Any ones I can find I stack up in front of the hole so when the dog comes out he won't rat on us. Emma's taking off her sweater and balling it up and trying to stuff it in the hole but that's just plain dumb, if you ask me.

"Don't," I say as I pull it out and throw it behind me. "Rocks," I quickly whisper to her, but it's too late.

The latch on the door clicks and we both freeze. Like a bullet from a shotgun the dog busts through the door and down the steps, barking like he's seen a ghost, which is funny if you think about it since he kind of has. We must look pretty ghostlike to a dog in the almost-dark, if he was watching through the window like I bet he was.

Right when we heard him scramble down the steps, me and Emma, we hurled ourselves to the far corner of under-the-porch. That's what I'm calling it here. It's like behind-the-couch. I cain't wait to tell Emma I've thought of this. I just hope I don't blow it and say it out loud when I'm only thinking it like in school, because if I do then we're toast.

We both stay real quiet like we forgot to breathe. How big is that dog, I'm trying to remember, since what's left of the hole isn't that much after the rocks we've stacked. He's barking like a big dog and I'm hoping he is because then he'll never fit. It sounds to me like he's circling the steps, so I hold on to Emma just as hard as she's gripping on to me. We must look like two starfish with all their tentacles tangled up underwater. I can feel her shaking. The barking's dying down and Emma tilts her head to my ear.

"I'm never going to go back, you know," she says. "Never."

The way she's looking at me I get the feeling that she'd kick me to the curb if I told her to come on back with me, not that I'm wanting to do that, let me tell you. But, let's just say I did want to go home. I bet Emma wouldn't go, not even with me. It doesn't seem right, you know? I mean, in most families it's the younger kids who follow the older ones around. But with us it's always Emma leading the way. Except for now, under this porch. I think we're both the same kind of scared about getting caught. No telling what Mrs. Godsey would do to us if the dog roots us out.

Speaking of the dog, I cain't hear him so either he ran off somewhere to look for us some more or he's just plain lazy.

"I think he's gone," I whisper to Emma right up against her ear just in case.

Not a minute later there's the sound of the latch opening again and then tin hitting the wood planks over our heads. If I didn't know the Godseys had a dog I would've thought someone dropped something, but my nose tells me different: they've put dog food out. And that's not even bringing Buddy or Spot or whatever his name is in — that's what I'm worried about. Where is that dog?

"Caroline?" Emma's whisper makes my neck go goose-stiff. She never calls me by my full given name. It's always been Carrie to her.

Slow-like, almost so slow you can't see me do it, I turn to where I feel Emma looking and then I see why the dog hasn't run up to get his breakfast. Just on the other side of the diamond wall is Buddy Spot, down there on all fours, looking like he's going to spring up and chase after a rabbit, staring right at us like he's looking down the barrel of a gun. Oh, Lord. Please, Lord.

Emma and I stop breathing at about the same time. It's like we both know that if we so much as move a muscle, we're toast. Burned toast. It's that time of morning when the day can't decide what it's going to be — sunny or foggy, happy or sad — so it's hard to know for sure, but if you ask me I think there's smoke coming out of Buddy Spot's nose. Like one of the Saturday-morning cartoons. We stare right back at him like we're in a contest. Oh, Lord, I think I'm going to sneeze. Oh, Lord, please don't let me sneeze. If I sneeze, we're done for. I'll shut my eyes! That's it! I'll squeeze them shut like this . . . and then maybe I won't have to sneeze so bad. I'm squeezing, squeezing . . . oh, Lord . . . it's . . . working! I think it passed me by! Phee-you.

But just then all three of us, all at the same time, jerk our heads up to the sound of footsteps inside *stomp-stomp-stomping* across the floor toward the porch. Buddy Spot looks at us and then back up to the porch and it's like he's wondering if he should rat on us or not. Oh, Lord. He's wanting to bark, I just know it. Emma's dirty nails cut into my shoulder even more and I feel sick.

Stomp. Oh, Lord. *Stomp.* Please, Buddy Spot, I think to myself, go away. *Stomp.* Good Buddy Spot. *Stomp.* Nice dog.

And just like that he gets up, shakes the dirt out of his coat and trots over to the bottom of the stairs to get pet by a hand that looks like it has no owner since most of the stairs cut off the top part of the body standing just about four cattails from us. Buddy Spot's my favorite dog of all-time. Even better than Lassie. I cain't wait to pet him myself to thank him for not telling on us.

The way Buddy Spot, his tail wagging like it is, takes up and follows the hand makes me all the sudden miss Momma. I wonder what she's going to do when she sees we're gone. I wonder if Emma really means it that she's never going back. I mean, never's a long time. What about if she's all grown-up and has a baby of her own and wants to show Momma? Will she still never go back? Or what about if she gets arrested and the police say the only way they'll let her out of prison is if she goes home to her Momma? Will she still never go back? Or what if she's in a horrible accident and she can't use her arms and someone has to take care of her all the time and feed her mushy food like babies eat? Who's going to do that but Momma? I guess I would do that. But what if I'm dead? Will she still never go back?

The ground we're sitting on hurts my rear end and smells bad altogether. Plus I'm starving. Emma, she can take going without food, but not me. I need to eat something. I really miss Momma. I can understand Emma doesn't miss Momma as much as me since Momma's not all that nice to her, but I sure do miss her already.

It's morning for real now. And that seems strange since we haven't really slept, so it feels like the end of the day and not the beginning. Richard must be getting ready to move on and up right about now. Me and Emma, well I guess you could say we're not moving up or on, we're just moving out.

Emma lets go of my shoulders and I look down to see four half moons carved into my skin, marking how scared my sister was. She looks at them, too, and then looks away, like she didn't need me so bad after all. We both know different, though.

"What do we do now?" I whisper to her. I'm tired of being the leader.

Emma squinches her shoulders up and then down again and keeps looking out through the diamond wall like that's where the answer lies.

"Uh-oh," she says under her breath, and I look in that direction and I see it sitting there on the other side of the diamond-patterned wall, just out of reach. The bottle of Jif, knocked over on its side! I must've dropped it when we heard the dog and hurried to get under here.

"We got to get it back," Emma says. I just stare at it like I'm working on a magic trick that'll bring it to us. "If someone sees it we're dead."

Before I can say or do anything, Emma is crawling over to the hole we've blocked and starts unstacking the rocks.

"What if the dog comes back?" I whisper over to her.

"That dog's gone for the day, if you ask me," she whispers to me as she pops her shoulders on through and reaches for the peanut butter.

"Hurry," I say.

"Jackpot," she says once she's crawled

back to me. She quietly twists the lid off and holds it in front of me so I can get a fingerful. Peanut butter never tasted so good, let me tell you.

While I try to lick it off of the roof of my mouth, Emma counts on her fingers.

"We've been gone about seven hours, I bet," she says. "It's seven in the morning, don't you think?" I nod back to her because that's exactly what time I'd have guessed.

"I'm starving," she says. I'm working on my third fingerful of Jif so I cain't even open my mouth, though I do hold the jar out for her but she just shakes her head.

"Why?" I manage to say through peanut butter. I don't understand. When Momma makes us fluffernutter sandwiches we peel the bread apart and Emma takes the fluffer side and I take the peanut butter, but I never imagined she'd rather *starve* than eat peanut butter.

Then Emma does something I never thought in a million years that girl would do. She crawls back over to the rock stack, unstacks them again, pushes her shoulders through, pulls her legs out, too, and disappears up the porch stairs. Just like that. I am sitting here holding the Jif jar, peanut butter still in my mouth, and I cain't even breathe I'm so nervous! She's real quiet but I can tell she's tiptoeing up the stairs. What she is planning on doing is the shockingist part. Before I can even crawl over to the hole to get ready to save her from a Godsey she's back by the diamond wall and I cain't believe what she has in her hand. The tin bowl full of dog food! She carefully places it just inside the hole then pops herself in and stacks the rocks neatly.

"What in the h-e-c-k do you think you're doing?" I ask her this clearly since the peanut butter melted in my mouth after getting tired of waiting for me to chew it down and swallow.

"What does it look like I'm doing," she says, just like she did a few hours ago when she unpacked her box in the Nest. Then she cups her hand and scoops out some of the kibble. She doesn't even sniff it before she tastes it! She just eats it like it's ice cream on a hot August day. I sit there watching her and wondering how I could be related to a girl that would eat dog food when, above us, a door opens and flip-flops slap against the porch.

We freeze.

Emma doesn't chew and I don't breathe. Step one — *slap*. Step two — *slap*. Step three — *slap*. Right now I think I'm going to wet my pants. Step four — *slap*. Oh, Lord. Step five — *slap*. Ground.

It's Mrs. Godsey. Holy cow. Her feet are pointing out like she's going to walk away from the house, and inside my head I'm praying that's the case, but there's a pit in my stomach tells me otherwise. Oh, Lord.

"Where is that damn bowl," she says to no one. Then her feet turn to one side of the porch steps. We're so close to her I can see the pink nail polish chipping off her toes. Her feet turn to the other side of the steps.

Oh, Lord, we're toast. I know it now.

She's walking toward us. *Flip. Flop. Flip. Flop.* "What in the hell . . . ?" she mutters to herself while she bends over, and then we see her squatting just a couple of feet away from us, reaching for something in the dirt. She's wearing a housecoat like Momma has, only hers isn't faded, it looks brand new. The flowers on it aren't the kind you ever see on the side of the highway. They're bright purple and yellow and red, like Dorothy's ruby slippers. I know for a fact she gets her hair done up and sprayed at Luanne's Beauty Parlor that's not really a beauty parlor, it's just a room off Luanne's kitchen with a bubble dryer and sink. Momma says Mrs. Godsey's so vain she's jealous of her own mirror. She always wears lipstick, but right now, I guess because it's so early in the day, she doesn't have any on, but it doesn't matter, she's still pretty. What is she looking at right there in the dirt and why won't she go away?

Oh. My. Lord. It's my stamp book! Just as I see this, Mrs. Godsey turns her head and looks straight in at us.

"What in the hell?" She says this out loud now so we can hear it. "Who's there?" She claws her housecoat closed at the neck but she needn't bother since it's zipped up so far as I can tell.

Emma shrinks into me and I remember I'm not watching this on TV. It's really happening.

"Who's there? Billy, that you in there? Come out right now!"

Emma's pushing herself even harder into me and I can hear what she said to me not so long ago: "I'm never going back."

"You hear me, boy? Get out here right now." Mrs. Godsey has straightened up — all we see are her feet and a little of her legs but she's still there and from the sounds of it, not likely to walk away now.

"I'm going to count to three and if you

aren't out by then I'll tan your hide so dark your friends'll think you're colored."

"One," she says with her right foot — no, I got it backward, it's her left — tapping in the dirt. Even with flip-flops on it makes a pretty grown-up sound.

"Two."

I inch forward into a crawl and try to move toward the hole, but Emma's holding my ankle so I can't get very far.

"Three!" Just as she says three she's down squatting again. This time she's pushing the rocks in and away from the hole and before I can back up her arm is in and her fingers are gripping my arm! "Get out here on the double!"

Emma lets go of my ankle and I'm dragged by five fingers up to the beginning of the hole. She knows she has to let go for me to fit my way back on through, and I do, after taking a huge breath in for courage.

I cain't see her face as I pull myself through but I can imagine it's all twisted up in surprise. For someone who thinks a Billy is coming out from under the porch, a Caroline is quite a surprise, I bet.

"Good Lord in heaven," she says out loud. When I look up from the dirt I see she's gripping her housecoat even tighter at the neck.

"What in God's name? Is that Libby Culver's child?" She asks this with her nose all crinkled up like I smell bad. Then she looks back under the porch. "Anyone else in there with you?"

Here's the tricky thing: do I tell her yes and risk her hauling Emma out or do I lie and say I'm alone and let Emma go on by herself? Jeez-um. What do I do?

"Answer me, girl!"

"Um . . ." But before I can say anything else I see that Mrs. Godsey is looking back at the hole for herself. She's not going to wait for me to answer. Oh, Emma.

"It's just me!" I try but I'm too late. Emma is at the edge of the hole looking out at the way things are going to have to go.

I feel colder than frog toes. Mrs. Godsey isn't saying as much but I know she's mean and mad and that's not a great combination in a lady like Mrs. Godsey.

"I don't know whether to box your ears myself or just let your momma do it," she says. I cain't bear to look at Emma, since I know she's going to want to make a run for it and I don't know if I can do that right about now. I'm tired and those little licks of peanut butter didn't exactly quiet my stomach.

"Git on up to the house so I can call your momma," Mrs. Godsey says.

"It's okay, we'll just head on back, Mrs. Godsey," Emma says in a voice I don't recognize.

"Oh, will we?" she says, trying to get her voice as high as Emma's.

"Yes, ma'am, we'll go right back on home now," Emma says, "we were just playing hide-and-seek."

"Hide-and-seek?"

She's never going to buy that.

"Yes, ma'am," says the squeaky-high voice. "But it's over now so we're heading home. Sorry to bother you."

"Where's my dog's bowl of food?" Mrs. Godsey is bending her fat body in half to try to see under the porch stairs.

"I don't know," Emma lies. And then she takes off running. Mrs. Godsey is staring after her when I run off, too, and we're free again.

I thought I didn't have it in me to run, but as soon as I start I forget how tired I am so we keep going until the Godsey farm is a distant memory. Emma finally stops but she's panting so hard she might as well still be running.

"Oh, my gaw, I thought we were done for," I say between gulps of air.

"Me. Too." She's breathing so hard she says those two words like they're two separate sentences.

"Where do we go now? You know she's going to call Momma and Richard," I say.

Emma is breathing regular now and is looking out at the woods in the distance. She doesn't say anything, she just points so that's where we're heading right now, into the woods. I'm not talking about the kind of woods where little baby deer nibble on moss and rabbits thump their feet while they talk to skunks. I'm talking about the kind of woods that make the sunniest day look black and the hottest day cool. These woods are the kind that take hold of your shoulders, spin you around, shove you in the direction you *think* you were going in and laugh when you don't get there. Momma always warned us not to go into these woods and we pretty much listened to her. The trees aren't any good for climbing, anyway, they're tall with spindly branches that have lots of needles attached.

"I told you I'm not going back," Emma says.

"I know, I know. Jeez, give me a break. I'm not going back, either, just so you know."

"You want to, though, I can tell."

Well, there isn't anything I can say to that so we both stay quiet until we get to the edge of the woods.

"You think we'll be okay?" she asks me without looking away from the darkness ahead of us.

"We'll be just fine," I lie.

She knows I'm lying, though, so it isn't much use.

"Let's get on then."

The first thing you notice when you go deep into the woods is how soft the ground is. The layers of pine needles are so deep it's like we're walking on a pillow.

"You figure this is what's it's like when they walk on the moon?" Emma asks.

"I bet."

"Tell the truth, do you think they'll find us?"

Honest to God, I don't know how to answer this question so I don't say a word.

"Carrie?"

"Yeah?"

"Do you think they'll find us?"

"I really don't know."

"What were you thinking just then?" she asks me, slowing down her springy steps so she can hear me better.

"I was thinking about Richard's guns, if

151

you want to know the God's honest truth. I bet he comes looking for us with that shotgun he keeps in the garage."

Now it's Emma's turn to be quiet.

"You asked what I was thinking about!"

"I know, I know," she mumbles back through the bad mood that's been building up in her. "Richard and his damn guns."

"I can't believe you just said that word!" Emma never swears. In fact, she always used to tell on me if I said "darn" because she thought *that* was a cussword.

"Who cares. So you think he'll bring the shotgun?"

"I bet he will 'cause Momma will be too busy looking for us to notice," I tell her. "He loves that shotgun, that's for sure."

Emma is balancing on a tree trunk that's cutting across the path we're taking. 'Course it isn't a path so much as it's just space between trees. But this tree looks like it fell a long time ago since it has moss growing over it like it's being swallowed back up into the ground.

"What I don't get is why he cleans it all the time if it stays in the cabinet," she says, jumping off the trunk and springing on the needles again.

I just shrug my shoulders 'cause I don't know the answer any better than she does.

"Why'd Momma marry him, anyway?" she asks me, crouching down and picking at a little mushroom growing on top of a moss-covered rock. She's just filling the air up with words since she knows I have no earthly idea what Momma ever saw in that man.

"I'll tell you what," Momma said to me, standing in front of the television blocking the Sunday morning cartoons, "you are too lazy to hit a lick at a snake."
Deputy Dawg! My favorite!
"Caroline! You better get on up and get ready for church or your daddy's going to beat you to a pulp."
But Daddy didn't look like he's ready for anything of the sort. He was coming down the stairs smiling at Momma and rubbing his glasses with a tissue.
"You better do something about your daughter if you want a seat," she said to him, heading for the kitchen so she could fiddle with something in the refrigerator.
"Caroline Clementine, listen to your momma and turn that off." He came over with a tickly look in his eye. "Or you'll have to stand up front with Bobby Bolker and help him light all the candles."
That's enough to get me to do just about

153

anything. Bobby Bolker is worse than baked possum. He has white stuff caked in his ears and greasy hair that's combed down and clammy skin that looks like it's got dirt on it from when he was three and pretended anywhere he sat down was a sandbox.

"All right, all right," I told Daddy, who was already pestering Momma for a kiss in the kitchen. She was swatting him off like he's a hungry mosquito.

I practice remembering other things about Daddy. How he used to smile all the time when he was around Momma. And how he used to pretend to spank me when she told him to but really he'd smack the bed alongside me and I'd holler like it was really hurting and then he'd wink at me and leave me alone in my room to think about what I did to deserve the spanking. Momma never knew about it. It was our little secret.

Plus he smelled good. And Momma said he used to take me along on days the carpets were put in because I liked to do somersaults in the middle of the room when they were done, before furniture was put back in. I think I remember that but to tell you the truth, I'm not sure. To this day, though, I love the smell of new carpet.

Momma didn't leave her room for a long time after Daddy died. I had to pull a chair from the living room into the kitchen so I could reach the cabinets and get food because she didn't cook a speck during that time. Her door just stayed shut like old Mrs. Streng's mouth stayed closed tight when she saw me in the country store in town picking penny candy out of the glass jars when Daddy gave me a quarter. And the food I could reach wasn't the taste-good kind. It was cereal — which didn't have milk to soften it up; flip-top cans of baked beans — which we ate cold; and a bag of sugar that I poured on the dry cereal but ended up eating straight from the bag after everything else was gone. I didn't care. I used to love sugar, but now I don't like it one bit.

Her room smelled like sweaty socks.

"Momma?" I always talked to her. Just because she didn't talk to me didn't mean she couldn't hear me, I figured. "Momma, it's me, Carrie."

Her body looked so little under the covers. The only thing peeking out was the tippy-top of her head.

"Just wanted to say hey and show you the frog me and Emma caught." I didn't bring Buttercup into the bedroom, not knowing how Momma would feel about it and all, but if she said she wanted to see her I'd have run to get her from our bedroom.

It looked like I wouldn't have to make that trip, though. Nothing from the bed. It was dark with the shades drawn and I don't normally do this but I pulled the string to raise the shades on the window to let some light into that hole. The sun cut into the room like a flashlight beam and suddenly I could see tiny little pieces of dust floating in the air like they're deciding where to land. Maybe that's why Momma liked it dark — so she couldn't see the dust.

I know! I'll dust in here. Then she can keep the shades open.

"I'll be right back, Momma," I told her even though I guessed she wasn't going anywhere.

I love the duster. It's like having a pet bird, the feathers are so soft and fluffy. I went downstairs and fetched it from the kitchen closet and raced back upstairs before Momma had a chance to close the shade again.

"I'm back," I said, closing the door quietly behind me. Even though Momma hadn't come out of her room to check on us I didn't think she'd much appreciate loud noises. Maybe they'd remind her of how Daddy died. So I'd been closing the doors by turning the handle first and letting it go once it's lined up with the frame.

Problem was, the duster only pushed more flecks into the air and made it feel suffocating in there.

"Hey, how'd you like the window open for a spell?" I talked to her in the same voice she used to use with me when I felt sick and needed ginger ale and smashed-up banana to settle my tummy.

"I'm just going to open it a tad, get some spring air into the room. I wish you could see how pretty it is outside," I told her. The breezes helped me out some and soon I had the bureau top all dusted off and the trunk that sits at the end of her and Daddy's bed.

The night table was right up by her face and, even though her head was mostly covered I didn't want to make her mad by interrupting her sleep. I thought maybe I'd skip it altogether. Then again, in a way, the night table's the most important thing to get clean since it's what she sees most. I tiptoed over to it, quiet as a mouse. Before I started I leaned over her to check that she was fast asleep. Jackpot. So I moved all the pill bottles off, and the picture of Daddy and me from when I was weensier than Emma is now, and the glass of half-drunk water and then I let the feather duster do the rest of the work. It erased all the round circles from where the bottles sat for I don't know how long and soon you could see the real color of the wood like it was new from the store. I couldn't believe my luck, Momma hadn't made a peep. She'll be so surprised when she sees it all fresh in here, I figured. After I put everything back the way she had it, I cleared away the Tab cans from the floor by the bed. Most of them have tons of cigarette butts floating in the brown sludge on the bottoms so I'm real careful not to drop any and then, bingo! I'm done.

I tiptoed out of her room, leaving the shade and window open so she could have a room that didn't smell like the washroom at school.

It took me two trips up and down the stairs to empty all the Tab cans into the trash, that's how careful I was about not tipping them over.

When Reverend Cleary came over soon after his eyes got real big, he looked at me all sad and then patted me on the head and opened Momma's door. I looked around and couldn't figure out what made him look that way except the kitchen was pretty dirty and messy, worse than Momma's room. Two things Momma never used to let it get. I felt so embarrassed I went in and tried to pick up some of the trash but it was too little too late. There was one pile I didn't dare touch: it was a stack of old pans of food people brought over but bugs had claimed it and I was afraid to shoo them away. I didn't dare talk to Emma about it 'cause I was trying to be extra nice to her since she's the one who saw Daddy die.

She won't talk about it but I heard Momma talking to Mrs. Godsey on the day we buried Daddy and Momma said it was real bad. The men were after money, she said. I remember Mrs. Godsey saying that if they'd only known we were poor as church mice, Daddy'd be alive today. She said being poor's what killed him after all, since I guess the robbers got fed up and mad when they looked all over and couldn't find any cash. That's when they shot him. Right in front of Emma. They figured she was too little to tell on them which I guess is pretty much true. She didn't make a sound after Daddy died. Not that she talked a whole lot before, but she was learning her words and could even say "ma." After that she hardly made a sound.

I was playing in the side yard with Forsyth. We were taking turns pretending we were horse and owner. Forsyth would whinny and I would comb her hair like it was a mane and then hold my hand out with an invisible sugar cube on it for her to nibble up. Forsyth heard the shots and turned to me to ask if I knew what it was and, stupid me, I said yeah it was just some car up on the road because I wanted to keep playing. But Forsyth's momma's voice reached across the air and pulled her back home. When I saw her tucked in between her parents at Daddy's funeral she looked over my head, like she was more interested in some bird flying in the sky than looking at me, and I just got a bad feeling like Forsyth Phillips and me would never be friends again. Momma said Mrs. Phillips won't let Forsyth come over to our house anymore, but we stayed friends on account of her mother letting us play over at her house.

The blood was all over the front room. I didn't see it, but it's a good thing we didn't have carpet because it'd never get clean. A lot of people came in and out of the house before and after the funeral, cleaning up and bringing food and they all looked sad when they looked at me, but it only embarrassed me and made me run to the bedroom to help cheer Emma up. I heard them, though, talking their hushed talk about "poor Caroline" and about how well I seemed to be holding up, "considering." No one dared talk about Emma, I bet, because they knew that would've made Momma cry even harder. But to tell you the truth I was more worried about Emma. And Momma.

Momma cried so much those first days I could feel the wall shake where her bed was. Even though I was one flight up my bed is right up against the same wall. So I would just lay there and feel my momma hurt. Over and over again. Especially in the morning like when you wake up on Christmas Day remembering there was something special going to happen and then remembering a second or two later what it was. But this was the opposite. I'd hear her rustle in her bed like she was waking up and trying to fix her brain to remember what was going on, and then, sure enough, the wall would shake when she remembered what was so awful about the day. Every day that happened. Every single day.

Emma didn't wake up to Momma's wall-shaking like I did. When she did finally wake up she'd just blink at the ceiling. I'd snuggle up to her so if she did want to talk to me it could be a whisper so Momma wouldn't hear her and remember how Daddy died. But as it turns out I didn't have to pull her into me after all since Emma didn't make a sound for a good long time.

I think Momma must have stayed alive by eating at night, when we'd gone to bed. Sometimes she'd leave clues behind like a wrapper or some brown paper that used to hold raw meat. And Tab cans. Always Tab cans. She and Daddy kept cases of Tab they got at the discount store so we'd never run out and I guess that was handy now that Momma stopped grocery shopping altogether. But I never saw her come out of the room. Not once. She didn't even come out to make us go to school. And I couldn't just leave Emma all alone to get herself food and water — she was just a little girl! — so I ditched school. At first it was great. I'd look at the plastic daisy clock in the kitchen and I'd think about what everyone in my class was doing and I'd be so happy knowing I wouldn't have to do homework or clean the blackboard or anything. The only thing I like about school is geography. Most kids would tell you they like recess the best but I hate recess. Balls hit me like I'm some kind of magnet pulling them to me. Everyone knows it. They don't even aim them at me anymore . . . they just keep playing whatever game they're in the middle of when I come out (red rover, softball, spud) and it's only a matter of time until the ball bounces off my head or slaps into my back. I always try to act like I think it's as funny as they do but that doesn't work. I try to act like I knew the ball was coming my way and I wanted to get hit by it but that doesn't work, either. So I went back to square one and I don't act at all, I'm just jumping like a goof every time the ball comes near me.

So I don't miss recess. Not a lick.

Since Momma stopped coming out of her room, the clothes have started to pile up wherever Emma and I decide to take them off. I like the pile at the bottom of the staircase because I can jump onto it from the third stair and it feels like a pillow. Emma copied me once and fell back onto her bottom, but there were enough clothes so she didn't hurt herself or anything. But she didn't smile. When she forgot how to talk she also forgot how to use her mouth for smiling.

One day Momma was at the kitchen table when we came down from the Nest. Just like that. Like it was normal. I smelled the cigarette smoke from halfway down the steps and tried not to get my hopes up but ran the rest of the way down just in case it was really her.

"Momma?"

She doesn't really look up so much as she straightens her back a little and pushes her head back up on her neck so I can see she is awake.

I hug her and even though her arms just stay down by her sides I know she's happy I'm there. At least I think so.

Momma's eyes are like a jack-o'-lantern's eyes . . . all carved out and hollow and dark. It scares me but I don't show it.

"You want me to get you some breakfast?" I ask her, but then I realize she's not much going to like what we have to eat.

Her pumpkin eyes fix on me and then move to every part of the kitchen, like she's seeing it for the very first time.

"How're you going to do that, I wonder" are the first words she says to me in I don't know how long. She says them real slow like she's just learned to speak English.

"I can, you watch," I say. Maybe she'll

164

like my breakfast. It's easy. I use the mug that's got a picture of Sacagawea on it from when Momma and Daddy drove out west when they were real young — I fill it up with flour and pour that into a mixing bowl I know I should've cleaned days ago. Then I hold the bowl under the tap and count to five and then I stir it together to make a paste. The frying pan's already on the stove from yesterday so all I have to do is pour a little bit in and watch it grow into a circle that'll fill our bellies until later. The pancake turner doesn't slide under it all that easy since I haven't cleaned *it*, either, but hey, no one's perfect.

While the paste is cooking I sneak a peek at Momma, just to make sure she's still there, in the flesh. I wish I hadn't done this 'cause I hate to see her cry. It's one thing to feel her cry, another altogether to see it in person.

I don't ever cry about Daddy. Maybe Momma cried enough for all three of us.

"Okay, here's the deal," I say to Emma, trying to take charge since it's going to be nighttime and we're going to have to find a place to sleep. "We got to find a little cave or something so we can hide and sleep a little."

"It's not even close to being dark out!"

"Yeah but if we're out walking around during the day they'll see us," I explain. Where this is coming from I do not know, honor bright. Thinking of Daddy makes me sure we're never going back to Richard. "Night's when we're going to have to make our move."

Emma squinches up her shoulders again and follows me. She seems so happy to be away from the house and I can't blame her one bit.

"Tell me about Daddy again," she says, peeling the bark off a pine branch so she can make a switch out of it.

"You deaf? We've got to start looking for a hiding spot! This isn't Picnic Day, Em," I say. Then my heart hurts like it does whenever I remember something about Daddy.

Picnic Day was Daddy's invention and Momma tried it with Richard once but I wouldn't let her. Picnic Day was as good as when the teacher says class is going to be outside under the sycamore tree because it's the first warm, sunny day after the cold winter. Picnic Day was as good as peeling the skin off an apple in one long curly strip. Momma would make fried chicken and start packing the wicker basket the day before Picnic Day. Just like in bedtime stories we had a red-and-white-checkerboard tablecloth and Momma packed it first, all folded up into a perfect square. Daddy's potato salad would be chilling in the ice-box, crunchy with sweet red pepper cubes, and I would practice my fake cough so when I went into school they'd see I was "coming down with something." I threw that part in. Momma and Daddy said I shouldn't do it, but it was all part of Picnic Day Planning.

For that one day of the year I would play hooky from school and Momma and Daddy would take me out to the Pine Barrens on the edge of the ocean and we'd lie around all day eating Momma's chicken and Daddy's potato salad.

After Momma married Richard, she got it in her head that he'd just take up where Daddy left off with Picnic Day. She started frying her chicken and she even made cole-slaw (to take the place of Daddy's potato salad), but when she pulled out the wicker basket from the basement that stays cold even through the summer heat I told her what for. She never tried to start Picnic Day back up again. It died with Daddy.

"Over here!" Emma calls out to me from up ahead. She is bending over something and swooshing her arm at me, as if I was

Helen Keller and couldn't have heard her voice.

"What?" Finally getting to her. I'd been walking much slower.

"It's perfect," she says. "We can lie down alongside each other and cover ourselves up with pine needles and they'll never see us."

"I don't know, Em," I say. I didn't want to make her feel bad but this is not exactly what I had in mind. "Let's keep looking. I bet we find a cave somewhere up ahead."

"Aw, come on." She sighs and rolls her eyes once but she follows me so I guess it could be worse.

"I'm starving," I say out loud.

"Me, too."

"Hey, how come you ate that dog food? That was so gross."

I watch Emma do the shoulder squinch. "When you gotta eat, you gotta eat," she says.

"Just eat the peanut butter like a normal human being," I say. But right then I remember: the last time I saw that jar of Jif was under the Godsey porch before we got found out.

"I'm so hungry I could gnaw my own arm off," Emma says, starting a game we always play.

"I'm so hungry I could walk barefoot on sap and then bite my own toes off," I say.

"I'm so hungry I could eat dog doo," she says, knowing she's beaten me. There isn't anything worse than eating dog doo. It's a short game today, that's how hungry we both are.

"Start looking for those mushrooms you were picking at back there at the tree stump," I tell her. We both study the ground ahead of each step like it's a test we're about to take.

We don't talk for a long time. Every time we see a white speck peeking up from under the needles we squat down and take turns eating it. Wild mushrooms aren't so bad when you're really hungry.

"This isn't making me any less hungry." She says what I'm thinking about now, too.

"I know."

"What was that?" Emma stops walking and whips her head around looking to right behind us. Oh, Lord.

"What?" I'm whipping my head around, too.

"Shh! Listen," she hisses at me.

We're standing like we've had a spell cast on us that's frozen us in our tracks. I'm too scared to move my arm back down to my side, even though it wouldn't make a sound.

"Do you hear that?" Emma whispers to me.

"No," I whisper back. "What is it? Whatdoyouhear?" And I do say it just like it's one word.

"There's someone coming." She's not whispering anymore. Instead, she grabs my hand and starts running. "Hurry!"

And, once again, I forget about being hungry. I forget about being tired. I run like it's a life or death situation.

"There!" Emma pants to me. She's let go of my hand and is pointing to an old tree that looks as out of place in this pine forest as we do. It's a perfect climbing tree.

We jump onto its trunk like we've got suction cups on our hands and feet. There's no time to think about anything but climbing as high up as we possibly can. It's easy to do because just when we've pulled ourselves up onto one branch the next one is so close it's practically bending down to pick us up for the higher level. The sap is already making little pads on the palms of my hands — I can't imagine how much turpentine it would take to get all this off!

Emma's climbing faster than me but I have to wait for a second. I'm hugging a branch that's almost as thick as I am, one leg is wrapped around one side of it and the other, the other side.

"Come down here, you little monkey." Daddy's holding his hand across his eyebrows to block the sun.

"Look how high I am, Daddy!"

"I see you, monkey. You're doing real good. But you better come on down before you give your mother a heart attack," he says.

"Caroline, get yourself down from that tree this very minute or there'll be hell to pay," Momma calls out from the back porch where she's pouring her preserves into clean jelly jars.

"C'mon, monkey." Daddy's smiling at me. "Come to Daddy."

"Psst," Emma hisses at me. "Can you see what it is?"

"Wait a sec." I answer her while I shimmy my rear end closer to the trunk. The bark catches on my T-shirt and pulls it in the other direction but there's nothing I can do about that right now. I look down through the branches and it's hard to say for sure but I don't think there's anything down there. So that's what I tell Emma.

"You sure?" she calls back from above me.

"Pretty much." And then I just wait. So does she, I guess, 'cause it's quiet as a church on Monday. Then I hear rustling and grunting and I can tell she's working her way down to me and my perch.

"Hey," she says from a branch just an arm's reach from me. If I wanted to I could push her out of the tree, that's how close we are. "I know I heard something coming. I know it."

I reckon it's sap that's gone and tangled Emma's hair worse than before. Now she'll most surely have to chop it all off. Looking at her I cain't think of what to say.

"Whatever it was it isn't here now, though" is all I say. I go back to letting my cheek rest on the bumpy bark. I wish I had a mirror so I could see the marks it's making on it.

"I heard it, Carrie," she says again. "I swear."

"All right, you heard something. It's gone now. The coast is clear so let's get down and get going."

"Go first," I say to her branch.

"No, *you* go first."

"*Jeez*, Em. I'm tired of doing everything first. Why can't for *once* you just do what I tell you instead of the other way around." But I'm moving off the branch and down to the next level. I'm so tired right now I think my arms might not be able to hold on if I started falling. We *have* to get out of this tree quick-like. Otherwise one of us will fall for sure.

"I'm going first, but come on! You can't wait for me to get to the bottom to start going down — you've got to start moving *now*, Em."

This is the part I hate the most about getting down from climbing a tree. It's the part where you have to jump the rest of the way to the ground. It always seems to me I'm going to break my leg or something. This time I'm so tired, instead of jumping, I just let myself fall to the ground and it's not as bad as I thought it might be.

"Hey, Em, let yourself fall at the end. It's so cool. It's cushioned so it won't hurt."

Thump.

Emma's down, too, and we're on our way.

We're walking along and I start thinking about how neat it would be if you could have a carpet of really soft pine needles inside your house. Wall to wall. For people who don't live near a forest but wish that they did.

"I knew it was y'all!" A voice cries out from behind us.

Emma and I both scream and whip around. Standing there with a weird smile on his face like he just won a contest is George Godsey, the youngest of the Godsey boys.

Emma seems as relieved as I am to see that it's only George, since he's more a pest than a bully.

"Go on home, *George*," she says real mean-like, and she shoves him in the chest. I had to keep from laughing since the sap on her hands stuck to his shirt and pulled him back to her like a rubber band.

"You can't make me," says George, and I swear he sounds like he's three. "This is my forest, anyway, so I don't have to do a thing you tell me."

"Grow up, George Godsey," I say.

Emma and I turn back and start walking again but we both know George won't be leaving anytime soon. His brothers pick on him for sport, his parents ignore him altogether, and his friends, well, they don't seem to notice whether he's around or not, so two girls tramping through "his forest" is too good to be true for George Godsey.

"Whatcha doing, anyway?"

George has this real annoying habit of using the word *anyway* in pretty much every sentence. It all but drives me crazy.

"Nothing!" Emma and I say at the same time.

"Why you all the way out here by our place, *anyway?*"

"None of your business," Emma says.

"Is too."

"Is not."

"Hush up! We got to keep our voices down out here." I say this part mostly to Emma but George sure does need to stay quiet, too.

"Where you going?" George whispers.

Maybe if we ignore him he'll get bored and trot off home. I can see Emma's thinking this, too.

"Aw, come on," George whines. "What's the deal? If you tell me, I'll tell you somethin' I'm not supposed to tell a soul."

We keep our mouths shut and our feet moving.

"It's good, too. You wouldn't believe how good it is. Come on. Tell me what's goin' on that's got you all the way out here. Tell me. I'm goin' to keep buggin' you till you do so you might as well go on and get it over with. Tellmetellmetellmetellmetellme . . ."

"Okay!" Emma spins around and slaps her hand across his mouth to shut him up. Before she starts talking, she winks at me but the trouble is she just learned how to wink and she can't do it real well so George sees her wrinkling one side of her face up and groans under her hand.

"I saw that!" he says through her fingers. She carefully takes her hand away and inches up real close to his face.

"You better hush up, George Godsey," she says, real low and slow. "Now, if you *really* want to know what's going on then you better *promise* never to breathe a word that you saw us to anyone else in the whole entire universe —" George is nodding his head real fast and his eyes are practically popping out of his head like in a cartoon "— not ever. You hear me?"

Now I know Emma well enough to know that she's not fixing to tell him what's *really* happening, but deep down I'm wondering real hard, like George is, to hear what she's going to say.

"You swear?"

"I swear." George is holding up his right hand, like that makes the swear official or something.

"All right then." Emma gives me a kindly grown-up look that's supposed to make George feel like she's telling him something reeeaaally important. "You better sit down."

George would jump off the highest tree he could find if Emma told him to right about now, that's how bad he wants to know. He plops to the ground and crosses his milky-white legs Indian style. He hasn't taken his eyes off Emma.

"We found out our daddy's killers live in this here forest and we're on a mission to hunt them down." She blurts this out without once looking in my direction. How'd she come up with *that?*

I can tell this is better than anything George ever dreamed of. He looks like he's forgotten to breathe. After a minute he musters up some words.

"Th-this forest?" he stutters. "Are y-you s-sure?"

He's struggling to his feet and I can tell that George Godsey won't be bothering us much longer.

"Yep." Emma nods her head like she's in church, real somber-like, as if she's at a funeral. "They're here somewhere. We just need to find 'em."

George never even said goodbye. We

watched those spindly little white legs of his run his body all the way out of sight.

"That fixed him," Emma says to me.

And we're back on track.

"How come you said that about Daddy?" I whisper to Emma, even though George is long gone by now but you cain't be too careful, I always say. We've never really talked about how Daddy died — I always figured Emma didn't think about it, her being so weensy when he was killed and all.

"I don't know," she says.

" 'His killers live in this forest and we're hunting them down'?"

"Well . . ."

"Well, what?"

"They might live here, you never know. They never did catch 'em, did they." But this is more an answer than a question, so I let it go. She does have a point.

"Still." That's all I have to say. Daddy's my turf and she knows it.

"What was that?" She whips around, looking real scared. This girl has eagle ears or something.

"What was what?" I ask.

"Shh."

"It's probably George Godsey coming on back," I say real soft-like.

"Shh." This time she hisses it like she's mad.

So I shush.

And sure enough I hear something, too. And you cain't mistake it: someone's feet are breaking branches. And the sound's getting closer. We both look up and around for a good tree to climb but there isn't a good one in sight. Just a ton of pines.

"Don't move or I'll shoot your head straight off your sorry ass self" comes the voice that almost makes me wet my pants. I'm paralyzed from the top of my hair to my toenails. This is worse than we ever dreamed of . . . worse than anything we were ready for, I can tell you that.

"Well, well, well. What have we here," he says, and his voice sounds like he's smiling.

I can't even look at Emma. I'm too afraid to move my head even a tiny, tiny inch. I almost want him to go ahead and shoot us since I know whatever he does will be ten times worse.

"You can run but you can't hide." The voice is right behind us now and it's just a matter of seconds before he circles around.

Please, God. Please look out for us.

Number one is seeping down both of my pant legs but there isn't anything I can do about that now.

And here he is, standing right in front of us like we're a buck he's just bagged. He's in his hunting costume, the paint-by-numbers spots of gray and green and brown just as ugly as his face, with all its craters and moles.

Richard.

"Look at you, you filthy shit, all full of piss in them there denims," he says, pointing his rifle down at my legs. "Turn." He motions with the gun for us to turn back around. "Move it!"

I look at Emma for the first time and it makes me want to throw up. It's like she's pressed up against a wall, her back is so straight. Her head's the same way. She's like a little soldier marching into war. There's nothing but a blank look on her face, like it's made of stone.

Richard's been talking but I haven't been listening, I've just been studying my sister.

"Ain't no more of that, now, I tell you whut . . ." he's saying.

"Eatin' dog food," he's muttering now. "You want dog food? You got it. Dog food's whatchur gonna get. Yessirree . . ."

He pokes the tip of the gun in my back, shoving me to walk faster. I look over and he's doing it to Emma, too.

"None a this home-cooked shit for you, you little dog . . ."

Emma's tuning him out just like a radio and so I'll try to do it, too.

And that's the way we walk out of the woods, past the Godseys', past the red barn and up to our dirt-packed front yard. Momma's standing up on the front porch with her arms crossed like the wood trim on the barn our bag's hiding in.

"Look what I bagged, Lib!" Richard shouts way too loud, and Emma and I both jump out of our skins all over again at the sound of his raised voice. "Got us some dinner!"

Momma shakes her head at us as we're marched up the rickety front steps.

Richard's still poking our backs with the gun so we go inside, even though I don't want to.

"Momma —" I reach out to her as I pass through the screen door, but she flinches and backs up like I've got cooties. I feel the tears boiling across my cheeks.

"Uh-uh-uh," Richard says in that sing-song voice grown-ups use when they wag their finger at you if you've done something wrong. "You do not talk!" he shouts. "You hear me? You shut your dirty little mouth!"

Momma floats away and a sick feeling churns in my empty stomach. A feeling I won't be seeing her ever again.

"Do not stop! Go right on through," he says, but this time it's not a shout at least. "I want you to see what you've done. You see all these things waitin' to be packed up? You see this?" Shouting again. " 'Cause I had to go looking for *you* it ain't done. Now I've got to be up all hours of the night doing shit that *would have been done by now* if it hadn't been for you, little Miss Caroline and little Miss Emma or whoever the hell you are. I *don't even know you!* You ain't my blood. Y'all ain't shit. 'Sfar I'm concerned *you don't exist*. Go on —" he shoves us again with the gun "— go on out back. I got a surprise for you."

Where's Momma?

Out back is our shed that's been locked since I don't remember when and our clothesline that's empty for the first time in ages, probably because the clothes are all packed up and ready to move. And there, right smack in the middle of the clothesline and the shed, sticking up out of the packed dirt like a metal tree that's trying to grow, is a stake like someone would use to kill Dracula. Snaking out of it is a fat chain.

"Git on over there and sit down." He shoves us one last time, this time toward the end of the mean-looking chain. "You little shit." The boot comes fast and hard. This time it takes a little longer for me to get the air back into my lungs. Next thing I know he's kneeling over us like he's going to gut us and skin us. Instead the chain *clinks* and I jump when the cold touches my neck. It circles around just like one of the serpents we saw a preacher hold up at church, but this feels much heavier than that looked. It's not quite resting on my shoulders. Once the two ends meet I hear a *click* and I know deep down where you just know things, I know I'm locked to this chain. I look to my right, which is not easy to do with this fat metal necklace I'm wearing, and he's fitting the same contraption around Emma's neck. *Click.* She's locked in, too. But there's a big difference I now see between Emma and me. This chain is weighing the top half of my body down, toward my crossed legs, and Emma, even with her being smaller and all, is sitting bolt upright and acting like someone's fastening a diamond crown to her head, like she's proud to be chained up. With me all hunched over like Igor I can smell the bitterness of the number one in my pants.

The dirt from the ground is caked on the inside of my jeans and I shiver, even though it's hot out here in the blazing sun.

And that's how we sit for the next I don't know how long. Me hunched over and Emma straight as an arrow. Every once in a while from inside the house I hear a door open and close and a thump here or there, like a full box hitting the ground. The sun that's baking us moves to the side and — finally! — behind the shed so it's getting late, that much I can figure out. Emma and I stay quiet. What is there to say, anyway?

"Where's my girl?"

"I'm up here, Daddy!"

"Come on down here and give your ole pa a hug — we're celebrating tonight!"

Daddy could catch me from any stair I jumped from — even the seventh one halfway up. When he did he'd grunt and say, "Whatchoo been feedin' this child, Lib? You tryin' to fatten her up for the fair?" But he'd laugh and hug me real tight and I'd sniff the carpet smell right out of his shirt.

"We got ourselves a bloodhound, that's what we got," he'd say. "What'd I put down today, sugar?"

I'd breathe him in again to make certain.

"Industrial!" I'd proclaim, and Daddy'd get this surprised look on his face.

"I'll be goddamned! You're exactly one hundred percent right! Did you hear that, Lib? Our girl nailed it again!"

And he'd squeeze me real hard and set me down careful like he was lowering me onto a bed of cotton.

When Daddy was in a good mood like that, he'd swirl Momma around the front room like they were at a dance hall. She looked so pretty in Daddy's arms, swirling under him, her dress puffing out on the air like a doll on top of a cake.

Then he'd spin me around and I'd feel like a ballerina, soft and delicate, tall and graceful.

"You're my little princess," he'd say. "Daddy's little princess."

It's dark now and I'm lying flat on my back in the dirt, staring up at the stars. The same dirt that was cooking up real good in the sun is iron cold right now. It's quiet inside the house but the lights are still on.

"Psst," I whisper across to Emma.

"What?" she whispers back.

"What's going to happen now, you think?"

"How should I know?"

"You think Momma'll come out here?" I ask.

"No."

"You *don't?*" It never occurred to me that Momma might not visit. I've been pinning my hopes on it, to tell you the truth. "Why not?"

"If she'd let him chain us up like this, she'd let him do just about anything."

She's got a point here.

"What about food?" I ask her. Like I said, sometimes Emma's like the older sister, what with her knowing stuff I don't. Richard she knows.

"Don't count on it."

"So they're gonna let us *starve?*"

"Anything's possible."

After about three shooting stars I whisper over to her again. "We've got to think of a plan. There's got to be some way out of this."

Emma doesn't answer me.

"Emma! Listen to me. We can get out of this if we just put our heads together."

Silence.

"What're you thinking about?" I ask her after a little while longer.

Still nothing back.

"Em?"

"Why don't you just hush up," she says, and I have to say, she doesn't say it nice at all.

"You thinking of a plan?"

"No-I-am-not. *Planning's* what got us in this fix in the first beginning. *Planning's* what's gonna do us in for good. You and your big ideas. *Let's run away. We can do it. He'll never find us.* I wish I'd never listened to you, that's what I'm thinking if you want to know the God's honest truth."

"You were the one who started packing to leave!"

"Only because you wanted to run away!"

"No one forced you to go along with it. Besides, I was just doing it for you."

"Well *I* was doing it for *you*," she says through her tears.

"So you'd have been just fine staying here with Momma and Richard. Whispering your little secrets behind his door. I should've figured you'd take *his* side —"

I can barely get this out when a big weight drops on me and starts pulling my hair and hitting my face. I hit her back and roll her over to pin her down but the chain is all tangled up and starts choking me and her both. We're coughing and I'm clawing at my neck, trying to pull some space between the metal links and my throat when

187

a huge triangle of light cuts across us there on the dirt.

"What in the hell is going on out here?"

I feel myself going number one in my pants all over again, but at least it's warming me up. Emma and I are real still, hoping he goes away.

"You have to lie still if you want her to come. Tossin' and turnin's what's gonna scare her away."

"But how will she know I lost it?"

"The tooth fairy always knows when little kids lose their teeth," Daddy said with a smile and a wink. "It's in the tooth fairy handbook."

"Honor bright?"

"Honor bright," he said, tucking the quilt right up under my chin how I liked it.

"So be still and go right to sleep and when you wake up there'll be a bright shiny nickel under your pilla where your tooth is now.

"Good night, Princess."

" 'Night, Daddy."

The cold water knocks the breath right out of us. It soaks our clothes like Daddy's blood seeped across the floor he died on.

"That'll teach you to keep it down out here," Richard says, letting the now-empty tin pan clank to the cement kitchen steps. "Next time it'll be my fist that shuts you up."

I start shivering before I hear the kitchen door slam shut and it keeps up for a whole long time. I can tell by the sound of the chain links Emma's shaking, too.

Richard came along when Momma's tears had just about dried up. He rolled into town from "nowhere in particular." You might not think that's an honest-to-goodness place but it must be, since that's what Richard answered back when folks asked him about his roots. Momma caught his eye like a bee locks on a flower and he never let her out of his sight. He came by the house every single day, bringing weedy wildflowers he picked from the side of the road, that tin can of nails, a jar of half-eaten jam (he said he just wanted to taste it first to make sure it was good enough for Momma), and once, a pot full of spoons — something no one could make heads nor tails of. Momma took all his presents with her mouth fixed into a smile, but her eyes stayed cold and sad. Richard didn't know what Momma looked like when her eyes smiled, too. When she left the room to put the flowers in water or the jam in the icebox, Richard fixed us with a mean stare that disappeared the minute Momma came back.

"Your momma's gonna get hitched to the beggar-man," Mary Sellers called out to me during recess one day. I didn't even have a chance to think of anything to say back, Emma flew at her so fast, pulling her hair and walloping her in the stomach until she ran crying to Mr. Stanley, who was recess monitor that day.

It hadn't occurred to me that Momma'd remarry but once Mary mentioned it, it kinda figured. The piles of clothes that'd been growing all over the house were shrinking. The trash was being sacked and carried out. The dishes were scrubbed so good they looked shiny new. It was like Momma was trying to prove she could keep house.

"We can't go on like this," she said one day out of nowhere. "The money's gone and I don't have training to do anything that's of any use. I can't even multiply. And I'm not winning a spelling bee anytime soon, either, let me tell you."

It's true — Momma never reads. Not to us at bedtime or to herself. She canceled the daily paper right after Daddy died.

"We got no options," she said. And that was that.

Momma married Richard two days later at the Town Hall, wearing the same dress she buried Daddy in.

I couldn't look Mary Sellers in the eye for a whole week after that.

"Rise and shine!" The metal pan slides from the tip of Richard's foot to about one Barbie-doll length from me, two from Emma.

There, heaped into a smelly mound still in the shape of a can, is a wet brown mess of dog food.

I blink over at Emma. She looks worse than I do, I'm sure. Dirt forms a birthmark along one side of her face and sticks are stuck in her sappy hair.

She blinks back at me and sidles over to the pan, dragging the chain with her. Then she cups her hand like she's about to drink from a crystal-clear stream and scoops out some of the mush and eats it out of her hand.

I don't know if I'm hungry enough to do it. Then again, I'm too hungry not to do it.

"He must've gone and gotten dog food

special, just to torture us," I say more to myself than to Emma while I work up the courage to eat it. Just thinking of touching it makes me sick.

"Where's Momma, you think?" I ask her, but she's too busy eating breakfast to answer.

She looks up at me while her mouth works on what's inside and then reaches her dirty hand, filled with dog food, over to my face and holds it real gently for me to sniff and, eyes closed and careful not to breathe through my nose, I nibble and swallow. I don't chew. No sirree. I barely let it touch my tongue. I just swallow it and then gulp the air to try to get the smell and taste out of my mouth. She scoops another handful and feeds me again. And again. After I move away she licks the pan clean.

I must have dozed off in the sun 'cause I jump awake when I feel a shadow staring down at me. It's Momma.

It's strange that it's her right eye that's black and swollen 'cause Richard's right-handed so left sides are usually the sore ones in this family. Her top lip is twice as big as it should be so now I know what all she's been busy with this past night.

"Why you doing this?" she asks, her

hands hanging useless down to her sides. She looks like she's got a chain around her neck, too. "You bring this on yourself, you realize." She bends down over my head and I think she's about to stroke my face but her hand goes to the chain gripping my neck. Her hand pulls back when she feels the hot metal cooking against my skin.

"Don't fight him," she whispers, easing her fingers into the links to pull a bigger gap between the chain and my neck. "Why you gotta fight him? Why you gotta sass all the time?" She's still whispering, but I can tell she's not waiting for an answer. "You just bricks weighing me deeper into the river." She stands back up, looks across I guess at Emma, who's still sleeping. "I'll be right back," she says.

My head's too heavy to lift so I lie there waiting on her to come back. What's going to happen then I don't know, but I got nothing else to do so I close my eyes against the sun and I cook a little longer. Next thing I know the chain's rattling and I turn my head to see her squatting in the dirt, fitting a key into the padlock at the stake, freeing the two ends of the chain. Even with the chain gone my head feels too heavy to lift and my eyes feel like they aren't getting all the way open even though

I'm no longer squinting. I think they're swollen.

"Get up," she says quietly. "Take care you don't use none of your back talk today." She walks back into the house and leaves us to stand on our own.

"Em? You standing yet?"

"Yeah," she whispers back to me. "Here." She's holding out her arm to help me up and it's all I can do to reach for it. I'm sore all over.

"Where're we going to go?" she asks. "We can't go inside. For all we know he doesn't know we ain't tied up anymore."

I'm aching to sit back down in the shade of the tree in the corner of the back, but Emma's got a point. We better be scarce today.

"What about Miss Mary?" I say. Emma nods.

"I'll leave a note so they don't think we've run off again," I say. I creep over to the kitchen door and listen for signs of life, and when I hear the ticktock of the clock that's still left hanging on the empty kitchen wall I sneak in. It takes me a minute to find a pen, and then on the top of a cardboard box marked Kitchen I write "At White's. Be back later. C and E" and then I let myself back out the screen door.

194

Slowly, slowly we walk down the same dirt road that looked so long and magical in the middle of the night last night. It's shaded with freckles of sunlight on the two lanes leading us away from the house on Murray Mill Road.

A few doors down from White's, I see Charley Narley, but when he catches sight of us, for the first time *ever*, probably in the history of Toast, he turns away. He doesn't follow us and call out what all we're doing. He just turns away and looks off in the distance at what I don't know.

"Oh, my dear Lord in heaven," Miss Mary says when she sees us. I haven't looked in a mirror yet so I guess we appear as wrung out as the dishrags Momma hangs from the clothesline after cleaning. "What in the world happened to *you?* Mr. White! You better come on out here right away." She's frowning all scary-like. Instead of patting her lap like she usually does, she comes over to us, kneels down and reaches out to touch my face like I'm made of glass.

"Oh, honey, what he do to you?" is all she says. I look into her eyes and I see they're filling up with tears.

"It's okay," I say. "I'm just worried about

Emma, is all." Emma's neck is ringed in red burns and her face has dried dog food on it from licking the pan like she did, so I bet she just looks a whole lot worse than she actually is. It's just that she's wavering on her feet like a tall daisy on the side of the road when a big truck races by, pulling it almost out of the soil.

"Oh, my God." Mr. White's kneeling in front of us, too. He stands up then and says, "I'll get the towels and ointment, Mary. Will you go and fetch the witch hazel so we can clean it out?"

And they're all busy, racing to fetch the things we tidy up along the edge of the shelves. Miss Mary grabs a box of Band-Aids even though Mr. White hasn't asked for them and then she leads us over to behind the counter and to the back room where it's darker and cooler 'cause the air-conditioning unit's on full blast against the burning-hot sun. The witch hazel goes on first and stings a bit but dries quickly and knocks out the burning feeling I have at the base of my neck, which I realize now must look just like Emma's. Mr. White dabs gently at other spots on my face and forehead and then he opens a small metal tube that squeezes out clear jelly. That feels so good on my skin I want to throw my arms around him.

"Don't cry, honey-bear," he says. I guess I'm just so happy about the jelly. "We just cleaned you all up. You cry it'll get all gooey and messy." He smiles at me like he's trying to convince my mouth to do the same and sure enough it works.

"Can you fix Emma up, too, like you did me?" I ask him.

"I sure will, honey, I sure will," he says. "But I want you to lie down for a bit while I work on her. Looks like you haven't done a whole lot of resting lately, so you just come on into my office and I'll fix a nice spot for you to stretch out on. I'll bring Emma in to do the same when I finish up with her."

I follow him back into his office, which I've never been in before, but I'm too tired to look around now so I crawl onto a blanket he's rolled out for me on the floor behind his desk and I don't even hear the door click shut when he leaves.

I wake up once to feel Emma curling up at my back a few minutes later (I think) and then it's back to sleep.

Even though it's still dark in Mr. White's office I have a feeling we've slept for a while 'cause when I open my eyes I feel better altogether. I guess the sound of

Momma's voice on the other side of the door is what pulled me out of sleep. I shake Emma awake, too, so she can be ready, 'cause I'm certain Momma came to fetch us on home.

Sure enough, a triangle of light slices into the room when the door opens and the shape of Momma is standing right in the middle of it, outlined in yellow.

"C'mon, let's go," she says, her hand feeling up on the wall alongside the doorway for the light switch, which she flips up and the light blinks on above us. I can't tell from the three words what the ride home's going to be like but I know we better hop to. I don't even stretch when I stand up, but I'd like to. Emma does and it looks like she feels better for it.

"Libby, you sure about this? It's no trouble at all," Mr. White is saying off from the side. "I've got plenty of room in that old house of mine. Plenty. I can drive over first thing in the morning tomorrow. . . ."

Then I catch sight of Momma's mouth, which tells me it'll be a quiet ride home, for sure. Her lips are tight. When they're in a straight line like that I know at least I won't be hollered at. She waves us over to her and steps to the side of the door so we can march through.

"We don't need charity, Dan," she says over her shoulder while she holds the door to the outside open, meaning we're supposed to go straight out to the station wagon running out front.

"Of course you don't. I just . . ." But Mr. White's sentence is cut off by the jingling shut of the door with the bells attached. I wish I'd known this would be the last time I'd ever see Mr. White or Miss Mary.

The car door is barely shut when she puts the car in reverse and backs out onto Front Street and points the car to Murray Mill Road. At the light she taps a cigarette out of its box and pushes in the knob lighter on the dashboard. She waits until she's held the bright red coils to the tip of her cigarette and inhaled before stepping on the gas — it doesn't seem like she cares Mr. Jackson's behind us waiting on us to move 'cause the light's turned green.

"I'm sorry, Momma," I say from the back seat.

If I hadn't of talked Emma into running away none of this would've happened. Momma doesn't look into the rearview mirror, she just stares at the road ahead of her.

"I'm real sorry," Emma says.

It doesn't matter that she doesn't answer

us back. In my head I promise her I won't be any more trouble ever again. I'll keep Emma from being trouble, too. She'll be so proud of us. Also, she doesn't know it yet but I'm going to give her all the money I've saved from working at White's. She can buy herself something real nice for once. I've saved twelve dollars and fifty-seven cents. I wish I hadn't of bought those stickers like I did . . . then I'd have even more to give her. But twelve dollars and fifty-seven cents can at least buy *something*. She'll see. She'll be so happy.

Seven

Richard's truck is all packed up and Momma's calling from downstairs so I take one last look around the Nest. Emma's already downstairs but I told them I'd forgotten something so I could come back up. Goodbye, fan. Goodbye, leaning ceiling.

Momma gave me a scowl when I started to cry earlier so I gulp twice and it works.

"Caroline, you as slow as a crippled turtle!" she calls up from below. "Get yourself down here and let's go!"

Momma doesn't like to think about things too hard. I wish I could be more like that. Seems like all I do is think on things and pretty soon they're worn out in my mind.

"Comin', Momma," I call back to her.

Goodbye, Nest.

Richard's riding in his truck all by himself, we're in the station wagon with Momma and the day looks promising. Momma turns on the radio as she pulls us on past the mill barn. Emma's looking out one window, I'm looking out the other, trying to memorize what all we had here. I s'pose the next family to live here will enjoy the flowers in Richard's boots but that's about the only thing I'm happy to leave behind.

Richard's arm is hanging out the side of the window and he points when he's going to make a turn 'cause his signal light's broken. Momma's is, too, but she doesn't bother to point.

"Momma?"

"Yeah?" She looks at me from the rear-view mirror.

"Why didn't you and Daddy ever move away from Toast?"

She turns the radio down a speck and thinks on my question. "We didn't ever have to," she says, flat like a pancake.

"Why do we have to now?" Emma asks.

"Why you asking all these questions all the sudden? You know why we're movin'," she says. "Richard's found a good job at a lumberyard out by Murchison and we got to go. Now, I don't want y'all all sad like fallen cake. You got to look forward, not back," she says, but I bet she doesn't realize she's looking from side to side as we pass through town like she's trying to burn it onto her brain, too.

"I got handed lemons, too, y'know —" she keeps talking "— but I learned how to make lemonade with them." She slows for a second while we go by Mickey's and then keeps on going. "No one ever told me I had to add sugar but that's life for you. It ain't sweet."

This must explain why Momma always has that look on her face like her jaw's tanging up from the sour lemon taste.

"We ain't stepping in high cotton," she says, "so we got to go where the money is."

"Is the money in Murchington?" Emma asks.

"It's Mur-chi-son and don't you sass me after what all you've put me through these past twenty-four hours."

The radio goes back up. I shoot Emma a drop-dead look. She always has to go and ruin Momma's mood.

Day turns to night and just before it turns back into day again we see a sign that reads "Welcome to Murchison . . . Timber!" It reminds me of Bugs Bunny sawing down a tree and calling out "Timberrrr" before it falls to the ground. I guess that's the point.

It's hilly here and I keep waiting for us to roll through town, but after the timber sign we haven't seen a flea on a dog.

Out of nowhere and for no real reason there's a flashing yellow light and Richard's truck pulls to a stop so we do, too. He gets out and comes up to Momma's window. It feels strange to be stopped right in the middle of the road but there's no one around to mind, I guess.

"It can't be too far longer," he says, pulling the smoke out of his cigarette. "They said turn right at the yellow light, but ain't no right turn to make."

His arm is propping him up to the roof above Momma's head. She looks at her map.

"I don't know what you're 'specting to find on that map, Lib." She folds it back up and turns off the radio. Nothing was coming in, anyway . . . just static and talk.

"Let's just keep on, and if you see it sound your horn," he says over his shoulder 'cause he's walking back to his truck.

"What're we looking for again?" I ask Momma.

"Turn River Road," she says, picking up a little bit of speed. "Keep your eyes peeled like onions."

A few minutes later the trees clear back from both sides of the road and we see an old gas pump with a food stand right next to it. It's boarded up, but at least there're signs of life. A bit farther and the roads start coming: Gumberry Road, Sunnyside Road, Downtown Road. Lottie's General Merchandise sits right on the corner of Downtown Road and . . . let's see . . . it's a handwritten sign so it's a little harder to make out . . . Turn River Road!

"There it is!" I call out just as Momma taps on the horn twice to alert Richard, but it's too late . . . he's passed it. He slows down and turns his truck around by pulling into the gravel space on the side of Lottie's. Momma's pulled to the side of Turn River Road so Richard can be the first to drive down our new road to our new house. I bet there's no Nest, though, so I'm not getting my hopes up.

My stomach's in knots and I can tell Momma's getting ready for whatever we'll find 'cause she shimmies up in her seat nice and straight. Richard's truck slows and then crawls along past houses that get smaller and smaller and farther and farther apart so that soon all you see are numbers on rocks or wooden boards tilted into triangles alongside dirt paths that barely look big enough for cars to fit on. Finally we stop in front of a piece of wood with number twenty-two painted on it. Emma scoots over to my side so she can get a good look.

"Here we are," Momma says, almost smiling. "Home sweet home."

The scrub branches take turns tickling then whipping the sides of the car as we inch past them. All I can tell about where we live now is there's a whole lot of green. We don't dare put our heads out the window for fear of getting our eyes poked out. The trees themselves have wide trunks, like the kind Mr. Grimm writes about. The kind fairies dance in rings around. The branches don't start till halfway up the trunk, about as high as all the trees I've ever seen grow to be altogether.

Soon the hill gets too crowded with bushes and fallen branches to drive on — a whole tree is upended a ways up, its roots tipped sideways like a giant mistook it for a weed — so Richard and then Momma come to stops right there, with barely enough room for us to open car doors and get out. I look up and can hardly see the blue in the sky, for the canopy the branches are making. Under our feet, sand mixes with moss and pine needles, and it feels like I'm standing on a trampoline.

"All right then," Richard says, reaching into the back of the pickup for a load we can hand carry the rest of the way. "We'll do it on foot. Man ain't meant to travel farther'n he can walk anyhow."

Emma takes hold of a pile of blankets from the wagon, I grip both ends of a box, and we start picking our way over rocks, tree roots, and needles, springing our way up the slope to number twenty-two Turn River Road.

"Listen? You hear that?" Richard stops a bit up the trail. "That's a hawk if I ever heard one. You hear that, girls?"

I didn't hear a thing but our own feet crunching broken branches, but I answer yes all the same. Emma does, too.

Right about when my arms start to shake from the weight of the box I hear a whistle let out from ahead of us. Richard's found the house.

"Woo-ee," he calls out.

The trees and shrubs clear back to make room for the house, but just barely. They look like bullies waiting for the house to crumble so they can move back to their spots. By my guess they won't have to wait long; the house looks like it's about to give in. The roof sways low on one side like a horse that's halfway to laying down. The tall, pointed part of the roof rises over the front door, above four or five steps and after a few planks' worth of a front porch. There're windows on both sides of the door but they look like they're made of wood, they're so dirty. I'm sure that'll be chore number one if I know my momma. "Clean them windows, clean them windows" is all we ever hear.

The bowed part of the roof looks like it's missing a board or two, but that'll keep Richard out of our hair for a while so I'm not worried. The door scrapes along the floor when Momma pushes it open. She ends up having to shove it with her shoulder to make it wide enough for us to carry boxes through. Richard's dumped his stuff and is headed back to the pickup for another load and I expect we'll be doing the same before long, but I'm dying to see where Emma and me'll build our new Nest. Also, if it's two sides of the room we're picking between I want to call the good one before she can. I'm no dummy.

After my eyes adjust to the dim light, I see there's dirt everywhere — on an old wood table left behind in the middle of the room we walked straight into, which, I think, is the living room, on the walls and, most of all, on the floor. All over the floor. There's more dirt in here than outside the house, for crying out loud. Mixed in are leaves and pine needles and I wonder how they could've found their way in until I look up and I see a big old hole in the ceiling right above the living room and then it all makes sense. Up by the ceiling are what looks to be a couple of bird's nests and a dead tree branch that accounts for the hole in the first place.

Momma is still. She's holding on to her box like she doesn't want to get it dirty on the ground. There's no way of knowing what she makes of our new house that's not so new after all.

"It's nice here," I say. "I'll clean it up, Momma. You'll see."

"Yeah, we'll make it look brand new," Emma says.

Momma doesn't even blink.

"I'll take that box and go look upstairs," I say to her after I put mine down. But when I go to take Momma's off her hands I find she'll have no part in it; she's gripping it like it's a floaty round life preserver.

"Okay, well," I say, taking Emma's hand so she can see we need to clear out of Momma's way, "we'll be back."

The stairs have holes in them, too, so it takes some doing to get upstairs. We walk on the sides, hugging the wall, as we make our way up to the second floor. I have to turn my head to the side so I don't get cobwebs up my nose or worse, in my mouth, while I'm gripping the wall. The light's real bad on account of the dirty windows so it's hard to find a place to hold on, there being no banister and all. At the top there are two openings that look like they used to have doors, and sure enough when we get up close I can see where they jimmied the old doors off their hinges. The room on the right is a big square with a single window and a shred of fabric hanging on to the top corner of the window frame for dear life. The room on the left is tiny, like a sewing room almost, and I know that's the new Nest. Emma does, too, 'cause she goes right in it and spreads her arms wide for measuring. If we're lucky we can fit our old mattress in it. It'll be cozy in here. There's a bitty half window that starts higher up the wall than we are tall — once it's cleaned we'll have light in here, no problem.

The other room's where Momma and Richard'll be and that's all that's up on the second floor so we go back down.

Momma's still standing in the front room so we go around her and back outside to the car to fetch our stuff. Richard's pile is growing so we better get a move on.

Each trip back and forth I'd notice something new I hadn't picked out before. Like that the walls in the living room (where Momma's growing roots) still have patches of faded rose paper on them. And the left-behind kitchen table was probably left behind 'cause it was too wide to fit through the doorway. Richard says likely it was homemade right inside the house; the maker didn't figure on its going anywhere. And there's a fireplace on the far wall in the living room that's made of smooth rocks Richard says were likely pulled from the river — the water's what polished them. They're so big it must've taken years for the river to do its work. They fit perfectly on top of and to the side of one another. "You gonna move your ass or'm I gonna have to move it for you?" Richard spits right onto the floor of the house and swats Momma's backside good and hard.

Momma stays quiet the rest of the day. She just put her box on down where she'd been standing and she set to work cleaning, like I knew she would. She hands me and Emma a bucket and tells us to go find water. We don't bother to ask where to look, she doesn't know any better than us.

"What about down that way?" Emma points to the left of the house.

Around the side of the swaybacked roof we discover a narrow opening of beaten-down earth, so we aren't the first to walk this way and for some reason knowing this makes me feel better.

"Who d'you think lived here before, letting it get all broken like it is?" Emma asks me.

"How should I know?"

"I's just asking."

"Probably some old people who couldn't do the work that had to be done," I say.

We're walking single file 'cause the trail isn't big enough to go side by side. Emma reaches out every once in a step to brush branches or touch leaves. It's hard to look straight up ahead or to the sides since we're not used to the ground yet, and we don't know when a root or rock'll trip us up. So for now we're both studying each step we take. That's why we're moving slower than molasses.

"You think we can get a dog?" she asks, skipping over a fallen branch that's covered in moss.

"I wish." The rocks are just big enough to twist up your ankle if you don't step square onto them.

The sound of trickling water gets louder and louder and pretty soon the rocks sparkle with water.

"We have our own stream!" Emma calls out. "Look!"

She's right about that — there's no one around to call it but us. "We better name it before someone else comes along," I say.

"I saw it first so it should be the Emma River."

"We can't call it the Emma River. That's stupid."

"I'm calling it that."

"I'm not."

Then there's quiet where I can tell she's wondering how strong a hold she has on the name since it won't be much of a name if she's the only one to use it. I know I can wait her out.

"What about the Toast River?" she says. I have to think about it a minute. It's really not much of a river since the water moves just a bit faster than a drippy kitchen tap.

If you laid five encyclopedias down on the ground and jumped over them with room to spare, you'd see how wide our stream is. The bucket doesn't go halfway down 'fore it hits bottom, but it fills up pretty quick so Momma'll be happy.

"I've heard worse," I say. "What about Sparkly River," I call up to her.

While I'm filling up, Emma's balancing

herself on the slippery rocks up the hill a spell. Like on the fence she doesn't even hold her arms out, she just naturally keeps herself upright.

"You look like one of those storybook fairies," I tell her. And she does. Those fairies that live in the woods and crawl out from mossy kingdoms and dance in the moonlight in sparkly dresses. Not that Emma wears sparkly dresses. Her pants are torn on one side from the time she climbed out onto Forsyth's roof and was about to jump off to prove she could land like a cat when she slipped and skidded to the edge and then hung there until Mr. Phillips fetched his ladder to carry her the rest of the way. Her shirt's stained from tomato sauce or syrup or berries or some other kind of food item. And her hair's still matted in the back, like it always seems to be.

"Or Diamond River," she calls back to me. "That's it! Diamond River. That's the name."

"We got to get back," I tell her after the bucket's full.

She jumps off the tallest rock she'd climbed and takes up behind me on the trail, which doesn't seem so long on the way back as it did on the way there.

"Your momma's looking for you,"

Richard growls at us when he catches sight of us coming out of the clearing between the trees. Like dogs, neither of us look him in the eye. Me and Emma, we haven't talked about what all happened out back of the old house, but it's like we know if we look at his eyes he'll attack. Or he could. And that's good enough reason to stay away for good. I wish I could make it all up to him like I'm going to do with Momma, but with Richard there's no telling what'll make him happy. Today, it's hearing hawks and I don't think we can top that. Emma doesn't seem to think about that kind of thing since being good's never paid off for her before, but I remember from Daddy days that it *can* work.

"Caroline Louise Parker, come over here this minute," Momma called out in her angry voice. I followed the sound and wound up in the middle of the kitchen facing Momma and Daddy both.

"Yes, ma'am?" I said, but just looking at them made my eyes sting with tears.

"You have something you need to get off your chest, Caroline?" Daddy said in that voice that never got used by him.

"What, Daddy?" I was just buying time, I know. I started to cry but that didn't change a lick about the look on Momma's face. It melted Daddy's.

"Your teacher called over," Momma said. "She told us what all happened today in social studies. . . ."

Momma's voice was getting harder and louder but Daddy interrupted her. "What happened, Butter Bean? Why'd you do something like that?"

The answer is, I don't know. I got a pass to go to the bathroom in the middle of us drawing pictures of the Indians who lived here before all of us did. I was the only one in the whole bathroom when I got there and the next thing I know I had it in my hand.

"It's disgusting's what it is," Momma was saying. "I cannot believe I gave birth to a child who'd do something like this. I don't know how I'm going to show my face in town anymore, I'll tell you what."

Daddy's eyes looked about as sad as mine were, only without the hot tears.

"Didja just get some on your hands? Were there no towels or toilet tissue around?" Daddy asked me like he really wished he could understand.

I shook my head, but the minute I did, I wished I could have gone along with the story he was painting for me. That would

216

have made sense. I went number two and wiped it on the walls of the washroom 'cause there wasn't any toilet tissue. But that wasn't the truth.

"You are in deep deep trouble, lady girl," Momma said. "Your trouble's deeper than the Yadkin River."

"You mind your momma." Daddy'd given up on me trying to explain what he knew I couldn't.

He walked out of the room and my ears listened to Momma's plan for me making it up to school, to her, to Miss Hall, but my heart left the room with Daddy.

I never did something like that again but I never forgot it, either.

From that moment on I dedicated myself to being the best little girl Momma ever laid her turtle-green eyes on. I swept the kitchen out after she finished her weekly baking, making sure all the flour dust made it neatly into the dustpan. I took apart the black iron trays that fit together on top of the stove like they're puzzle pieces and cleaned each one by hand. I beat the front room rug over the porch the way Momma liked, watching the flecks of leaves and hair and dust catch wind and float away in the beams of sunlight that hit. I tried to do everything right so Momma would kiss me on the forehead at night before bed just like she used to.

It took a while before I could face Daddy, but it wasn't too long before he was calling me "Pea Pop" again and patting his lap for me to climb up.

So making things up to people works. Just not, probably, with Richard.

I've been trying real hard to keep the water from sloshing out of the pail but I tripped on a root and didn't count on the ground being so springy so I lost some of it on the way in. There's still enough in there to clean with so I think we're okay. My fingers have formed to the hollow wooden section at the top of the handle that is s'posed to keep the metal part from digging into your hand. My fingers went from hurting real bad to having no feeling in them at all many many steps ago. When I set the bucket down on the porch outside the front door my hand opens just a breath, just enough for the handle to fall out. It's in the shape of a claw, my hand. Opening my fingers one by one is like pushing a heavy door when it hasn't been pushed in a while, they creak with each bending try.

"Where have you been?" Momma flies

out from the outline of a screen door (it's an outline since the screen isn't there anymore, just the wood that holds it remains). She doesn't wait for our answer, she just grabs the bucket handle and, making it look like it isn't heavy at all, carries it inside the front room, which looks about the same as it did when we left, only I'm squinting now that I know it's dark inside the house.

"You need to be cleaning up these windows now that you're back from your little nature walk," she says, and a bristle brush splashes into the pail. "Soak the glass first with water, use this wet rag on the bar of soap to clean it, and then take the bristle brush and get all that dirt off. Mind you work on the crevices. Get busy." And she's gone.

"What're cre-vic-es?" Emma whispers to me, sounding out the word.

"Beats me," I say. "I guess we best scrub the whole window frame down while we're at it — that way we're covered."

Every once in a while Momma breezes through. She starts to unpack a box and disappears for a spell and then reappears mopping her way out of the kitchen into the front room where we're finishing up the last window. Richard clomps around upstairs, no doubt unpacking all they brought with them. He took a can of beer up there with him and hasn't been back down for another so I reckon that's a good sign.

I wonder about school and where Emma and me will go out here in the boonies like we are and then it hits me. Momma said before we don't need to worry about schooling and so that's what I start doing. Worry.

"Momma? What're we going to do about school?" I say over my shoulder. I felt her come back into the room from the front porch, the air sucking past us like it did.

"Don't you be thinking about school," she says. "I see a streak in the upper right corner of that middle one."

I back up to take a look and there it is. My rag rubs it out like it's a mosquito needs to be killed.

"But where're we gonna go?" Emma asks.

"Don't start," she says. And she's gone again.

Some days are talking-to-Momma days, some days aren't.

"Leave her be, child," Gammy is saying, "just leave her be."

Daddy's away again selling carpet and Momma's door's closed up good-n-tight.

My grandmother — we call her "Gammy" on account of the fact I couldn't pronounce "Grandma" when I was a bitty child and the name Gammy stuck — is staying with us for a while.

But she's not good with tears. Daddy told me that before he left town. ("You be good, Butter Bean," he said, squatting down so he could look me square in the eye, "and remember, your Gammy's not good with tears so you better dry up and mind your Momma, all right?") Daddy's good with tears usually, but this time they didn't stop him from leaving. Momma's door had been staying closed for a while before he left, even.

"I want my Momma," I'm saying, but I cough since I'm trying too hard to keep the tears back and some of them fall inside my nose, not outside like they should. "Momma? Momma, can I come in? Momma?"

"I *said* leave her be." Gammy's hands are at my back and I can tell if I don't move away from the door on my own those hands'll get a lot stronger. "Now, go on outside and play."

"Momma!" I try one last time, but Momma's door isn't budging so the hands show me where I'm supposed to go.

That's when I learned there are not-talking-to-Momma days.

By the time we finish cleaning up the downstairs windows Emma and me hug the walls and pick our way up the broken staircase to look at our Nest upstairs.

"Hey! The mattress fits!" Emma says. She makes it up the stairs much easier than me on account of her ability to balance.

Sure enough, the mattress is waiting for us across the small room, fitting perfectly between the two walls on either side with a bit of room to spare. I can even fit my stamp collection on my side of the bed so I can look at it anytime I want. There's a pile of sheets folded up at the foot so I unfurl them and crawl up to the top of the bed where our heads go, to tuck the corners in underneath. Emma takes the foot of the bed and before we know it we've got ourselves a place to sleep!

"Let's try it out," Emma says, crawling herself up to where she'll be laying in a few hours.

"The ceiling is much higher than before," I say. It's cozy in our room. My eyes trace the shapes the peeling paint has made up over us. "Hey, squinch your eyes almost closed and look at the ceiling — doesn't it look like it's clouds above us?"

"Yeah," Emma says.

The sheets are cool underneath us. Nothing better than cool sheets on a hot day, Momma says. And she's right.

"Why don't you leave well enough alone?" Momma says it more than asks it — in a low voice outside our door. I blink all the way awake.

"What did you just say to me?" his voice isn't near as low. There's no light coming in from our half window — no telling how long we've been asleep.

"Can't you see she's tired?" Momma answers back. I turn my head slightly to look at my baby sister, who just got stuck up for by Momma for the first time I can think of. But then the sounds move farther away, words bumping down the stairs angrily. A few make it to our ears and when they do I know we won't be leaving our airless room. The heat's trapped itself in here so we're lying on top of the sheets with our arms and legs spread as wide as they can get without overlapping onto one another, so what little air there is can move all around us. My nose is stopped up, even though it's far from the time of

223

year when that usually happens. My mouth is open and I soon realize I am panting like a dog.

"Emma? You awake?" I barely whisper, in case she isn't.

"Yeah," she whispers back.

"What do you reckon we'll be doing about school? It's weird how Momma didn't say where we'd be going."

I'm picking at my nails again. Bad habit. I don't need Momma to tell me that. I chew on my nails, but then they get so short there's nothing left for my teeth to work on so I go to the skin around the nails. Whenever Momma's around you can bet you'll hear "stop it" now and again. If I don't pull my hand away from my mouth right then, Momma yanks it so when I hear her, I stop right away. Even Emma's had enough. Lying on the sheet that's now sweaty, she hisses at me to stop, so I do. For a second.

"I don't want to go to a new school, anyway," she says. "Fine with me if we just stay here."

"Yeah, I s'pose," I say. But I don't really agree with her. Like I said, I was hoping to be the popular one at my new school. Plus, who're we going to play with out here in the boonies like we are?

224

Then, just like that, we fall back to sleep. Hot sleep where you turn over and you're cool for a second and then you realize you're just baking on the other side. No position's comfortable for very long. It's the kind of sleep that's just filling time until daylight.

"Hey there," says the woman carrying something square with a dish towel draped over. "Orla Mae, stop that scuffling — you're kicking holes into my legs with all them rocks flying, I swear to Sunday," she says to the girl who's walking a few steps behind her.

"Your momma home?" she calls out to me and Emma.

"Yes, ma'am," we say at the same time, and Emma pushes past me to go get her, spitting the word "jinx" out on the way. I run after her. I want to see for myself what Momma thinks of the friendly lady and her daughter.

"Be right back," I say to the two of them, standing at the foot of the front stairs, trying not to look like they'd love to come on in.

"Momma!" Emma's calling out through the house. "We got company!"

Momma comes out from a back door I

225

don't remember noticing yesterday. She's wiping her hands on her apron and pushing the pieces of hair that've fallen in her face back behind her ears. "All right, all right," she's saying to us. "Here I come. Now, go on upstairs and make yourselves presentable."

Richard cut boards the size of stairs and nailed them on top of the broken ones so it's easy to get to the second floor now.

"Hurry," Emma's saying to me, pulling one leg out of the ripped pants she's still wearing from yesterday and reaching over into a pile of our clothes that're all mixed up in a heap at the foot of the bed. "Come on."

"Don't! That's mine." I grab her hand just in time — she's trying to make off with my yellow button-up shirt. "I'm wearing it."

"Fine. Jeez-um."

We race back down the stairs to get a good look at this Orla Mae who kicks stones when she walks. They're out on the front porch with Momma.

"It's just down a ways, no more'n a mile and a speck . . ." the lady's saying. Now Momma's holding the square dishcloth-covered pan. "Take him maybe ten minutes on foot ev'ry day."

"Come on in, why don't you," Momma says when we open the screen door frame. I can tell from the tone in her voice she doesn't want them to take her up on it.

"Oh, no," the lady says. "We're on our way. Orla Mae here was dying to see who kindly moved in. We see your truck and car drive through town yesterday and ev'ry-one's wanting to put out the dog for you."

She looks down at us and shoves her daughter in our direction. "This here's Orla Mae."

"Hi," I say. Emma raises her hand like a wave. She gets shy with new people some-times.

The way Orla Mae looks us up and down makes me realize not everyone wears their pants until they're sugar-soft and high up above their ankles. She makes me feel funny about the fact that my toes are peeking out from the tips of my shoes.

"Want to see our stream?" I ask Orla Mae. She nods and follows us down the stairs and over to the trail by the side of the house.

"Well, I guess you best come in then, looks like they've taken a shine right off," Momma's saying to Orla Mae's mama.

"How old are you?" Emma asks her while we jump our way on the cushiony ground to the Diamond River.

"Seven," Orla Mae says.

"What's your family name?" I ask her.

"Bickett."

"You go to school?"

"Of course I go to school," she says. "I go to Donford. That's where everybody from round here goes. How old are you?"

"I'm eight, my sister Emma's six," I say.

"I've got a baby sister," Orla Mae says. "And four older brothers. They work up at the lumberyard where my mama says your daddy's gonna work. I ain't never to see them, though. They's much older. My sister's two, though. Ain't no fun to be around, just cries all the time. I helped her be born."

"First off, he ain't our daddy, he's our *step*father, our daddy's dead, and second of all, what do you mean you helped her be born?" Emma says all in one breath.

"I's at the foot of the bed with the lady who came to help Mama. I pull her out."

"Did not," I say.

"Did, too." From the way she says it, I almost believe her.

"Here's our stream," Emma says loudly, sweeping her arm toward the water.

"What do you mean it's *your* stream?"

she says. When she talks her upper lip curls up like she's sniffing dog doo.

"It's the Diamond River," she says right back to Orla Mae, not noticing Orla Mae crossing her arms against her chest like she's waiting for Emma to stop talking so she can prove us wrong. "It's on our property so it's ours and no one's going to tell us different."

"My daddy says your daddy's gonna work the smoke shift," Orla Mae says.

"*Step*daddy," Emma corrects her again.

"Your *step*daddy's gonna work the smoke shift," she says, minding Emma.

"What's the smoke shift?"

"It's the worst one," she says. "They got to be careful not to let the sawdust catch fire overnight. Your stepdaddy's got to keep stirring the pile and stirring the pile so's it don't catch on fire."

"Stirring sawdust?" I say. This doesn't sound right, either.

"Yeah," she says. "You gonna be working the boxes?"

"Huh?"

"For turpentine," she says in the way you do when someone's stupid. "You'll be working the boxes, I betcha. I work 'em. Summertime's when the flow's the best but the smell's the worst. I wear a cloth that's made from one of daddy's old shirts. It's tied around my mouth so I don't cough to'n much."

"Orla Mae Bickett! Orla Mae!" her mama calls through the trees. "We got to get a move on, girl. Come on now."

"Bye," she says, and she flies away like a bee after honey.

"Turpentine," I say to Emma.

Emma squinches her shoulders up and jumps down from the rock she's been sitting on above the Diamond River.

"How're we gonna know what to do?" I ask her, but really I'm not waiting for an answer since I know she doesn't have a one.

We take our time coming out from the stream, so when we get to the house the Bicketts have already gone and Momma's nowhere to be seen.

"Let's go up behind the house that way," Emma says, pointing.

I can tell we've been gone awhile 'cause my belly's growling at me to put something in it.

"Let's go back. I'm hungry," I say.

"Oh, all right," Emma says. And once again it takes us a much shorter time to get back to the house than it did to get away from it.

"Momma?" I call out while we're fitting

through the door off the kitchen.

"What?" she hollers back at us.

"We're hungry," Emma says.

The kitchen is much smaller than our old kitchen and it isn't near as bright on account of the window facing the tall trees. In a box on the floor there's some bread and a jar of honey so I figure we can start there and see how far that gets us. Trouble is, I cain't find any silverware to use to get the honey onto the bread slices, so we're going to have to do our best without them. I hope Momma doesn't come in — she calls us savages when we use knives and forks so no telling what she'd think if she saw us ripping the bread into sections, rolling it between our palms into little balls and then dipping the balls straight into the jar. A long string of golden honey stretches from the jar to my mouth. It's all over my chin and half of the dirty counter. Emma laughs and copies me and then it becomes a game — whose string stretches farthest from the jar without breaking. I take a step back and the honey stays attached. One . . . more . . . step . . .

"What the hell do you think you're doing?" Momma's voice makes me jump clear out of my skin and the fine thread is broken, falling gently onto the counter, where it melts into the puddle that's already formed.

"Huh?" I say with my mouth full. I turn around but Emma's run for cover. Where I don't know.

"Don't you 'huh' me," Momma says. And she swats my rear end to make her point. Trouble is I wasn't ready for the spanking so I tumble into the counter and knock the honey jar clear over onto the floor, where it rolls a few feet, spilling gold honey, before I can get back upright and get my wits about me.

"After all the cleaning I've done I've got to follow up after you like a damn maid?" Momma's voice is louder than I've heard it in a while.

"I'm sorry, Momma," I say, choking on the last of the honey ball still lodged at the top of my throat, waiting for a good gulp to slide the rest of the way down. "I'll —"

"I'm sorry, Momma," she gets her voice up high, "I'm sorry, Momma." And she wallops me good again, in case I hadn't picked up the point the first time around. Only this time I *really* wasn't prepared so my head bounces against the counter on its way down, which makes it a little harder not to cry. But I don't. Cry. That'd be the kiss of death with Momma.

"Get up," she yells at me. "Get up!"

I do as she says.

"Now get your sorry ass out to the front and get that mop. You're going to clean this floor till it looks new, that's what you're gonna do."

I make for the door but I stumble again on account of the fact that I'm clumsy that way and it's hard to get my balance after hitting the floor so fast. I swallow the blood from my lip and that helps the honey ball go down.

"I hate you, you little savage," she yells after me. "You hear me? I hate you. I hate the way you look, I hate the way you walk, I hate everything about you. . . ." I don't hear the rest 'cause I'm trying to hurry with the mop.

I know Momma doesn't mean this. She's just mad and when Momma gets mad she has trouble with her mouth — it won't stop moving, is what the trouble is. That's why Emma takes off if we're caught in the act of doing something Momma won't like. Emma acts all tough and grown-up but when Momma says that hate stuff to her I can tell it kills her inside. Emma's really not grown up enough to know Momma doesn't mean it.

The mop's just where Momma says, tilted up against the front porch railing, with the wet side up so it can dry. But when I carry it back into the house the pole part bumps the wall and makes a racket that I know will set Momma off again so I stop and lower it a bit and tiptoe the rest of the way into the kitchen to set about cleaning up the honey.

Momma's gone but I hear her footsteps over my head so she's probably back at work in the upstairs bedrooms, scrubbing down walls and floors. Emma peeks in through the kitchen door.

"The coast is clear," I whisper to her. She's careful when she opens the screen door, closing it carefully behind her.

Without saying anything more to each other, we clean up together. Emma picks up the jar and tilts whatever's left of the honey back in and I push the mop around over the spill. When you dip a mop into a bucket of water you have to do it slowly so you can stop pushing it down when the water rises up to the edge of the bucket. I forget about that the first time and water sloshes out across the floor before I can help myself. It's okay, though, since the floor's still gluey with honey so the water helps in the clean-up.

"You think you can just come in and fix yo'self anything your little heart desires."

Momma's voice makes me jump all over again. "A little honey on toast, please," she says in a higher tone, making fun of me and Emma. "Oh, thank you, don't mind if I do." She's leaning up against the door to the kitchen, smoking a cigarette, watching us clean. I'm careful not to look her in the eye. I don't want her to think I'm sassing her.

She starts pacing. Back and forth on the part of the kitchen floor that's clean already, her bare feet slapping against the wetness. "You think you can just come and go, pretty as you please." Back. "Not a care in the wind." And forth. "No troubles a'tall."

Emma's head's down, too, concentrating on the counter, even though that didn't need as much concentration.

"Get out!" Momma shouts.

This time I do look in her direction, but not into her eyes. I want to make sure she's talking to us, which, come to think of it, she must be since Richard's nowhere to be seen.

"Momma?"

"I said, get out." She's stopped pacing. "You deaf? Get out of here right now! I don't even want to look at you! Get out!"

I drop the mop pole and it clatters onto the floor. Emma leaves the rag she's been wiping with and we hightail it out of the kitchen, through the back door and onto the trail in back of the house.

"Get out!" Momma's still hollering from inside. When we're safe onto the trail we stop at the same time and listen to hear if she yells anything else. All I can make out is her crying.

"Let's go find Orla Mae," Emma says after a spell.

"How we s'posed to know where she lives?"

"I don't know, but we can try."

So we set out off the trail, along the side of the house with Momma crying inside, down the path that brought us here in the beginning and out to the main road where we saw the Bicketts drive in from. I cain't believe it took us this long to find our way out of the forest into the real world, but I'm glad we finally did.

At the edge of the road the sand mixes with soil and then the blacktop starts up, nice and smooth like it's just been tarred over. Clean yellow lines cut down the middle of it.

"Right or left?" I ask Emma, since this was her big idea.

"Let's shoot for it," she says.

"Rock, paper, scissors," I say, turning my

hand from fist into flat for paper.

"Scissors!" she says, her two first fingers chop-chopping into my hand. "We go left, since we ain't been that way yet."

"It's 'haven't,' " I correct her.

"Huh?"

" 'We *haven't* been that way yet.' "

"That's what I said."

"You said 'ain't.' "

"No I didn't," she says.

"Did, too."

"Did not."

"Em-*ma.*"

"Car-*rie!*" she whines right back at me, stubborn as a mule.

"Oh, come on," I sigh, "let's go to the left then."

It doesn't take long before we come up on another opening in the trees big enough for a car to make tracks through, but there's no telling whether this is Orla Mae's road.

"You can't see anything from here," Emma says, standing on her tippy toes in case whatever there is to see up the driveway is higher than her head. "We better just walk up and see what we see."

Three steps in and the barking starts.

"Dog!" a man's voice calls out from far away. "Brownie! Get!"

237

I've turned to leave but Emma calls out, "Sorry!"

"Who there?" the voice is getting closer yet. "Brownie, get up front. Brownie!" The dog's still barking up a storm.

"It's just us," Emma says. I roll my eyes at her. Like he'd know who "just us" is.

Then he's standing there. Right in front of us. Holding a shotgun that's almost as long as his whole body. He's the kind of old where you have no idea what his birth age is. He could be a million years old as far as we know. His hair's greased back, all shiny and gray, and his face has more lines in it than there are blades of grass in the world. If he's wearing a belt you wouldn't know it 'cause his belly hangs so far over where his waist is s'posed to be. He's scary-looking, especially the way he's scowling at us, which makes his eyebrows almost meet in the middle, above his nose, which, by the way, takes up a whole lot of his face. It's the fattest nose I've ever seen and it has bumps all over it.

"Brownie! Quit!" And, just like that, the dog shuts up good. "Who you? Whatchoo want here?" He's still scowling, but his eyebrows are working their way back to where they belong.

"I'm Carrie and that's my sister, Emma,

over there by that tree, and we just moved in a bit up the road."

He doesn't speak or move. He just looks at us, waiting. "Who's your family?"

"Our momma's Libby Parker and our stepdaddy's Richard Parker."

"You the Rutherfordton Parkers? Now, what was his given name? Sam, I believe."

"Not sure, sir."

"What you mean you not sure? You don't know who your family is?"

"It's not that," I explain. "It's just that we don't know who my stepdaddy belongs to. My daddy was a Culver. From Toast. His daddy, my granddaddy, sold farm supplies out of there, too. Anyway, that was our name, too, till he died and Momma got a new husband and then made us get a new name."

"Culver," he thinks on the name. "Culver. From near the Yadkin side?"

"Yes, sir."

"I knew of your granddaddy — he used to play a mean banjo, he did."

"I remember Daddy talking about that. He kept his banjo after Granddaddy died."

"Sure enough! Jordan's his given name?"

"Yes, sir, that's right."

"So, this Parker fella, you don't know

239

who his family is? Where he come from?"

"No, sir."

"I see."

"Number twenty-two. That's our house. Number twenty-two."

"The old Farley place." He nods like he knows it. "Whatcha want here?"

"Um, well, we were just looking around," I stammer.

"We looking for the Bicketts'," Emma calls out from behind a tree.

"They down the road farther," he says. I can tell he's still suspicious of us. He's looking at us like we's ghosts.

"Okay, well, we'll just be going on then," I say. Brownie the dog's back and sniffing my hand. I haven't looked down at her because I'm scared to take my eyes off the old man in case he changes his mind and points that shotgun at us square. He looks at his dog and his face softens up, the lines unfolding a bit, so I look down at her, too.

"What happened to her leg?" I ask him. Brownie's two front legs are fine, normal. Same with one of her back legs. But strapped across her back, right above her tail, is a harness thing that's holding up a wooden leg to take the place of a missing one.

"Got caught in a trap," the old man says.

"Years back. Had to saw it off her."

I kneel down to pet her, since now she seems like she wants to make friends with me. Emma's by my side, petting her, too. She's cooing her name over and over again and she looks like that's just fine with her.

"Ain't never seen her take to strangers like this," the old man says. He's tilted the shotgun away from himself, forming a triangle with the ground. "I tell you what. You got pig fat in yo' pockets, something?" And then he smiles. And just like it was the scariest frown I ever saw, his smile is the sweetest on account of all the lines framing his mouth, highlighting it.

"Just like a human, that dog is," he says. "Ain't got no one else round but her and me and I'll be damned she doesn't make the best comp'ny I ever had. I fashioned that wood leg for her after the accident. Couldn't stand seeing her try to get used to skippin' around the yard out front. I got's one, too," he says, lifting his pant leg for us to see his own wooden leg.

"Are you a pirate?" Emma asks him. I'm glad she does 'cause I'm wondering the same thing. Then again I don't know if pirates are for real or just in stories.

The old man smiles again. "Naw. Just lost m'leg is all. Name's Wilson."

"Nice to meet you, Mr. Wilson," I say, knowing Momma'd be proud my manners are getting better.

"Y'all come on by see Brownie when you want since she's taken a shine to ya, from the looks of it. Aw-right, dog. You let them get on their way, hear?" He pats his good leg so the dog'll come to him. She does, but not without some more pets from us before we straighten up.

"Which way to the Bicketts'?" Emma asks him.

"End of this path you turn left, pass three more of the same, and on the fourth you'll see 'em. Can't miss 'em."

"Bye!" we call out.

He doesn't say anything, he just turns to go back where he came from, but Brownie sits and watches us go, her tail wagging a half circle in the dirt. If a dog could smile that one'd be doing it right now. And I don't have any earthly idea why it makes me mad that a dog can be so happy but it does.

"Let's go to Orla Mae's tomorrow," I say to Emma when we're back by the blacktop. "All the sudden I don't feel much like going over there."

"So what do you want to do, then?"

"We better go back and see what's what," I sigh.

"Aww," she whines, letting her head flop back up at the sky, her arms dead against the sides of her. "But I don't want to."

"I know. Neither do I, but we have to."

"You reckon we'll be gettin' a proper supper?" she asks. "After the honey thing?"

"How should I know?"

We walk along the blacktop a spell and then she speaks up, her voice sounding old. "Hey, Carrie? You think Momma'll ever like me as much as she likes you?"

I don't reckon she will but I can't exactly say this to Emma without her feelings being hurt. I mean, it's one thing to know in your heart your momma doesn't like you that much, it's another thing to have someone like your sister spell it out to you clear as day.

"Sure," I say, wishing it were true.

"What do you think it'll take?"

"Huh?" I say over my shoulder.

"For her to like me," she says.

I cain't come up with anything so I just keep my mouth shut, like Gammy says to do if'n you ain't got anything good that can come out of it. After a spell of walking some more I look back at her.

She was almost finished wiping the tears off her cheeks.

Eight

"Hush!" Momma hisses at us from across the kitchen table. "You be waking Richard up with all your chatter. Now. Look at what I've written. Two-hundred and fifty minus ninety-seven. How you suppose we get that?"

"Mom*ma*," I whine at her. "That's so *easy!* Take one from the five, making it a four and the zero a ten and then minus seven from the ten, which is three, and carry a one over from the two to make the four a fourteen and minus the nine from the fourteen. Then carry the one that used to be a two down and the answer is one hundred and fifty-three. See? Easy."

Momma puts her forehead into the palms of her hands and doesn't say anything. But then, from her bowed head she says, "Miss Caroline Parker, I have one nerve left and you have worked it to the bone."

Her head tilts up and out of praying position. I know this look on her face means she's starting to forget me again, starting to creep back into the world inside her head. So I talk fast while there's still a chance she'll hear me.

"All I need is for you to sign the sheet that says I did what I was s'posed to do," I tell her. I swear, Emma has it so easy, all she has to do for homework tonight is draw a picture of our house and the four of us out front. Then she has to count how many chair legs there are in our whole house. That's so easy.

Momma reaches for the sheet from the teacher. "Give it over." And she signs it and I'm done for the night.

Donford Elementary School is about half the size of our old school, with half the number of kids there, too. Every morning since school started four weeks ago, we walk to the blacktop and turn left and wait for the bus in front of Mr. Wilson's house. Brownie waits with us every day, rain or shine. I watch from the window seat of the second row while she turns and waddles back up like an old lady, hobbling on her wooden leg back to her spot at the foot of Mr. Wilson's front stairs until we get home at the end of the day. Mr. Wilson says she knows the sound of the bus and heads down the path to wait until we step off.

"Carrie Parker? You pay attention, now. I saw that note you passed and I will not embarrass you by reading it out loud, but next time I won't be so kind," Miss Ricky says.

Here's what I wrote: *Orla Mae, do you like Johnny or what? He keeps looking back at you to find out. Check yes or no at the bottom.* And then I drew two boxes, one with "yes" spelled out on top and the other with "no." But now I'll have to wait until after math class to find out what her answer is since I can't risk Miss Ricky getting hold of it and reading it out loud.

Orla Mae rolls her eyes at me from across the row, but I can't tell if that's a yes or no. I hope it's a no on account of the fact that I like Johnny but she knew him first so if she likes him then she has dibs on him.

"So that's how we do long division," Miss Ricky says, closing her teacher's workbook. "For homework y'all need to do practice sections fourteen and fifteen *all the way through*. If you don't show your work I will count off of your homework grade. Is that clear?"

"Yes, Miss Ricky," we answer her.

The buzzer sounds and we're free.

"So? Do you?" I ask Orla Mae while I

pile my books on top of one another in order of their size — biggest on the bottom, smallest on top.

"What if I do?" she says.

"That means you do! I *knew* it!"

"I didn't say that," she says, shushing me so Johnny won't hear on his way out of the room to the hallway where it's loud and echoey. "I think *you* like him."

"I do not!"

"Do, too."

"What?" Emma scoots up to us outside of the main door to the outside. She always catches up to us when we're in the middle of a conversation.

"Nothing," I mutter to her, hoping she'll scoot away. Now that I'm popular it isn't so much fun having a baby sister tagging along everywhere I go.

On the bus Orla Mae and I sit together and Emma climbs into the seat right behind us so she can spy on everything we do and say. She sits by herself since there are only three other people on the whole entire bus and they spread out across the rows by themselves. Orla Mae and I are the only ones who sit two to a seat. There's Starlie Tilford, who lives kindly close to school but not close enough to walk. And there's Will Lawson, whose father is the big boss at the lumber mill. Finally there's Oren Weaver, who smells bad and had to go to the principal's office because he threw the chair that almost hit Coralie Coman in the head one day during snack.

Orla Mae's daddy is one of the bosses at the mill on account of the fact that his own daddy worked there all his life. Turns out she was right about Richard having one of the worst jobs of all.

Richard leaves for work every night after supper. We're careful not to say a word during the meal 'cause these days there's no telling what'll make Richard madder than he already is. Momma doesn't sit with us. She's at the sink or wiping the counter-top or passing over some plate of vegeta-bles that won't get eaten by Emma or me but will get shoveled down by Richard. Then she's packing up some food for him to eat later on at the mill.

"Don't put that shit in there," he says to her when he sees her wrapping up a tin of peas from the other night. "You know I hate them peas. Put the greens in from last night."

Momma doesn't turn around. "No more've the greens. I'll find something else in the icebox." She's real quiet, too. Her eye's healed up but her arm's still not better. It feels like it's been a month of her favoring it like she is, but it's probably only been a week. One morning we came down for breakfast and there she was, her right eye swollen up, her left arm black and blue with a cut down the middle. ("Oh, Momma!" I said. "Don't you 'oh, Momma' me. I'm fine. Got stung by a bee's all. Eat your corn cakes.") I just wish it'd go on and heal 'cause Richard gets all stirred up when he sees her wincing if she knocks it against something or if she has to lift something up with both hands.

Richard stabs another piece of chicken from the platter in the middle of the table and then lets it fall onto his plate.

"What're *you* eyeballing?" he says to me.

Without even realizing it I'd broken the rule of not looking at Richard during mealtime. "Nothing," I mumble to my plate.

"You didn't want this last piece of chicken, didja?" he says with his mouth full. "Boy oh boy, is it tasty."

I did want the chicken, but no way am I going to tell him that.

"Still hungry?" he asks me.

"No," I lie. My stomach is still growling on account of the fact that Richard only let me have the chicken leg tonight and that chicken was pretty scrawny.

"No, what?" he says.

"No, sir."

"That's better. 'Smore like it. A few more sirs and ma'ams round here won't hurt a bit."

After he sucks all the meat and juice off the bones of the last piece, Richard pushes his chair from the table.

"Where's my sack?" he says over his shoulder to Momma. He's gulping down the last of his beer and when he finishes he drops the can on the ground and steps on it, making me and Emma jump in our chairs at the sound. He gets a chuckle out of startling us like that every time he does it.

"Ah," he says. Then he burps real loud. "Aw-right then." He takes the paper sack from Momma's good arm and leaves.

We didn't hear about Richard's job from him, of course. We heard about it from Orla Mae's daddy one day when we were over at her house. He pays us a penny for every ten rocks we clear out of the front garden.

"Y'daddy does good work keepin' that stack movin' like he does," Mr. Bickett says to us. We're crouching down counting up the rocks in our three piles. I've got to be careful or Emma will steal one or two (or more) from my stack, but I want to know if Orla Mae's fibbing about the pile catching fire all on its own so I look up at him. Not square in the eye, just in case he's cranky like Richard.

"Does it really fire up if no one stirs it?" I ask him, careful to look beyond him to the woods.

"Sure does," he nods, spitting the brown juice from his tobacca into a cup he holds up to his lower lip. "In fact, that's why I come to let go've the last guy we had in overnight. Fell asleep right there with the iron stick in 'is hand. That pile of sawdust was so big you had to stand up and put both-a yo' arms into it. Shouldn'ta let it get that big in the first place. I know that now, yessir. But there it was all the same and Chancey Dewalls asleepin' like a baby when the flames swallowed up the dust faster than a hen picks feed."

"What happened then?" Emma asks him. She's crouching over her pile, too — like I'm gonna steal from her!

"What happened then is Chancey Dewalls went screaming outta the mill, half his body all burned to a crisp —" he spits again into the cup "— and it took a whole troop of us all night long to put out that fire. Lost a lot that night, mmm-hmm. Four cabinets for Asheville and thirteen chairs for a family over in Raleigh. Now, why you'd want thirteen chairs and not twelve or fourteen is a mystery to me, I'll tell you what, but thirteen's what we lost. Just like that. Took a while for us to find someone willin' an' able to keepa good watch over that pile. That's how we come to your daddy."

"*Step*daddy," Orla Mae corrects her father. "Her daddy died when Carrie was little."

"Hard luck," Mr. Bickett says, patting me on the head with one hand and reaching into his pocket for pennies with the other. "Sorry to hear that, child. Now, here's your pay. Good work, girls. Good work."

Four pennies for me. I love dropping them into the china piggy bank I got from Gammy back in Asheville. The plastic stopper that keeps the money from dropping out of the bottom was lost a long time ago so now a heavy piece of tape closes it up, but the pennies clang in against the others down in there.

When Richard stumbles up the front path to the house with the hole in the roof, his hair's the color of snow, there's so much sawdust stuck to it. We're just getting ready to leave for school so it's a bit noisy what with Momma calling out for us to get moving faster than we already are.

"Y'all're hollering all over the hill," Richard says, dropping into the chair in the front room. Momma fetches him a beer out of the icebox while I stack up my books to carry to school. Social studies one is the heaviest so it goes on the bottom for the others to rest on top of.

"Go on and get yo'self outta here," Momma says under her breath to me and Emma. "I'll see you when you get back."

"Bye, Momma," we say one by one, taking our lunch sacks from her good arm. And then we race out the front porch door frame that still hasn't got any screen tacked up in it.

"Jesus, look at you." I can hear Richard starting on Momma back inside but there's nothing we can do about it now. Brownie's waiting and that's all I can think about since I picked some leftover meat from the icebox to give her a treat this morning. I sneak that in whenever Momma isn't looking.

Mr. Wilson's waiting with Brownie.

"How'd you like to do some target shooting after school," he says to us while

253

we stoop over the dog.

"Target shooting?" Emma asks.

"Tin cans and all. You mean yo' daddy never taught you target shooting? P-shaw," he says to himself, looking out on down the blacktop to where it disappears over the hill. "You come on up after school lets out and we'll be takin' care o' that."

"But we ain't never held a gun," Emma says to him. I'm still petting Brownie, but she stopped the minute Mr. Wilson started talking.

"Don't matter," he says. "I teach you everything you need to know. Just do as I say and come on up offa the bus."

"I don't know," she says, toeing the dirt. "Momma's 'specting us right up after school. We got chores."

"You gots time for a lesson or two, won't take much."

The bus is coming at us so I pick up my books out of the dirt and brush off the bottom so the crook of my arm stays clean.

"See you then," I call out to him after Emma climbs up the first and steepest step. "Bye."

He just nods and Brownie wags her tail across the dirt. As usual.

"My daddy says you's nothing but white

trash comin' in here thinking you ain't."
Fred Sprague spits in Emma's path after
he says this loud enough for her to stop in
her tracks.

His friends laugh and that just makes
him bolder.

"Y'all think you better than everyone
else coming in from out East but you ain't
got two pennies to rub together to make
fire," he says.

"She can use her daddy to make fire
since he's gonna start one worse'n
Chancey Dewalls did up the mill, he so
drunk all the time!" Lex Hart says, slapping Fred, who's bending over laughing
hard like he's in a play.

"Take it back, 'fyou know what's good
for you," Emma says through her gritted
teeth. She doesn't spit but she might as
well have from the way she says this.

"What, you gonna make me?" Fred
taunts her.

"I'm so scared I'm wettin' myself," Lex
says.

"Take it back," I say to them. They have
no idea who they're dealing with.

Then, before anyone can say or do anything, Emma flies at them like a bat out of
the attic, swinging punches at Fred and
Lex both. Fred falls to the pavement with

Emma attached to his neck and Lex is so surprised he takes some time before he realizes he should be pulling Emma off of his friend. When he does reach for her she turns her head and bites him. Hard.

"Ow!" he shouts, shaking his hand. "She bit me!"

"Get her offa me!" Fred's shouting, trying to hold her back and protect his face at the same time. Emma's still swinging. To buy her more time, I get behind Lex and pull him back so he cain't reach Emma. This backfires, though, 'cause he whips around and wallops me so hard across the middle I gotta let him go. The wind's knocked so far outta me I fold in half and gulp like a dog trying to get molasses out of his mouth. I look over at Emma's hand and it's bloody. Funny thing about Emma is even though she draws pictures with her right hand, she punches with her left. That's the hand that's all red.

"There!" she says. She pushes herself up and off of Fred and brushes the dirt off of the front of her shirt. "I took it back for you." And, just like that, with Fred staring up at her through his one unswollen eye, Emma marches off, paying no mind whatsoever to her crushed hand. I wish I could ignore my sore middle where I got hit but I feel it every time I take a breath in.

I run like a cripple but I finally catch up to her. "You're gonna get it," I tell her.

"I don't care," she sniffs. " 'Sides, you were in there, too, so *you're* gonna get it."

"Why'd you stick up for Richard like that? Who cares what they say about *him?*"

"They weren't talking about *him*," she says, "they were talking about *us*."

"You're still gonna get it."

She shrugs and keeps on walking. "So're you."

By the time the bus stops in front of Mr. Wilson's driveway, Emma's punching hand is twice as big as the other one.

We both look down at it.

"Guess you don't feel much like target shooting today," I say.

"Yeah I do," she says. "I'd use the other hand, anyway. . . ."

"I don't know," I say. "Let's just tell him we got to get back on home. He won't care." Truth is, I don't feel like shooting anymore.

"Come *on*," she whines to me like I'm her momma and not her sister.

Emma steps off the final step and pets Brownie with her good hand, holding the other one behind her back in case Mr. Wilson walks down to meet us.

"Let's go home," I say. "He's not even here."

But he isn't so we walk up the blacktop a ways till we see the clearing that leads to number twenty-two. Emma takes in a deep breath and then follows me in. Just in front of the house is a pickup truck we never seen before.

"Who's that?"

Emma sighs and shakes her hair out of her face. "It's Mrs. Sprague."

"How do you know?"

"It's bound to be her." She sighs again.

"Wanna go back to Mr. Wilson's? We can wait her out over there and then sneak back when the truck's gone. C'mon."

"We got to get it over with," she says, walking toward the house with the hole in the roof. "Let's meet back out here after. We can go back over to Mr. Wilson's."

"You sure?" I cain't believe she'd still feel like shooting after the whipping she's about to git. But I wait for her, anyway.

"Well, well, well," Momma's saying as we march up to the steps in front of the truck. "What do you have to say for yourself before you get your whipping?"

I don't hear what Emma says but I hear Momma clear as day.

"You damn well *better* apologize or you'll

get yourself ten extra licks!"

That's enough for me. "Sorry," I say as loudly as I can without having to take too deep a breath.

Emma's voice is too faint to make out, but pretty soon Mrs. Sprague climbs back into the truck with Fred scrambling up on his side and it sputters to starting.

Momma and Emma are gone when the truck clears out. "Git on over here," Momma's calling to me from inside the house. "Why you got to act up every single time I turn my back? Huh?" The sound of the strap catching wind on its way to skin is probably the worst sound in the universe. I guess we'll be sleeping on our bellies tonight. It takes a while for Emma to finish up after me, but here she comes, walking careful the entire way down to me. Before too long our feet are taking us right back down the blacktop and over to Mr. Wilson's.

"Seems to me sumpen's wrong wit' you kids today when shooting at a tin can is sumpen you ain't been doing since birth," he says.

"I'm only eight," I say. "My sister's six. We ain't too growned up yet."

He just shakes his head and walks over

to the fence to put the cans one-two-three right in a row. Emma hangs way back watching since her backside's no doubt sore as all get out right now. So's mine but I'm older. I've had way more experience with it.

"Now —" he spits and picks up the gun "— I'll show you what I'm talking 'bout and then we git to know the gun a little."

He puts the gun against his shoulder and *pow!* He fires the first shot without even telling me he's gonna do it. It's so loud I feel like it split my head clean open.

"Go on over an see if I made my mark," he orders at me. He talks a bit loud and I figure it's 'cause his ears are ringing, too.

Up at the top fence rail the two cans sit tall and proud but the third's down and I have to climb through the bottom rungs to fetch it.

"You did it!" I call out to him. Right there in the middle of the curved can is a big old hole where the bullet pushed through. I look through it back at him like it's a telescope. Brownie must know he did it right 'cause she's wagging that tail of hers in the dirt.

"Git back over here and I'll do it again," he says. And I scramble back through and run across the dirt and rocks toward him before he fires again. This time I'm not taking any chances. I hold my ears the whole way.

Pow! Pow!

I hustle back over and pick up the last two cans and sure enough: holes right through the middle sections of each.

"Wow," I say to him as I get back close. "Can I try? Can I try?"

"Sure can," he says. "But first you got to learn to respect the gun. To respect it, you got to learn it good. My pappy taught me just like I'm teachin' you. It's not too hard but you got to learn it good, you hear me, girl?"

"Yes, sir," I say.

"This here's the chamber." He holds the gun out to me like it's a towel draped across his hands. "Ain't got no bullets left in it right now so it's okay if you hold it. That's right, hold it careful. With respect. Don't ever aim it at anyone like you doing right now. That's bad. Aim it out to the fence while I'm talking to you else the lesson's over. Now, this here — put your finger right there — good. That there is the catch. That's got to be off if'n you mean business. Once that catch is off the bullet knows it could be called on at any minute. That there's — no, feel right here. That's right — that's the safety. That's on in case the catch comes undone by mistake. That safety gets pushed off and then you're good to go. This here, this is the most dang'rous part of all — it's the trigger. So you gots the catch, the safety and the trigger. They all there to make it happen for you. Slide your finger in against that trigger and feel what it's like. That's right. You got a nat'ral stand right there. That's good. That cain't be taught good. You either got it or you don't. Do like I did and hole it up to your shoulder — no, the other way . . . that's right — and feel how heavy it is. This one here's one of the heaviest of guns they making. My pappy done shot a good number'f white tails wit' this here gun and I reckon I add to it ev'ry coupla weeks in season. Now. Bring it back down and give it over. I s'pose you ready now for a bullet in that chamber. I just cock this part open and slide a bullet in it — see how it fits in there? I slide it in like that. There. I click it back closed and the bullet's aimed down the shoot like it s'posed to be. Now put it back on your shoulder . . ."

"Am I gonna shoot now?" I feel sick at my stomach. The gun feels much heavier with the bullet in it, even though the bullet weighs no more than a pin.

"Yep, you gonna shoot off at the fence. But first you got to hand it back to me so I can set up the cans fer you."

I do as he says. He walks over to the fence, swinging his wooden leg out in front of his good one slowly with each step.

One, two, then three cans are set back up on the top of the fence rail.

When he comes back he gets behind me before settling the gun in my hands from over my head and shoulders.

"Now. Remember what I taught you, girl," he says. "Look through the crosshair until that can is right in the middle of where the two lines meet up. Once you get it there slip the safety off and slide your finger in front of the trigger . . ."

"I'm scared. . . ."

"You should be," he says from behind me. " 'F'you weren't scared I would be. 'Snormal to be scared. Fear and respect. That's what you got to have when you holding a gun. Now you ready. Pull that trigger when you see the can 'tween them two lines . . ."

Pow!

The gun slams back into my shoulder so hard I yelp and drop it right there in the dirt in front of Mr. Wilson. Brownie looks down at it and back up at her master.

He spits into the dirt and after a second or so he slides his wooden leg out to the side so he can bend over and pick the rifle back up.

"I'm sorry," I say, stepping away from him. I get ready to run just in case. "I'm so sorry, sir. I didn't mean to drop it. It hurt my shoulder so bad I couldn't help but drop it. I didn't mean —"

"Quiet, girl," he says, patting me on the head. "You making more racket than that ole dog does at dinnertime. 'Sal'right you let it drop. I forgots to tell you about the pain. Guess I'm numb to it by now. You did good. Now, don't you be crying like a sissy-girl. I hope I ain't wastin' my time on a sissy-girl. Stop your crying. 'Sal'right, I tell you."

I sniffle and wipe my tears with sweaty hands that smell smoky and metallic.

"Now, take the gun back," he says, trying to hand it back over to me, but I'm shaking my head. I don't want it back.

"What? Again? But . . . but I dropped it in the dirt," I sniff. "I didn't respect it any." Plus my shoulder is throbbing like a heartbeat, but I don't want him to think I'm a sissy-girl so I don't say nothing about that.

"Take the gun back," he says with a gruff voice. "You never get past your mistakes if you leave 'em right there. 'Sides, there's a can missing on the top rail and I think you and me both know what that means."

I squint out to the fence and he's right! I hit the can!

"Easy, girl," he says to me, but Brownie thinks he's talking to her so she starts wagging again. "Remember, this'll be a strong punch in the gut again but this time you got to hold on to the gun no matter what. Let it push you back. Relax into it and it won't hurt but a little this time. You'll know it's coming. Look for that can in the crosshair. You see it? Good. Now you're ready to pull that trigger back. Anytime now you're fine."

Pow!

The pain shoots sharp through my neck this time, but once I open my eyes back up I see the gun's still in my hands. Mr. Wilson lets out a low whistle and Brownie gets up and hobbles out to the fence like she knows that was my last shot — *which it is.* If I shoot again I feel like my head'll blow clear off my neck, the pain's so bad.

"I'll be a bumpy toad on a clean white lily pad," he whistles again, calling me out to where he's standing by the fence. "Git on out here, girl. Come see what you done."

Only one can is left teetering on the edge of the top of the wood fence. The other two are lying on their sides in the dirt on the ground. And there, right below his holes are two clean ones in each shiny can.

"Looks to me like I got myself a shooter here, what you think, Brownie?" He pats the dog's head like it's her who shot that second can clean off the fence. He whistles again.

"I shot *both?*" I see it but I cain't believe it.

"You shot both, sissy-girl."

"Don't call me that."

His laugh sounds like a chicken clucking. He spits again. "Guess you be wanting me to call you Annie Oakley after this!" He laughs again. "Now, come on back to the house and wash your hands off'r you' momma'll take it up wit' me and I ain't in no mood to fight wit' some sissy-girl's momma."

Somehow knowing I shot the cans on my first try at target shooting makes the pain in my shoulder go away almost altogether.

"Can I do it again tomorrow?"

"We'll see," he says, clucking alongside me. "We'll see."

"Please? I got to do it again tomorrow," I say. "Please, Mr. Wilson?"

"I told you we'll see," he says. "Now git."

I push open his screen door like it's my own. Walking through to the kitchen takes some doing since his whole front room is crowded up with stacks and stacks of papers. There's a little trail carved through the stacks so you don't have to step over anything, but it's hard to focus on the trail since there's no light coming through. Now I think I know why Mr. Wilson's always out on his front porch . . . he doesn't have any chairs, any furniture to speak of. Just stacks and stacks of newspapers, magazines and white papers with writing all over them. I wonder what he does in the winter when it's too cold to sit up on the porch.

"There's a bar of soap right by the faucet," he calls out after me, once the porch door slams telling me he's in the house, too, now. "See you wipe off some a that blood while you at it."

I look down and sure 'nuff there's blood on my hand and some just starting to dry up on my arm. Twisting my neck good I see that the gun carved a little cut clean into my skin up where my shoulder meets my neck bone. Momma'll kill me, I just bet. She's always after Richard, telling him to "git that thing out of here" when he pulls his gun out. She never lets me or Emma go near it, even when he takes it apart to clean it.

The faucet squeaks and squeaks when I turn it, which I have to do a lot of before any water even trickles out. When the water finally does come out it's rust-colored and I give up waiting for it to turn clear after a minute or so. The soap Mr. Wilson told me to use is a brown square and I can't tell if it's brown from dirt or just plain brown to begin with. I use it anyway. After pushing it to and fro between the palms of my hands I get a good lather up and wipe that all over my hands and as much of my arms as I can hold over the sink. There's nothing else but a rag by the tap so I use it to dry off, dragging it up my arm to my shoulder where I dab the blood off real good so Momma won't have a fit when she sees me. Sometimes she doesn't say anything when I come home hurt — or when I used to come home hurt from my old school where I got beat up a bit — but I can tell that inside she's having a fit. She turns away slow and tightens her lips into each other and that's Momma's way of being fit to be tied.

★ ★ ★

"You tell me who did this to you and I'll take care of 'em," Daddy said, his hands on his hips right where his belt looped carefully into his pants. "Go on, now. Tell your Daddy."

"I . . . cain't . . . tell . . . you," I said when I came up for air in between sobs, "they . . . said . . . not . . . to."

"They cowards, that's why they said that," he said. "Now, put these frozen peas on your eye and set yourself down here and tell me exactly what happened."

The cold bag felt good against my eye.

"Leave her be," Momma said from the kitchen. "She'll be fine. How's she ever gonna toughen up with you babying her all the time?"

"Hush, now, Lib. Our girl's got a shiner and I'm gonna take care a who gave it to her 'fit kills me. Now, go on, Butter Bean. Tell me."

He stroked the hair that'd got caught up in my tears and stuck to my cheeks. By the time I got home from school so much of it was stuck there it felt like my face was flattened in a web. Daddy knew just how to push it back to behind my ears, the way I liked it in the first beginning.

"They started by calling me crazy girl,

Scary Carrie," I said to him, pressing the bag on and off my face since the cold hurt if I left it too long against my eye. "And then," sniff, "and then they said after school they gonna knock some sense into me," sniff, "and then when I came out the back door on my way to the bus I see 'em waitin' for me."

"Who?" Daddy cooed to me like a turtledove does to its chicks. "Who's waitin' for you?"

"Tommy," sniff, "Bucksmith. And Floyd Cunningham. And I couldn't see who else."

"Who threw the punch?"

"I don't know." I was telling the truth since I was looking down to my scattered books when the fist came.

"Why can't you just leave it be?" Momma asked Daddy from the doorway, her lips all tight after her question.

"I'm going over to the Cunninghams and then to the Bucksmiths and I'll be back after that." Daddy stood up, smoothing the wrinkles he got in his pants from sitting down next to me. "Don't give me that look, Libby Culver. It's a coward that hits a little girl."

When Daddy left the house it stayed quiet, so the only sound I heard was the

270

rattling of the frozen peas when I'd re-adjust the bag over my swollen eye.

Momma stayed in the kitchen and I stayed in the front room next to the imprint of Daddy in the cushions next to me on the couch.

That night the smell of carpet got up close to my face and I felt Daddy kissing my forehead.

"Ev'rything's all right, Butter Bean," he whispered, stroking my hair again like he did earlier. "And don't think your Momma ain't fit to be tied. She just got a diff'rent way of showing it than me."

"Where you been all this time?" Momma asks me, inhaling on her cigarette and blowing smoke right into my face. "This in't some diner you can come in an' out of, orderin' food whenever you please. Supper's over. You better find something to put in your stomach 'fore you get at your homework. But don't be expectin' me to come wait on you hand and foot. You miss supper, you get something for yourself later on. I swear, Carrie Parker. You working on my last nerve." The smoke lifted delicately up into the air. Two ribbons of it stay right above her head and for a second it looks like Momma has horns. Emma goes straight up to our room and I know why: sometimes, even if Momma's already long done with a whipping, if she sees your face again it reminds her of how mad she was and she'll start hollering all over again. Emma doesn't want to take that chance and I cain't see as I blame her.

I love the color of the drink Momma's sipping on, it's cat's-eye orange. When she gets to drinking on it, it's a good idea to do as she says.

"Go on," she says, flicking her head toward the inside of the house.

"Momma?"

"Yeah?"

"Do you like living here?"

She takes another gulp of her drink and brings her cigarette up to her mouth but pauses for a hair of a second before she inhales smoke. She's still looking out at the forest. Then she inhales and blows it out.

"Some things aren't a matter of like or hate," she says, the wispy smoke floating away from her. "Some things are just a matter of fact. Nothing you can do to change the facts."

"We gonna live here forever?" I ask her.

Her arm stops before it rests back on the arm of the unraveling wicker chair she's settled in. I can see her head's cocked to the side while she thinks about my question.

"Libby!" Richard's voice shatters the still air between us.

She steps on her half-smoked cigarette and sets her drink down under the chair.

"Go on and get at your homework," she says, pushing past me into the house with the hole in the roof. "I'm coming, I'm coming," her voice getting farther and farther from my ears.

I look out in the direction she was staring in and I see that she's nailed up the old wooden birdhouse Daddy made way back before I was born. I guess that answers my question.

Sure enough, up in our room, Emma's lying on her belly when I come in the door. She's propped up on her elbows, drawing whatever picture is her homework tonight.

"Hey," I say.

"Hey." The tone in her voice tells me the licks are feeling worse.

"Whatchoo doing?" I say, lifting my shirt up over my head so I can put on my pajamas.

"Drawing." She yawns and then inches up some more so she can ask me what I knew she'd been stewing about the whole way back from Mr. Wilson's. "How'd you know how to shoot like that?"

I shrug my shoulders but deep down I admit I'm pretty pleased with myself.

"How'd you do it?" she tries again.

"I honestly do not know." And that's the truth of it.

"Who's Annie Oakley?" She cocks her head to the side and looks just like Momma when she does it. Up until now I haven't ever noticed that.

"You don't know who Annie Oakley is? Annie Oakley? The cowgirl who could shoot better than a man? She's part of the Old West or something. She wore cowhide skirts with lots of fringe along the bottom and matching cowhide jackets with fringe along the arms and a bandanna round her neck. She was the fastest gun in the West."

"You don't have fringe skirts and jackets." She says it like she's accusing me of lying.

"Huh?" I say. "Who said I did?"

"Mr. Wilson's calling you Annie Oakley," she says. "But you ain't got no fringe."

"It's a *nickname*," I say to her. I swear. "Remember those? *Nicknames?* Gaw."

"Can we go there again tomorrow so I can try?"

I think about this while I pull my pajama bottoms on. Just pulling the elastic band over my feet and then up to my knees causes me pain in my shoulder.

"I don't know," I say to her. "We'll see."

It's tough saying no to a girl with red strap marks cutting across her backside.

"Mr. Wilson? Why you keep all those old newspapers?" I'm watching him shake three bullets out of a tattered old box that he lets drop to the ground when he gets the right number out. Several of them fall out when it hits the dirt so I kneel down to round them up.

"Why you nosing around my business?" He slides the first bullet into the little round chamber. "Last time I checked, a man's home was his own business." The chamber clicks turn, making room for the next bullet.

"I'm not nosing around, I'm just wondering, is all," I say to him, putting the bullet box a little ways away so no one kicks it during our target practice. "I never seen so many newspapers all in one place."

"Now, today you gonna prove yesterday wasn't jes' beginner's luck," he says, motioning for me to come stand in front of him so he can lower the gun over my head like the day before. When I settle it against my shoulder the pain takes my breath away. But once it's in there good I can breathe normal.

"Hurts, don't it?" Mr. Wilson spits into the dirt just off to the side and I realize I must've made a face. "Goes away after a spell, don't worry. Hunker down in your feet for traction. Good. 'Member to get that can in the middle of the lines 'fore you take a shot. Anytime after that, fire away."

But my arm's shaking from the weight of the gun so I can't hold the can in place in the crosshairs.

"I cain't do it." I put the butt of the gun into the dirt to rest my arms for a second. "It's too heavy. I cain't do it."

"Hold on," he says. "Let the blood rush back down t'your fingers and then we try again."

"But it's heavier today than it was yesterday."

"Ain't heavier, girl, your arms tireder, that's all. Now, hoist it on up and try for it again."

The minute I get the can in the middle of the lines I pull the trigger back, but it's too fast and my arms are too weak and the gun slides right out of my hands and onto the ground again after the shot explodes.

This time I think I might've gone deaf from the sound.

"What in the hell?" he says. "Get that gun out'f the dirt, girl. I thought you said you ain't gonna do that agin. Dust it off real good and hand it over. That's right."

The tears are stinging in my eyes.

"Aw, now, don't go with the waterworks agin," he says, rolling his eyes up in his head. "This sissy-girl stuff's got to git old sometime. Cut it out and let me show you how it's done."

He sets the gun up onto his shoulder and squints into the viewfinder and fires off a shot all in one breath. Someday I want to get that good. One then two shots ring out. I don't even need to run up to the fence to know there're two cans rolling in the dirt, fresh shots in both of 'em.

"You figure I can do that someday?" I ask after him. He's hobbling out to the fence to collect the cans.

"You don't crap out like that again and sure," he says, swinging his wood leg out and in front of his good one with each step. "You jes' gots to work on that shoulder. Build it up. House ain't worth nothin' if'n it ain't settin' on good strong bricks."

"How's it gonna get stronger if I cain't even hold the gun up?"

He shakes his head and spits to the side. Then he shrugs up his shoulders and when he does his whole overalls rise and fall back down again, they're so loose on him.

"Can I try again?"

"What makes you think your arms can take it after only five minutes have passed?"

Now I shrug and he laughs. Cackles, really.

"Aw-right," he says. He goes to behind me and I reach up for the gun that's being lowered over my head. "Remember —"

"I know, I know," I sigh, "git the can in the crosshair, slide my finger in front of the trigger and pull once the can's in view."

My arms shake but this time I make my brain tell them to quit and they almost do. At least long enough for me to settle the can in the middle of the circle of the viewfinder.

Pow!

I smile even before I set the butt down on the ground like I watch Mr. Wilson do. I know I hit that can. I just know it.

He pats me on the head.

"Now go on out there and tell me what you got," he says.

I tilt the tip of the gun to him so he can hold it and I run out to the fence. Bull's-eye! I hit the can after all.

"How old you say you are?" he asks me.

"I'm eight, sir."

"And you never shoot a gun 'fore this?"

"No, sir."

"You daddy have a gun?"

"My daddy's dead, sir," I remind him. "My stepdaddy's got a gun but I ain't never even touched it 'fore."

He scratches his chin just like in storybooks, but usually in books it's the evil villain who strokes his chin while he's dreaming up some torture for his victim. But I don't think Mr. Wilson's an evil villain.

"Hmm," he hums more to himself than to me. "I just trying to figure out what to do 'bout you, kid."

"Will you let me shoot again?"

"I reckon. But if you do the good stuff you gotta do them hard stuff that gets you there. You gots to learn how to take care of the gun so it can take care of you later."

"What's that mean?"

"Come on," he sighs. "You best see for y'self what I'm talking about."

It's hard to know what to do when you're walking with Mr. Wilson. I could out-walk him any day till Sunday but I get the feeling he wouldn't like that all that much so I walk behind him and off to the side like it's by choice that I'm moving in slow motion.

Over to the backside of his house is a shed I never noticed before. It's rusted-out tin from the looks of it; same material as those cans we been shooting. Through two metal loops attached to the double doors is a chain that's held together by a giant padlock. He pulls a jangly ring of keys from a pocket in those overalls of his and sifts through them until he finds a small one that looks fake setting there like it does between his big, rough hands. Mr. Wilson's hands look like baseball mitts.

A little turn and the lock pulls down from the U-shaped bar that's looped through the chain links. "There," he says.

I didn't know what dark was until I saw the inside of this shed. I blink so my eyes can focus faster but even that's hard since Mr. Wilson's blocking the doorway and keeping any of this daylight from falling inside. When he goes in farther I can start making out different forms. A lot of shelves. A lot of cans, maybe paint cans but I can't be sure. A lot of old pots and pans. A mower, which is strange since there isn't any grass around here. Glass containers for what I don't know. And a case that hangs on the side where Mr. Wilson's fiddling around. After a few more blinks and some good old-fashioned squinting I can see there are more guns in the case.

"Wow," I say. "You got a lot of guns."

He looks out at me and looks back into the case. "I guess so," he says. "But not nearly as many as some others out here in these old woods."

"How many guns do other people have?"

"Dozens," he answers back, pulling a rag from a shelf right above the case. I look closer and see he's taking his gun apart. "Ole man Plemmons had 'bout a hundred. He died and they had trouble finding 'nuff people to divide 'em up between."

It's funny hearing Mr. Wilson calling someone else "ole man."

"How many you have?"

"I got six. This here's my workin' gun. That one there's my squirrel gun. They all got they reason for being mine, I reckon."

"What's a working gun?"

"Workin's going out and hauling back food. That's workin'."

"Can I try that one?" I point to a littler gun that looks like it wouldn't hurt my shoulder none.

Mr. Wilson looks to where I'm pointing and shakes his head. "You best stick with this rifle and learn it good. After this ev'rything'll seem easy, don't worry. Now, come on over here and help me wit' this cleaner. We gonna bring it back over to the front so I can set in the light and show you how to clean up a gun good and proper."

I must be making a face, the face I always make when Momma tells me to help her clean, 'cause Mr. Wilson says, "Don't be givin' me trouble, chile, or you ain't touching no gun never agin."

"Yes, sir." I wipe the look off my face as easy as pie.

He hands over a metal can that smells like gasoline for a car, a handful of rags stiff with brown dirt, a bucket and a brush.

"How ya daddy die?" he asks me while we walk over to a tree stump by the front porch. "He die from the drink?"

"Robbers," I say. "My sister saw him laying there after they kilt him but she was real little at the time and Momma says she kindly won't remember it."

"How come you livin' out here if'n you rich 'nuff for people to steal from?"

"We ain't rich," I say. I don't know what else to add to that.

He makes a "harrumph" sound like he

doesn't believe me.

"We ain't!"

"They kilt you daddy for *something*," he says. "Must be they took it all wit' them and now you be living out here close to the country."

I don't know what Mr. Wilson means by "close to the country," but if he means we're living out in the middle of nowhere then I guess he's right. We ain't rich, though. I know that for a fact.

"Come on and help me with the dishes," Momma says to me. Her chair scrapes against the kitchen floor when she pushes back from the supper table.

She carries her plate over along with Daddy's and sets them on the side of the sink.

Momma puts the stopper in the drain to catch the water and make the sink fill up while I pull a chair over so I can stand on it to make suds.

The water runs through the tin can Daddy punched holes in the bottom of, but there's not enough soap to make suds.

"Momma! We need more soap," I say above the sound of running water.

"All right, all right," she says. "I s'pose we've gotten enough use out of our bar upstairs by now. Run on up and fetch it for me."

Once the soap gets to be a sliver it goes into the suds can. The bar that we been using isn't quite a sliver but it'll do.

I run down the stairs and into the kitchen, where Momma's putting away the salt and pepper shakers from the table.

"Here." I try to hand her the soap but she juts her chin out toward the suds can so I climb back up onto my chair and drop it in. Sure enough, when the water runs through, soapy suds come out the bottom and the dishes can get clean after all.

"Careful you don't use too much water," she says. "When you're done you better carry that piece of soap you fetched back up to the bath."

"Why?"

"We got to get clean somehow," she says, closing a cabinet door.

"I thought the soaps in the can are for dishes."

"They are. But t'ain't near the end of the month yet and we can squeeze s'more use out of that one there."

I hurry home after Mr. Wilson shows me how one big gun can turn into millions of tiny little pieces.

Richard's truck's still in its spot by the side of the trail that leads to number twenty-two and along the front porch rail Momma's set out the little rugs that dot the floors so they can come to air out. I better tell her it's fixing to rain. Brownie lies on her right side when rain's coming. That's what Mr. Wilson said when he spied her that way on our way out of the shed from putting the gun cleaning stuff back in. He didn't lock our gun back up. Says he keeps it by his side in the house "in case." In case of what I do not know. But if Mr. Wilson's scared then I guess we all better be.

"Where the hell *you* been?" Richard sneers at me and makes me jump back from the door handle I's reaching out for.

"Nowhere," I say to him. I'm trying to figure out if there's enough room on either side of him so I can squeeze by without him grabbing me or *something*. It's the or something I'm more worried about since he doesn't just grab, he grabs and twists.

"You thank I'm dumb enough to buy that? You been *nowhere*. *N*owhere. Now where in the hell you reckon *nowhere* is?"

Nope. No room on either side.

"I'm talking to you, girl," he says, pointing the tip of his beer bottle at my chest. "You look at me when I'm talking to you. That's better. Now you're gonna tell me where all you been."

"Just down the road a ways," I mumble.

"Just down the road a ways *where?*"

"Where's Momma?"

"Don't you be asking them questions. I'm asking the questions round here," he says, taking a swig off the bottle and then swallowing it and belchin' real loud. "You been tomcatting round these woods since we landed here and I got a right to know where you been. You answer me or I'm gonna have to find out the hard way."

I cain't believe he could hear me. I's talkin' real low, just to myself. I didn't mean for him to hear. It's just that he don't have a *right* to know where I been. We're studying the difference between rights and privileges in school and when Richard knows where I been it's a *privilege,* not a *right.*

"You sassin' me? 'S that what you doin'?"

The boot kick comes hard and fast and before I know it, I'm flat out on the floor, doing the one stupid thing I should know better 'bout by now.

"Momma!" For a second I feel like I'm on the ceiling, lookin' down at myself. My voice doesn't sound like my own, it's a hollow holler that comes out before I can help myself.

See, calling Momma is bad in two ways. One, she never comes but if she happens to, she just gets mad at me and Emma for hollering for her like she's a dog so then they're *both* mad and that's never good. Two, it just makes Richard worse off if he thinks we're being whiney little babies.

Sure enough, he's got a handful of the backside of my pants and pretty soon I'm lifted off the ground and shoved to the stairs.

"You git on upstairs, you little shit." Even though I'm sure he's right behind me, his voice sounds like it's coming from far away.

"Emma?" I cry out.

"She ain't here," he says, kneeing my backside up the next stair.

"Where is she?" I'm whispering 'cause talking louder will need more air in me and to get more air I'd have to take a deeper breath and that just plain hurts around my middle.

"Emma?" I tilt my head up and whisper as loud as I can, so the sound can float past Richard.

"I done tole you," he says. By now he's got me cornered in my room, blocking the doorframe. "She ain't here." He tilts the beer bottle all the way in the air to get the last drops from it. "Now come 'ere." He motions with the bottle for me to come up close to him but I don't wait any longer.

Like a bullet from Mr. Wilson's gun I shoot out toward him, pushing him off balance to the side so I can get past him to the stairs, which I leap down, almost three at a time. The door slams shut after me so I can have more space 'tween me and him if he comes after me, which he is 'cause from the trail that leads to the Diamond River I hear him hollering.

"Git on back here, girl!"

I tumble over a tree root.

"You better watch out," he yells. "I'm gonna git you when you come back here!"

I'm not even out of breath, jumping over rocks and the fallen tree in my way. Funny how the pain goes away when you got the chance to be free.

"Emma?" I call ahead so she doesn't run from the sound of footsteps, thinking it's Richard, like I would if'n I heard someone running at me.

At the edge of the creek I bend over 'cause now I *am* out of breath and bending over seems like the best way to catch it without causing too much trouble to my insides.

"Here I am," a little voice carries over to my ears.

My head jerks up at the sound. But I don't see her at first.

"Where?"

"Over here."

And there, on a smooth rock that's half in the water, half out, is my baby sister, hugging her knees and rocking to and fro. At first the bruisin' doesn't look so bad, but when I come closer I see there's dried blood caught up in it and my stomach does a nosedive.

So before I reach her I squat down and hold the end of my shirt into the water so I can clean her up.

"I couldn't find you," she says, not even wincing when I dab at her forehead.

"I's over at Wilson's," I say. "Hold still. Where's this comin' from?" I'd started from the bottom of the dried trickle and traced it up into her hair where there's a round patch of darker blood. It's up above where the worst of the bruisin' is. That's when she does flinch when I dab at that.

"Hold on, lemme git some more water," I say, jumping off the rock and picking a fresh part of my shirt to get wet.

"You okay?" I ask her when I get back close.

She's as still as the rock she's sitting on. Her shoes have come untied so I tie 'em back up, double knotted the way she likes it.

"Say something."

But she won't.

I cain't run my fingers through her hair to make her feel better 'cause her hair's all knotted up so instead I stroke her arm.

"He lost his job," she says quiet-like.

"What'd you say?" I lean closer to her mouth so I can hear better. She's being that quiet.

"I said, he lost his job."

"Richard?"

"Who else?"

"Why?"

"How'm I s'posed to know?"

"Does Momma know?"

Emma shrugs her shoulders. "I don't even know where Momma is."

"Me neither. How'd you know he lost his job?"

She doesn't say anything so I guess it isn't important how she come to hear.

"Guess we'll be stayin' up here at the Diamond River a whole lot more" is all I can think of to say.

And then it comes to me. "What if we write to Gammy?"

"What?" Emma raises her head a bit.

"We could write Gammy and ask her to come out here for a while," I say. As I talk it sounds like a better idea than when it first popped into my head a second or two ago. "She might like it better'n where she is now and then she could live here with us."

"But what about Auntie Lillibit? Gammy's already takin' care of her," Emma says.

Auntie Lillibit is Momma's little sister, whose real name is Elizabeth but everyone just calls her Lillibit after what Momma nicknamed her when they were kids our age. Gammy lives in a room in her house near Asheville and does all her laundry and cleaning for her, like she's sick or something, which she always seems to be. When they were little Auntie Lillibit started wheezing when she ran out to play and the doctor told her momma, Gammy, she wouldn't live long if she overdid it, so from that day on she underdid it. And she's lived ever since. Momma and her never did get along on account of the fact Momma says Gammy spoils her rotten and she doesn't like to be around rotten things. So Momma's steered clear of the both of them for as long as I can remember. Gammy came to visit us a few times when we were little, but when I close my eyes I cain't even remember what Gammy looks like, it's been that long.

Still, I cain't think of a better idea so I'm clinging to it.

"Gammy could help Momma the way she helps Auntie and then Momma'd be a whole lot happier, I bet," I say. Emma's head's stopped bleeding, but if you look hard you can see a big bump right past where her hair hits her forehead.

"I'm gonna do it," I say. "I'm gonna write her."

"Where're you gonna get a stamp?"

"I'll ask Mr. Wilson where the post office is and I'll go in and buy one, stupid," I sass her. "That's what you do when you want to mail something. You go to the post office."

"What about her address? You don't know where she lives."

"I know for a fact she lives on Sycamore Street," I tell her, " 'cause she used to say she was sick-a-more streets popping up around town and I remembered it that way. I don't know the number but Avery

Creek is a small town — the mailman'll know her for sure."

"She'll never come," Emma sighs, and goes back to hugging her knees. "Not in a million years."

"She will, too."

"We'll see."

We stay by the stream until it's hard to see to the other side and then we know it's time to go on back home. Standing up and stretching feels good — my bottom is sore from the rock I was on.

The floor of the forest is spongy and I wonder why it never occurs to us to sit on it instead of hard rocks.

"Okay, so this is what we're gonna do," I say to Emma from over my shoulder since she's walking slower behind me. "I'll go in first to see where he is and find out if the coast is clear and then I'll whistle for you to come in. If you don't hear a whistle, don't come in, I'll take myself out the back door and meet you there and we can come on back to the stream. Got it?"

"Yeah, okay," she says in a whisper. "I don't feel so good standing up and walk-ing."

"Just get to the house and then you can lie down."

"My head's swimming."

"I know," I say. And I do. My head swims like that when it gets hit, but after I sleep for a spell it's all better.

"I can't go any farther," she says.

"Stop your whining and hurry up," I say. "We're almost there."

I don't whine half as much as Emma is after this whipping. Most times she's good and keeps it to herself, but I guess tonight's not one of those times.

There's a light coming from the back of the house, the kitchen, so it's anyone's guess who's in there. Momma, okay. Richard, not okay.

"Remember to listen for the whistle," I hiss back to her. I hope she hears me, she's pretty far behind me.

I slow way down when I get to about a hundred Barbie lengths from the back door. I listen for a clue to who's in there but I don't hear a thing. A few steps more and I can make a dash for the bottom of the window where I can peek in. One. Two. Three . . . and I'm there, below the kitchen window that's right above the sink.

I didn't think about the fact that the window's set up higher than my head, so I have to push . . . this . . . rock . . . aah . . . to a spot right here so I can stand up on it. There. Perfect. The edge of the windowsill is so dusty and dirty my fingers slip off at first but then I grip on and slowly . . . slowly raise my head up to the corner of the window.

I can see the table with the smooth metal edges in the middle of the room, Momma's ashtray's in the middle, and, right in front of me, the flies licking up the leftover crumbs on the plates stacked up for cleaning. I think Momma's waiting for more soap slivers to go in the can 'cause the dishes've been piled in there for a few days now. The flies dart from one to another, stuffing themselves. The bigger ones are the ones that bite real hard and leave red marks on my skin.

Strange that the light's on but no one's in the kitchen. Momma's always after us to turn them off — wait! Here she is. She's coming straight at me and I duck, in case she sees the top of my head. I hear clinking that's probably her shifting things around in the sink and after it goes quiet for a spell I inch back up to see what's what.

Scrape. The chair's being pulled back at the table and there's Momma, lighting up another cigarette. She takes in a deep breath and blows the smoke up to the ceiling. I'm about to turn to give Emma the whistle that the coast is clear but I stop when I hear the floorboards rattle with the weight of Richard coming into view. He's standing in the doorway, taking a swig of his bottle, like he did with me earlier.

"Just go on," Momma says. I can hear her clear as day.

Richard looks over the top of Momma's head and for a second I think he's caught me in the act of spying, but then I see he's looking to the sink.

"When you gonna start acting like a real woman an' git to cleanin'?" he says. When he does his top lip curls up toward the bottom of his nose.

Momma says something I cain't quite make out since she says it 'fore she takes another breath of her cigarette.

"Whut?" Richard looks back over to her with the top of her head resting on the palms of her hands, her cigarette in the fork of her two first fingers on her right hand.

"About the time you fix the hole in the roof over our heads," she says to him, raising her head up to his.

"You're lucky I'm goin' out or I'd put a hole in your head the size of my fist," he says. He tilts his bottle up, drains it and throws it through the air right toward the sink . . . toward me. It shatters onto the top of the heap, bits of glass clink against the windowpane. I duck down just in case it breaks through, and while I'm squeezing my eyes shut the picture of Momma, sitting at the kitchen table smoking, is burned against my eyeballs. She didn't even flinch when his arm hurled the bottle across the room. Or when it hit the sink.

The front door slams shut and I feel the wall I'm leaning up against rattle. Now, at least, the coast is clear. His truck rumbles up and coughs away from the house.

I turn away from the house and whistle into the air, but I cain't make out any bushes moving where Emma'd be pushing through, so I whistle again. Nothing.

She probably fell asleep waitin' on me like she was.

"Hey, Em!" I whisper-yell to her. It's quiet all around so I follow the cut of light on the ground outside the window to the edge of the woody trail. "You can come up now!"

"Hmm?" I hear a tired little voice from practically under my feet.

"Where are you?"

"Here," she says. My eyes adjust to the dark and there, curled up like a dog, is Emma, about three Barbies from my foot.

"C'mon." I crouch down to help her up.

I know her head's throbbing so it's making her more tired than she is in the first beginning. Last time my head was hit, anytime I stood up too fast it throbbed like my brain was going to beat its way out of my skull. So I know what she's feeling like right about now. "C'mon and put your arm over my shoulders and I'll help you in."

She does as I tell her and we wobble back up to the house, breaking sticks under our feet along the way.

I don't get worried until her head rolls back onto my arm that's holding her across her shoulders. *Now* I'm scared.

"Momma!" I call out to her while I try moving Emma sideways through the front door, propping it open with my foot at the same time.

"Momma, help!" And then we both collapse inside the door, our arms tangled up like they were when we were standing. After a few minutes that seem like hours, I try to get my arm out from under Emma, but her deadweight makes it near to impossible so I just leave it be.

"What in the hell?" I hear Momma saying over us. "What've you gone and gotten yourself into?"

I keep my eyes closed because opening

them will mean having to heave myself and Emma up off the ground and I just don't feel I have the strength for it.

"Get up," she says. And I can hear her sucking the life out of her cigarette again. "Go on, get up. I know you ain't asleep," she says to us. And she's half right — I am not asleep but Emma sure is out cold.

The floorboards squeak and squawk with the weight of her walking away and I figure that's for the best, anyhow. She ain't strong enough to pick both of us up, anyway, so I was just putting off the inevitable, I s'pose.

"Emma." I rattle her back with the arm that's still stuck underneath it. "Come on, Em. Move up just a little. Emma."

I turn my head completely sideways and see that her eyes are blinking open.

"Just move a little so I can stand up and then I'll get you up," I say. "That's good. Okay. That's real good." She arches her back up so I can slide my arm out and hop up.

"Okay, now give me your hands and I'll pull you up and we'll get you up to bed good and quick. There. Now give me the other arm. That's real good. On the count of three I'll pull you up. One. Two. Three!"

And just like that game where you swing

a baby over a puddle, I swing Emma up off the floor.

"Let's go over to the stairs," I say, holding her left arm across my shoulders again. "Good. Little baby steps. That's real good, Em." I find that when I talk to her like she's a baby I get a whole lot further than when I get mad at her.

"Good girl, that's real good. One more step. There. We're at the top of the stairs now. A few more steps and we're on the bed. One step. Two steps. Good! Three steps. Four. There!"

I let her fall facedown onto the top of the bed so I can pull her shoes off before I set her in there proper. Pine needles are stuck to the back of her shirt so I pull that over the top of her head by kneeling on the bed right over her. It's messy but I get it off. She's gonna have to sleep nekked on top 'cause I cain't get her sleep shirt onto her, but that's fine since it's real hot tonight, anyway.

I walk on my knees to the top of the bed where our pillows go and I pull her up so her head's on one of them and then I shimmy the sheet out from under her so I can let it fall on top in case it gets drafty overnight.

Phee-you.

Now I can go down to see about some

food in my belly 'cause I know I won't be able to sleep with it empty.

Momma's at the kitchen table, smoking, and I know better than to ask her about supper so I go to the icebox to see what's what.

"There's chicken from Sunday in there," Momma says. "Don't eat standing up — how many times I have to tell you that? You sit and eat proper."

I spoon out some of the chicken stew onto a plate I take right from the top of the pile in the sink . . . no use dirtying up another when I know it's me that's gonna clean 'em all, anyway.

Momma sets back in her chair and crosses her arms in front of her like she's inspecting my eating habits.

"What happened to the stage star I saw all passed out on the floor in front, begging to be carried in?" she asks me, fixing her lips tight around the cigarette. "You want me to spoon-feed you, too?"

"Wasn't me that needed carrying in," I say, "it was Emma."

Momma pushes her chair back from the table and crosses over to the cabinet to the right of the sink, where the glasses are.

"Caroline Parker, I am so sick of Emma this and Emma that," she says, helping herself to a bottle she keeps under the sink. It's so quiet I can hear her Adam's apple move up and down, pushing the drink faster into her belly. "That's all you whine about — Emma needs this, Emma needs that. Every single goddamned day. When'm I gonna get a break, huh? When?"

She's sitting in front of me again, the glass in between us like a silent relative that's gonna ruin the night whether you like it or not.

"I'm sorry, Momma," I say, trying to keep the glass as filled up as possible.

"Ah, but you didn't answer me," she says, reaching for it. Her Adam's apple goes up and down again but when the glass is set back down the level isn't too much lower so I've still got time. "When'm I gonna get some peace around here?"

I push the last of the stew onto my fork with my left finger and hope she doesn't notice. I don't know how anyone can expect to get the last bite of stew onto a fork without their free hand helping.

And while I chew I think about how I can answer my momma.

Thank goodness she starts talking again so I don't have to think too hard. "Things are gonna change round here," she says. "I'm gonna be taking in some cleaning and whatnot and you're gonna be helping me with it after school. I don't want to hear a peep from you in the way of whining, you hear me? Not a peep."

"Yes, ma'am."

"None of this Emma needs this or that, you hear?"

"I cain't help it if Emma gets in trouble," I say, trying to keep the whining out of my voice, but I swear it's hard to do 'cause it's not fair I'm getting blamed for what Emma does.

"Emma can fend for herself," she says. And from the way she stubs out her cigarette I can see the subject is closed.

"You better get the crack on with those dishes," she says. "They ain't gonna do themselves."

So I go over to the sink and pull the can of soap slivers out from the cabinet below the sink and turn on the water to let the suds settle where they can in the canyon below the spigot.

One by one I wash each plate and fork and knife, setting them on the counter beside the sink for drying later. My old button-down shirt (minus the buttons, which Momma snipped off when I outgrew it) is the dishrag I use for drying. The crickets are so loud outside it's like they're singing along with my hands.

Slam!

The screen door bangs shut, footsteps stumble in.

"Aha! You a good girl, doin' them dishes fo' yo' momma," Richard says, working his mouth around each word with more than a little effort since the drink makes them slide into one another like a dream. "Tha's mo' like it."

I'm almost finished stacking the plates, but then I'll have to dry the silverware so there's no escaping him.

"Wher's yo' momma at?" he slurs.

"I don't know," I say.

"You forgot to call me sir," he says. "I deserve sir, don' you think?" He's feeling for a chair to fall into like he's in the dark but the lights are on.

"Sir."

"Wha?"

"I don't know where my momma is, sir," I say.

"Tha's better," he says, plopping into the chair at last. "Now I got to look at this shit?" he says, looking at the casserole in front of him.

I go over to it but he grabs my arm hard when it reaches out to take the glass container. I try not to wince when he twists it up to the ceiling.

"Give y'daddy a kiss," he says, holding his cheek out for me to kiss.

"You mean my *step*daddy," I say, real quiet-like.

"What did you say?" Richard's head snaps straight.

"Nothing," I say.

"You sassin' me, girl?"

"No, sir."

Then *whap!* The slap comes from the other hand that's not grabbing onto my wrist.

Whap! Whap! The slaps come faster.

"Why you gotta sass me?" Richard's voice is higher than I've ever heard it. But maybe it just sounds that way 'cause I'm holding my one free arm over my head to keep my face from being hit too hard.

"Why? Why you always gotta back-talk me?" His voice cracks, almost like a girl's. "I feed you," *whap,* "I give you a roof over yo' dirty little head," *whap,* "and whado I git? Sassin' all the time," *whap.* "Day an' night, night an' day." The slaps let up and I look out from the space underneath my elbow and see that Richard is folded over, his shoulders heaving up and down, his sobs loud. He lets go of my wrist.

"Things are gonna change round here." His arms dangle, tired from hitting. "Y'all won't know what hit you. Things gonna change. . . ."

I could run. I could. I could make it up to our room, crawl alongside Emma, who's soft in sleep by now. I could even make it to the Diamond River if I wanted. But my feet won't move. I've never seen Richard cry.

"Get out of here!" he hollers, even though he's resting his forehead on the edge of the table. "Go on and get." He cries and cries, not caring whether I do go or not.

And for once . . . just this once . . . I stay.

"I'm sorry," I whisper into thin air. But it drifts away like Momma's smoke.

"Go!" he sobs. The veins running up and down his arms look thick, like river lines on a map, squiggly. His hand is un-curled and limp when it waves out blindly in my direction.

And I do.

Emma's breathing hard and heavy when I come in and I almost hate to have to move her but I have to; she's sprawled out sideways on the bed, taking up the whole dang thing.

I crawl up along the one side that's got a bit more room and shove her over some. Seconds later she's back to snoring.

Lying on my back, blinking so my eyes can get used to the blackness of the room,

I picture Richard crying at the kitchen table. Gammy's just got to come out here and fix things. If she could make Auntie Lillibit live she could make things right here at number twenty-two, I just know it.

I cain't fall asleep on account of the fact that I'm writing the letter in my head.

Dear Gammy,
   It's me, Carrie. How are you? I am fine. We're wondering if you'd like to come on out here to visit us. It's so nice and pretty here at our new house. You'd love it. There's our own stream, for starters, and a whole lot of trees — too many to count. Momma really misses you and Emma and I do, too. Please come out to see us. Please? Okay, well, got to go. Love, your granddaughter, Caroline Parker.

She could even bring Auntie Lillibit! I just thought of that. With the two of them here things'd be even better. I know Momma's gonna whip me good when she finds out I wrote Gammy, but it's worth it if it works.

I must have fallen asleep 'cause the next thing I know Emma's shaking my foot to wake me.

"Carrie, c'mon," she's saying from the bottom of the bed. "We're gonna miss the bus."

I jump up and into the first clothes I can pull on and two minutes later we're running out the front of the house, without even hollering bye to Momma and without anything in the way of lunch.

"There it is!" I can see the yellow top of the bus chugging toward Mr. Wilson's path and I run faster than Emma so I can flag it down and tell it to wait on my baby sister. "Hurry!" I end up not having to do it, though, 'cause Emma keeps right at my heels the whole way.

"That was close," she says, falling into the seat bench alongside me. She's panting hard, too.

"Did you get something to eat?" I ask her.

"Just some bread."

She's lucky. It's gonna be a long day. "Hold my books for a second," I tell her. I have to tie my shoe.

"Hey, Carrie." Orla Mae Bickett weaves past our seat and settles down in the one right behind, ignoring Emma like she always does. She ignores everyone but me, practically.

"Hey, Orla Mae," I say back to her, once I straighten up.

"I brought you something," she says, unhooking the two clips that keep her lunchbox good and tight. "My momma made it last night."

It's a piece of corn bread almost as thick as my flattened-out hand. The plastic wrap is stuck to the top of it, there's so much butter — just the way I love it.

"Thanks, Orla Mae," I say. The only thing keeping me from digging in right away is I sort of want to cry — I don't know why. I guess it's on account of no one ever bringing me corn bread before.

"Y'welcome."

I balance it on top of my books and then pretend to be appreciating the scenery out the window. Inside my head, though, I'm figuring out how I can wait until lunchtime to eat it. I don't think I can. My finger pushes into the top of the plastic wrap — the corn bread's so soft it leaves a dent where my finger was and that just makes my mouth water.

The bus squeaks and lurches over the hills to school. Past a sign pointing to Johnson's Farm tipped over onto one sign so there's no telling where you're s'posed to turn in. Past hundreds of pine trees, thousands, maybe. Up a long stretch of hill that promises something good's gonna lay on the downhill side, but when you get up to the top there's just more of the same, blacktop with double yellow lines, sometimes broken up, sometimes straight. Finally we slow in front of the long, low building where we go for learning. Donford Elementary School is carved into the stone above the single front door, which has a handle that's worn from years of hill children pulling on it, dragging themselves in for a few hours each day. The windows on either side of the door show the backs of pictures taped up, no telling what's on the other side, unless it's your classroom you're going into. Inside the dark hallway there's a poster that reads "We're *yearning* for some *learning!*" and has a smiley face dotting the letter *i*. I like coming in and seeing that smiley face every day.

"Carrie, wait up!" Orla Mae's calling after me once we're inside the door.

So I do.

"I hear you been shootin' over at Mr. Wilson's." She leans in to me, her arms hugging her books into her chest.

"Where'd you hear that?"

"You kiddin'? My daddy says round here you can scratch your ass on one side a town and the ladies on the other'd talk about how many strokes you used," she says. I keep walking, not saying anything.

"Well?" she keeps at me. "Is it true?"

"What if I said yeah?"

" 'Tain't no big thing, I's just wondering," she says, straightening up. "Mr. Wilson tole my daddy you the best shot he's seen since Harry Maphis, and my daddy says that's something since Harry Maphis could shoot a squirrel's eyeball out from a mile away if'n you tole him to."

"I ain't shooting no squirrels, I can tell you that right now," I say. "Hey, where's the post office?"

"Whatchoo want with the post office?"

"I just wanna know, is all."

"Just keep on the same blacktop school's on and you'll hit it on the right side of the road. It's the general store. Same place. Hey — where you going?"

"I'll be right back," I call to her from over my shoulder. I'm walking one step slower than running. I can barely hold on till I get to the girl's washroom.

Inside the first stall on the left, the one I always use, I test the metal latch that swings over and fits into the fork on the fixed part of the door to make sure no one can push the door open by mistake (I've done it sometimes, not meaning to), which is why I always choose this stall. The next stall down has no latch and the two other stalls on the other side of the bathroom have bent latches so that it seems like the door's gonna stay shut, but then once when I was in the middle of going number one the latch came loose and I had to reach and hold the door closed until I could pull my pants up. I bend in half and scan the bathroom floor for feet in case someone was in a stall and I didn't notice it when I came in. No one's here. I've got the place to myself and about five minutes until I've got to be in the classroom. That's plenty of time.

The plastic wrap on the corn bread is all tangled into itself so there's no neat way to open it up. I tear into it from the top and break off a piece and drop it into my mouth, tilting my head back so I don't waste any crumbs. Mmm. This is good and I know I'd think that even if I did have breakfast. Mrs. Bickett scrapes off real corn from the cob to put into the bread along with the cornmeal and that makes it nice and crunchy in parts.

When Gammy comes to see us I'm gonna ask her if she can make us some of this corn bread. She maybe could get the recipe from Mrs. Bickett, even. I hope I remember to ask her.

With my mouth still full I roll the plastic wrap up into a little ball and throw it out on my way out of the washroom.

Time for school.

"One, two, three . . ." our teacher, Miss Ueland, calls out while she switches the lights on and off above our heads.

"Eyes on me!" we answer her all together.

"Two, three, four," she says back, leaving the lights on and walking to the center of the room.

"Close the door!" we say together again.

Now we're all quiet, like she wants us to be. Miss Ueland picks one or two words out of a sentence and says them slower than the rest of the words, like she's giving us all a chance to catch up to her. I didn't mind it at first but now it drives me crazy trying to figure out why she chooses the words she does to slow down.

"I hope y'all did your *homework*," says Miss Ueland. "We got a lot to do today so we won't be going *over it* like we usually do, but I trust you're ready to move *forward*."

The blackboard's all clean, the chalk beaten out of the erasers, and a new pack of white chalk waits in the long well that runs along the bottom of the board. Miss

Ueland opens it up and breaks a piece in half, blows on it and writes *presidents* up on the board in pretty cursive.

"Washington, Adams, Jefferson, Madison, *Monroe*," she says, "Adams, Jackson, *Van Buren*. Now, I know you can't *believe* this but you'll be able to recite those *back to me* — and more after them — by the end of the day *today!* It isn't all that *hard*, Oren, now don't roll your eyes at me. The first thing we *do*," she says, turning to face the board, "is break down each name to its *first few letters*. Like this."

Now she writes *wash* then *ad* then *jeff* and *mad* and on like this and it hits me I can write all that down and write Gammy at the same time. That way when school's over I can tell Emma to go on without me and I can run to the post office and drop the letter in the mail and still be home for supper.

"Caroline!"

The class laughs.

"Yes, ma'am?"

"Nice of you to *join* us," Miss Ueland says. The class laughs again and it occurs to me they're laughing at me. "Now that I have your *attention*, Caroline, can you tell me what the next word in this pattern will be?"

I look up at the board and see all the words shortened below the whole names and a space still to go underneath "Tyler."

"Um?" I'm buying time. Why do teachers always know when your mind wanders?

"I'm afraid 'um' is not the *answer* I was looking for," she says. But before I can say what I think it is, she calls on Orla Mae, who gets it right away and then smiles at me like she did me a favor. Which she didn't. 'Cause now I look even worse off that I didn't get it right away, too. Thanks a lot, Orla Mae, I say back to her with my eyes.

"That's right, Orla Mae," but Miss Ueland says that to me, not Orla Mae. " '*Ty*' is correct. Carrie, will you tell us what comes *next*? What's short for *Polk?*"

"Po?" And the class laughs again for some reason so I turn around in my desk and say "what?" to all of them. That quiets them up good.

"You've got the *right* idea, Carrie —" Miss Ueland's being nice since she sees I'm really trying "but it's 'pol,' like the north *pole*. That's enough, class, now quiet down. *All right,* let's keep going. Everybody got all this down or should I leave it up a little longer? Yes? Okay then." And she erases the words before I've copied them down — I couldn't tell her I didn't have it yet or she'd know for sure I'd been day-dreaming. I'll just get it later from Orla Mae.

Miss Ueland writes the next batch of names on the board and this time I write them down as she does, but not as pretty. No one writes as pretty as Miss Ueland.

Pretty soon it's clear I'll be copying the whole dang lesson from Orla Mae after school, but I don't care. I gotta write Gammy while the letter I wrote in my head last night is still fresh.

Dear Gammy,

How are you? I am fine. Emma's fine, too, in case you were wondering. We're hoping you can come on out for a visit and soon. Momma really misses you and we do, too. I have a friend named Orla Mae, isn't that a funny-sounding name? She's real nice, though. You'll like her a lot. There's a dog down a ways named Brownie, only she's black and has three legs.

Please come out to see us. We need you.

Love,

Your granddaughter, Caroline Parker

P.S. Maybe Auntie Lillibit wants to come on out, too.

I write all nice with the cursive letters I learned last year in school back home. I feel better already. When Miss Ueland turns to erase the board again I fold it up square by square until it's real tiny and I can squeeze it into my pocket, where it'll stay the rest of the day till I can mail it in town.

"Carrie? I need to have a word with you, hon," Miss Ueland is saying to me while the others in class push past me on both sides to get out of the room for recess.

"Yes, ma'am."

"Where were you today?" she asks me once everybody's gone.

"Ma'am?"

"I know you weren't paying attention in class," she says, looking down at me through her glasses, "so I'm wondering where your mind was today. It's not like you to drift off so much."

I shrug my shoulders. What'm I supposed to tell her? She wouldn't understand I had to write my Gammy.

"Ahem." Miss Ueland clears her throat. "I also wanted to inquire after your arm."

Without even knowing for sure what

she'll say next I push my sleeve down, but it only goes halfway down the last part of my forearm. Momma always says long-sleeved shirts can be worn till they've become short sleeves, but mine're not quite there yet.

"You don't need to hide it, Carrie," she says, pushing her glasses back up to the ridge that's built into the crook of her nose for them. "I've seen it all week. What happened?"

"Nothing, ma'am," I say, crossing my hand over to cover what my sleeve cain't.

We both blink at each other, waiting to see where this conversation's going.

She breaks first. "Are there any more like it anywhere else?"

"No, ma'am."

She cocks her head to the side and I can tell she's deciding whether to believe me or not.

"Now, Carrie . . ." She clears her throat again and points to the desk that Freddy Sprague sits in, so I use it and she squeezes her grown-up self into the one next door to it, where Ellie Frenden sits. "I know you may not believe me but I was once your age. I know how hard it is when you're, ah —" her throat clears again "— living in a tough place. I had marks like that, too."

Then she stops talking. I'm supposed to

say something. Jeez, what am I supposed to say?

"So if you ever want to talk to anyone, someone who's not your parents, I mean, well, you can come and talk to me."

The talking's stopped again.

"Do you have anything you'd like to tell me?"

"No, ma'am."

"You sure?"

"Yes, ma'am."

There's quiet between us, but it doesn't feel like the quiet there was a second ago.

"Well, all right, then," she says, squeezing her hips back up through the space between the seat and Ellie Frenden's desktop. "I guess that's all."

I shoot out of the room like a bull pushes out of the gate at the rodeo.

"Hey, Orla Mae, wait up."

"What'd Miss Ueland want with you?" she whispers to me. She's arranging her books on the desk in the science room. The smell is all vapors and metal.

"Aw, nothin'," I lie. "She just chewin' me out for not payin' attention in her class."

Orla Mae nods her head. "Hey, can I come up with you to Mr. Wilson's after school, watch you shoot? Maybe he'd teach me some."

"Yeah, maybe," I say. "But you cain't come today 'cause I need to get to the post office, remember? Plus Mr. Wilson don't like new people. He didn't even like us when we first met him. And his dog, Brownie, well she's just a mean old dog," I lie again.

"What kind of a dog is she?"

"She's of the three-legged variety."

"Ain't no such thing."

"Is, too. It's how come she's so mean. She's mad she ain't got four legs like all them other dogs."

"All right, all right," she keeps on, "I'll steer clear of the dog. I just wanna see you shoot, is all. Please?"

Before I can say anything back, Mr. Tyler the science teacher pushes his way into the room like we've got some answering to do.

"All right, now," he starts class, "who's the wiseacre who thought it'd be funny to soil all my glass slides? Huh?"

Nine

"Hey, Mr. Wilson," I call ahead on my way up to his rickety house. "It's me, Carrie!"

But he ain't nowhere to be seen.

"Hey, Brownie," I pat the dog's head as she hobbles down to greet me. "Go on, now." It's annoying when she keeps on shoving her head under my hand to be pet. "Go on." But she won't go.

"Mr. Wilson?" I holler up loud enough for my voice to carry through the screen door at the top of the steps but still nothing comes back.

"Brownie, git," I say, but she doesn't mind me. "Go *on!*" I didn't realize she was lighter than she looks so when I kick her to the side she yelps and goes a lot farther than I thought my foot would take her. She lowers her head and looks at me from the side and then limps over out of my way. That'll teach her I mean business, as Richard would say.

At the top of the stairs I put my hand in a salute over my eyes so I can see in through the screen door to check if Mr. Wilson's there and just cain't answer for some reason, but no sign of life. What'm I gonna do for a stamp?

Before I realize it I'm tiptoeing through his front room, looking around for where he might keep them . . . or maybe some change so I can buy one at the post office. It's impossible to think of where either might be in this mess. I need to get going so I get there before it closes, so after a minute or so I give up.

"Whatchoo doing in my house, girl?" Mr. Wilson's voice booms into my bones, which I practically have to scrape off the ceiling since he startled me so.

"Um, um . . ."

"Um, um, what? What you need?" he says, a bit softer, seeing how scared I look.

"I'm sorry, sir," I manage to say. "I called up but you didn't answer and I need a stamp to send this letter to my Gammy and I wanted to get it in the mail today, 'fore the post office closed, and you weren't around so I thought I'd just come on in and see if you had a stamp laying around, but I wasn't gonna just take it. I'll pay you back, I promise I —"

"Now, slow down, sissy-girl," he says, spitting his chewing tobacca into the plastic cup he's always carrying around for that purpose. "I'll git you your stamp just to git some peace and quiet around here."

He hobbles over to the sideboard with three drawers and rifles through it till he comes out with a brand-new stamp and holds it out for me to take.

"Here ya are," he says. "You can have it . . . ya ain't got to pay me back or none if'n you can tell me who 'tis on the face of that stamp."

It looks familiar, this face with a dark beard. Stovepipe hat. "Abe Lincoln?" I say slow-like in case I see on his face that I'm wrong and then I can take it back and try again.

"Bingo!" he says. "Man who brought this country to its knees. I reckon you be hearing all 'bout the war 'tween the states in school so I ain't gonna start wit' you now. Plus I want my house back to myself after the day I had, so go on and git to the post office."

"Thank you, Mr. Wilson!" I lick the stamp on my way out the door and fix it to the corner of the envelope I lifted from Mr. Tyler's desk on my way out of science class. He was too busy taking care of Alver Quinten, who took the fall for the slides 'cause Odie Rice pointed to him behind his back when Mr. Tyler was scanning the room.

Just like Orla Mae said, the blacktop leads me right to the post office and I get there in plenty of time 'fore it closes. My mouth waters when I pass the jar of lemon sticks, but I keep on going, seeing's how I don't have any money to buy none, anyway. Emma'd be mad as the Nutrena rooster if I came home without one for her, so I guess I'm better off all the way around.

The clothes on the man behind the counter hang on his thin body like they would a hanger. He says nothing, just reaches out his bony hand with knobby knuckles for my letter and peers at the address and stamp by tilting his head back so his eyes will match up with his half glasses. He puts it with care on top of a pile of other letters sitting in a box with Outgoing written on it in perfectly shaped black letters. Then he turns to me and waits.

"Is that it?" I ask him. Seems to me it must be harder than this.

He nods slow-like.

"Thank you," I mumble so I can still consider myself polite even though I doubt he heard me.

Now we just have to wait.

On the walk back home I feel lighter for a bit, but by the time I've passed Antone's department store with the faded Closed sign in the window next to the sign for Human Hair Wigs, I start thinking I should have written "don't tell Momma I wrote this" on the letter somewhere. She'll be hopping mad if Gammy lets on I begged her to come. Shoot, I'll be whipped no matter what so I might as well leave it be.

Ten

"You're lucky I got too much to do today, little miss," Momma says to me in a snarly kind of way, "otherwise I'd tan your hide darker than it's ever been in your sorry little life. Now, go on. Take that rug outside and beat it good and hard. When you're done, fill up the bucket and help me with these floors."

Momma was surprised about Gammy coming, all right. When I heard her holler for me after hanging up the phone I knew it was Gammy who called, and Emma and me, we stayed clear of her altogether for a whole day and a half.

Gammy got my letter and called straight away to say she and Aunt Lillibit were gonna make the trip to see us. Now, I don't know for sure if she told Momma I'd written her, but the meanness in Momma's voice these past two days tells me she did. It's the first time in my life I'm happy there's a lot of housework to do. Momma's puttin' out the dog for Gammy. She pulled out the fancy nuts and everything.

The fanciest thing I've ever seen is Mr. Peanut, with his eyeglass and cane and that big ole smile. I love how his stick legs look about to dance. And I love his fancy top hat. People here don't ever dress up. Momma has a real pretty dress, but she almost never wears it because she says it makes her look like she's expecting. Expecting what, I don't know.

I've decided I want to get this label that's stuck on the can off so I can keep Mr. Peanut. After I do this I'll do the rugs real good but first . . .

There's only one ridge of glue holding it on so I'm trying to slide my fingernail right up close to it so it doesn't tear and then I can peel the rest off no problem. But the paper is getting jagged because the glue isn't in a straight line.

Almost there, almost there. I'm a little over halfway down the can from the plastic top you can pull off and put back on "for lasting freshness." If I quit now, Mr. Peanut will get ripped off tonight and then he'll be thrown away and who knows when Momma will buy nuts again. We've had this can for years, it moved with us from Murray Mill Road. Momma pours a handful of nuts into the milky white dish my grandmother gave her — a house-warming present she said, but someone should've told her dishes don't make you warm — and if some are left over she carefully pours them back into the can and puts them back up on the shelf. My cousin Sonny once touched all of them after he scraped dog doo off his shoe and then didn't even wash his hands (and I know for a fact Momma saw this, too) and Momma *still* poured the leftovers back in the can.

"Why doesn't Momma want Gammy to come visit us?" Emma asks me. She's squeezing the suds out of the rag she's been soaking in the bucket. We've got a floor-cleaning system: Emma rinses and squeezes and I rub the floor until the rag's dirty and then we do it all over again in a different spot.

"I guess we'll be finding out soon enough," I say.

"She's not going to tell us anything."

"I know, stupid," I say, pushing some of my hair back behind my ears so I can see better what all I'm doing. "But it's bound to come out once she's here, don't you think?"

"That the way you greet your kin?"

Gammy says, pulling her body out of the car. She's talking to me and Emma. We're hanging back closer to the steps to the house in case Momma decides now she's really gonna cream us good, now that all the housework's finished.

"Come on over and give your gammy and your auntie a hug, right proper," Momma says toward our direction. I can tell her voice is fake nice, but I don't think anybody else could.

Gammy's traveling dress smells like Clorox bleach. Aunt Lillibit doesn't lean down for us to hug her but instead reaches out to pat us on our heads and then pulls her hand back like she's having second thoughts about that, too.

Momma's chattering up and down to them like a raccoon at a garbage can: How was the trip? You all tired? You hungry? I got corn bread, Momma, I can fix you up a slice. What about you, Lil? Ooh, looky your hair, all done up like it is — ain't no place round here to get that done, I'll tell you what. That too heavy, Momma? Lemme get it.

Chattering away, she is. And me and Emma, well, I guess we feel like the dog that chases the car and finally catches it. We don't know what to do now that

Gammy's come on out to see us for her ownself. The way she's looking at us, I reckon she's feeling the exact same way.

"Ow!"

"Hold still, child," Gammy says. "Hold ya head *still*."

"You're *pulling* too hard. Ow!"

"This hair of yours . . ." She doesn't finish the sentence but stands up from the edge of the bed and pushes me to the side so she can get up from behind me. When she leaves the room I look back onto the bed. She left the brush, with my hairs stringing through it.

When she comes back I do not like what I see.

"Gammy, no!"

"Hold still or it'll be a lot worse'n what I have in mind," she says, snipping the scissors into the air to get 'em all warmed up.

"I'll pull the brush through." I try to slow her down, but fingers are gripping the top of my head, keeping me from turning and reaching the brush.

"Your momma," *snip*, "should've done this," *snip*, "years ago," *snip*, " 'stead of lettin' it git this bad." *Snip.*

"Gammy!"

Snip.

"*Please,* Gammy," I cry. But it's too late — the chunks of rats' nests fall into my lap and, soon, to either side of me.

"Hold still."

The snips match my sobs.

"Why'd you have to come out here, anyway?" I ask her when my tears dry up.

"Oh, hush," she says. "You know as well as I do why I came, so just be quiet." The cold metal of the scissors slides against the back of my neck and gives me shivers. "I'm just evening up the bottom here and you're all done."

I never look in the mirror 'cause I'm too scared to reach up and tell how short it is.

"Don't look too bad, if I do say so m'self," she says. "Now, run on and show your momma how clean you look."

I close my eyes and think of that blind and deaf girl we read about in school, Helen Keller, 'cause I'm feeling the way I look instead of rushing to a mirror.

"It's short as a boy's hair!" And the tears come back like they never dried up in the first beginning.

"Now, hush," Gammy says, scooting me aside so she can get up again. "You look just fine. Now, run on . . . I got to git supper started."

"What're we having?"

"Nothing if that whine stays in your throat," she snaps back at me. "Now, clean this room up and come on down and give me a hand when you're done."

"How come you don't cut Emma's hair?" I holler after her, but she's already on her way down the stairs. It's not fair Emma doesn't have to have a haircut, too.

"Shh, little baby," he says, stroking my hair, "quiet now. You just had a bad dream. I'm here now. Shh . . ."

"Daddy," I say into my pillow, breathing hard after the word. "I keep seeing it."

"The same thing?"

"Yeah, it's this little-bitty house with nothing but shelves in it — rows and rows of chickens . . ."

"Shh, now," he says again.

"and they all have sacks over their heads but you can still hear the clucking. Clucking, clucking. It's so loud. . . ."

He strokes my long hair over and over. The next thing I know it's morning time.

"You ask me, it's white trash lets her child run all over town looking like that one does," Aunt Lillibit's saying to Gammy. They think we're too busy playing jacks with the shells I saved from a beach vacation we took when Daddy was still alive to hear what they're talking about. Emma's been saving rubber bands for years, adding to the ball she started when we were back in Toast. It's pretty bouncy now, her ball is. So it's perfect for jacks.

"Your turn. You have to beat fives," she says, but I shush her so I can hear what all they're saying.

"That man'll be the death of her if she don't keep her head down and her mouth shut," Aunt Lillibit's saying.

"I tried talking to her about it, but she don't listen to her momma like she should," Gammy says. "Never has. I s'pose she never will."

"You see the back of her head where the hair bumps out over that cut? She got to stop back-talking like she does."

They're saying more but I cain't make it out, and because I'm trying to hear I mess up and the ball hits the ground before I can swipe up the six shells I was fixing to swipe up.

"And that Caroline takes right after her momma, you ask me," I can hear Aunt Lillibit saying. "She's got the welts to prove it. She and her momma need to take a lesson from Emma and be scarce."

"Hush, now," Gammy says. "That'll

be enough of that."

"How come you never around in the evenings?"

Mr. Wilson's setting in his armchair that looks like it belongs inside instead of here on the front porch, whittling wood like he sometimes does when he's thinking real hard on something.

"How you know I'm not round come evening time?"

I shrug, thinking he sees me but then I add, "I just know, is all. Where do you go?"

He turns the hand-size piece of wood around in his big hand, looking at it like he's seeing it for the first time.

"You know a man can work on his carving his whole life," he says to the nugget of wood, "and not git any better at it. Did you know that? Other things, well, you git better at 'em if you do 'em over an over again through the years. Not wood. You can stay just as bad a carver as you were the day you were born if that's the way it's s'posed to be."

"What do you mean, 'the way it's s'posed to be'? How do you know if something's the way it's s'posed to be?"

"You jes' know." He shrugs, and when he does I can see what he must've looked like when he was young, before age drew lines 'cross his face. "Like you shooting that gun. That's the way it's s'posed to be. Like me playing on that six-string. I ain't 'shamed to say I ain't half bad at it. It's the way it's s'posed to be."

We sit there, me with my legs dangling over the side of the porch, him with his knife flicking wood shavings off onto the floor, while I think about what's s'posed to be and what ain't.

"You never told me where you go come evening time."

"If it was yer business I'd tell you I go to play hill music down the road at Zebulon's, but 'tain't yer business so I won't be telling you that."

"Can I come watch you play?"

He shrugs again. "If you like. Don't your momma need you do chores 'fore bedtime?"

"What's Ze-boo-flan, whatever it's called?" Here's a trick I learned from Orla Mae: answer a question with a question and everyone wins.

"Zeb-*you*-lon is a feed-and-grain store at the edge of town we likes to go. The sound's good, what with them feed bags soaking it all up so it don't sound tinny, and, anyway, Sonny can't move that easy so we come to him, not the other way round."

"Who's Sonny?"

"You a nosy one, ain't ya? Sonny Zebulon's the oldest living man in town. You come on down sometime and meet Sonny. He'll like you. Yeah, 'sgood idea, come to think of it."

"Can I've a drink of water?"

"You know where the kitchen is."

When I get up to go inside Brownie cowers and Mr. Wilson looks over at her. "What's got into you, dog?"

I go get my glass of water.

Aunt Lillibit waits for people to mess up like she knew all along they were going to.

"Go on up and get me one of those extra blankets I see your momma has in the closet between the bedrooms, will you?" she calls over to me from the bed Momma's put together for her and Gammy to share in the front room, as far from the hole in the roof as a body can be.

"Take care you don't let it drag on the floor on your way back here!" Aunt Lillibit hollers up to me.

But there it is, the one corner I didn't double-check to see was tucked into the crook of my arms before I made my way back down to her, trailing after me like a tail.

"What did I just say to you? Huh? Give it here." She grabs the bundle from me and inspects the blanket corner for dirt, nodding her head like I just did exactly what she thought I'd do.

"Sorry." Nothing more for me to do but stare at the floor and wish she'd release me.

"I can see why your momma can't keep her house, what with you trailing dirt everywhere you set." She turns back to the bedding and snaps the blanket into the air so it falls across the other two that're already spread out on top of the mattress we hauled with us from Toast. Momma and Richard are sleeping on the box spring that fits underneath this one, and, oh, Richard was fit to be tied the first night of sleeping on *it*. He hollered up a storm at Momma about how we aren't a way station for her meddling family and how come he's expected to give up the soft mattress for the hard spring one when they're the ones lucky to have a roof over their heads.

"Why don't you go on and see to your gammy," Aunt Lillibit says to me. "Your *momma* sure isn't." She thinks I don't hear that part.

Gammy's busy scrubbing the kitchen counter.

"Hi," I say. "Need any help?" I say it quietly 'cause I don't want to scrub the kitchen, that's for sure.

"Go on and fill up this pail with outside water, will you?" she says, motioning to the river bucket setting by her feet.

"Yes, ma'am."

"Watch it! You got to be more *careful,* Caroline. You just got dirty water all over the floor there, you yanked the bucket up too quick! Now, dry that up before you set out. Well, I don't know where your momma keeps the dishrags. Go look under the sink. No, to the left. There. Now, come on over an' get the part right in front of my right foot. That's right. Take that rag outside with you and squeeze it out. Good. Now, take care with that bucket, you hear me?"

"Where's Emma?"

"Get *going.*"

"All *right.*"

"Don't you talk to your grandmother like that," she hollers after me.

Holding the bucket up in front of me like it's a bouquet of flowers, I walk straight and slow toward the river, my flowing white dress almost as beautiful as my veil. On either side of the path people are crammed into the pews, craning their necks to get a look at me, the bride. Oh, hey, Betsy! And there's Perry Gibson. He's always had a crush on me but I never gave him the time of day. Poor Perry. And there's Mary Sellers. She sure looks jealous of my dress, it's written all over her face.

"Carrie! Jeez, I been hollering at you for about a *year!*" Emma trots out from behind me. "Wait up."

"Where've *you* been?"

"Lookin' for you."

"Not lookin' too hard, since I've been Gammy's slave inside. I notice you didn't show hide or hair *there*. Move, I got to fill this bucket or she'll be so beside herself she'll hold her own hand."

Emma jumps across to the rock in the middle of the stream and squats to pick at the moss, like this movie we saw in science class where a wild monkey picks bugs out of her babies' fur.

"Why's Gammy always in such a bad mood?" she asks.

"How should I know?"

Emma shrugs and picks some more. "You think she likes us any?"

Now I shrug 'cause I have no earthly idea.

The bucket's full so we go back up to the house. Just before we get to the back door, the one that opens into the kitchen, I look down and see my shoes untied. I set the bucket down to tie them so I don't have to hear all about how messy I am from Aunt Lillibit and that's when I hear them.

"Wait!" I hiss over at Emma, who's reaching for the door. She backs up toward me and turns her head so the sounds'll go straight into her ear without having to turn sideways at her face.

"I told her about that one and I told her about this one," Gammy's voice carries to us. "But she's hardheaded. I've said it from the day they had to pull her out of me — stubborn child wouldn't even leave her momma's belly when she was told to!"

"With Henry she was up against other women," Aunt Lillibit says. "And with Richard she's knocking against a brick wall, day after day. This one makes the other one look trifling."

"I know it," says Gammy.

"Folks in town here all sayin' he dipped his hand in the till of that store, Annie's or Auntie's or whatever it is," Aunt Lillibet says.

Antone's? I mouth over to Emma, who's stretchin' her neck even farther out to get closer to the voices but right this second I cain't even make out what they're saying. Wait! Now they're talking normal again.

"How'm I supposed to know?" Aunt Lillibet is saying. "He like to have made off with a good-size sack, though, 'cause folks is spittin' mad. Lost his job over it, didn't he?"

Me and Emma, we just stare at each other like in a cartoon when they get hit on the head with something and they get big eyes before they tip over.

"By the way, I ran into Nellie Lamott the other day back in Toast when I went through there to gather up what was left and she said Selma Blake was asking all about Libby. A little too much, according to Nellie. She said the rumor's *still* sticking to Selma about being a home wrecker and all. That Selma never did know when to leave well enough alone without going and stirring up her own pot of trouble for her own self. Asking all over town about Libby. Takes nerve. Nobody'll give that good-for-nothing husband of hers a job after that high drama. She needs to look after him a little more, talk about Lib a little less."

"I know it."

"You ask me, Libby traded up," Aunt Lillibit says.

"With this one? You're crazy."

"That Henry was no more faithful to

Libby than the one that turned all them others 'gainst Jesus at that supper. Everybody knew it. Even Libby. Prowling round like he did. This one, well, so he's got a temper," Aunt Lillibit says. "You find me a man *without* a temper and I'll show you a miracle from God. Look at Daddy. He had a temper but he held a job and all. Didn't drink himself half to death every night."

"And that's a fact. Your daddy kept a roof over our heads through the worst of it. Times we didn't have a scrap of paper to suck on but your daddy kept that square of land, that's for sure. You girls might'f gotten a belt now and then, but your sister was harder than a horse in need of breaking. You, well . . ."

Their voices drop to where we cain't hear them no more.

"Carrie!" I hear Emma calling out to me. "Where you going? Carrie! Wait up!"

But I'm gone. Over the fallen tree. Across the stream. Up a steep scattering of rocks. Gone. To where I cain't hear them talking no more.

"I'm ready to go to Zebulon's." I'm panting wors'n Brownie.

"What's that?" Mr. Wilson looks up from the electricity cord he's fooling with.

"I'm ready to go to Zebulon's," I say, clearer for having caught up with my breath. "Can we go today?"

Mr. Wilson's clicking his tongue to the roof of his mouth and shaking his head back and forth, and even though I cain't see his face straight on 'cause he's bending over the cord I know it doesn't look good.

"First off, it ain't nighttime, last I checked," he says, more to the plastic covering he's peeling off them colored wires, "and second, since when am I lettin' a five-year-old kid tell me what I'm doing."

"I'm *eight!*"

"Just the same. No eight-year-old's gonna come on over here and tell me what all I'm to be doing, 'stead of asking real nice. Like bossy-the-cow, you are."

"I'm sorry," I say, smiling 'cause now I know I might sway him on taking me there. "Mr. Wilson, could you please-oh-please accomp'ny me to Mr. Zebulon's so's I could hear y'all play? Please?"

He's shaking his head again, but this time I'm pretty sure I can make out the crinkles on either side of his eyes.

"Please?"

"Best be patient and I'll think on it while I finish up with this here cord," he says.

So I slide my fingernail under a bubble

of chipping white paint on the boards next to his front door. When it comes off nice and clean I do it again. And again. Until he coils up the cord and puts his screwdriver back in the tackle box he uses for nails, tools and what all else I do not know. I do think he's got a ruler in there. And a couple of dulled pencils he sharpens with a knife.

"All right, girl," he says, standing up. "You wore me down with yer waitin' so I guess we best git on our way. Lemme go in and get my six-string."

He settles the guitar in the middle of the long front seat of his bro-ken-down old truck. It's facing out, the neck reaching up taller than I am.

I like that he doesn't talk much. I mean, it's not like I'm wanting to think about home or Gammy or Aunt Lillibit, 'cause I don't.

"Mr. Wilson?"

He's got one hand on the wheel, one elbow resting on the open window. "Yeah?"

"What's a home wrecker?" I look out my side of the truck while we drive along so he cain't see I'm about to cry thinking on the words. I feel him looking at me, though.

"I reckon a home wrecker does jes' that

— wrecks yer home."

I look over at him now. "You mean busts everything up? Like furniture?"

"I mean souls," he says, straightening out the arm that's been in the window, signaling to the driver behind us he's turning left, I s'pose.

"Busts up *souls?* What's that mean?"

"A home wrecker breaks yer spirit. Breaks the family up. Why you asking all them questions?"

I don't answer him. He doesn't seem to need me to, anyhow.

A few minutes later we pull up sideways alongside a big barnlike building with a rusted sign that reads "Ze lon's" on account of the *b* and *u* being all worn out. Mr. Wilson turns to the outside and swings his bad leg so it's in the same direction as the good one and then he hops out of the truck, taking his guitar with him.

"I cain't open my door," I call out through my window. "Wait! I cain't open my door." But he's going in through the open barn doors and cain't hear me so I slide across the seat and go out through his side.

"I got locked in the truck," I say when I catch up to him.

"Your side don't work."

"How come you left me?"

"You can't figure out how to git out of a truck," he says, hobbling past the sacks of flour and meal, "there's no hope for you a'tall."

"Wilson." A man about the same age's Mr. Wilson holds his hand out to be shaked.

"Walles," Mr. Wilson says back.

"How come we got to see your ugly old face in the daylight?"

Mr. Wilson smiles, picks up a tool that's lying there on the table, hoping someone'll take it home, and says, "Oh, you know . . . someone's got to scare away the vermin running through here."

"Who's this riding shotgun?" He looks me over like he's thinking I might steal something.

"Don't need to pay her no mind," he says, like I'm deaf, "she's along for the playin'. She's a Culver. She got banjo in her blood, God help her."

The man Walles nods and falls alongside Mr. Wilson, heading to the back of the store where the shelves clear out and up-side-down wood milk crates become stools. A couple even have old flour sacks on top — the five-pound sacks — for your back-side. Mr. Wilson takes one, Walles the other, and then I see a raisin of a man hunched over his guitar a stone's throw away. I reckon he's Zebulon, since he's in a real chair with arms and a back, 'cause if you're the oldest living soul in town you shouldn't have to sit on a milk crate.

"Zeb," Mr. Wilson says softly. He's so quiet I'm not sure Zebulon hears him until I see him nodding his head, picking out notes up and down the neck of the guitar.

"What we doing today?" Walles asks, shimmying his backside into the flour sack.

"How 'bout some Mississippi John Hurt?"

"Naw. Blind Willie McTell."

"I could use some 'Mama 'Tain't Long 'Fore Day.' Or what 'bout that left-handed woman who plays the right-handed strings? What's her name?"

Before they can settle that, Zebulon starts playing something on his guitar and the other two join in and sure enough they make the most beautiful sounds in the world. I close my eyes and imagine my granddaddy pulled up alongside them. I bet *he* wasn't a home wrecker.

I come back up the trail that leads to number twenty-two and there it is, the sheriff's truck in front of our old house. If

I wasn't sure whose truck it was all I'd have to do would be to look at the writing on the door that opens to the steering wheel. In big block letters Sheriff is written, so there'll be no mistake.

"Emma?" I holler out in case she's not inside and can come tell me what all's happening. But she doesn't answer.

They've come to take Richard away. I can feel it.

There's a big rock that's made for sitting so that's what I do. Sit. And wait. I wonder if they'll use handcuffs.

I don't have to wait too long until the door opens and out of the darkened house comes the sheriff, not holding Richard, but holding a piece of paper that, when the door closes behind him, he tacks up, front and center. I don't know what the paper says, but I do know the sheriff doesn't look like I thought he would; he's wearing blue jeans and an old shirt that looks like it's made for winter, not summer. When he comes down the front steps to his pickup truck I can see he's got a star pinned to the front of it, so I guess that's the only uniform he's got to wear out here in the country.

Wait! Here's Momma.

"What're we s'posed to do now?" she

calls out from the porch to the sheriff, whose one leg is already climbing into the truck.

"Maybe you got family you can go to," he says.

"Please don't do this," she says. And she's close to tears 'cause I can hear her voice catch them and hold them back. "Please."

"I'm sorry, ma'am," he says. "The law's the law."

With that he climbs on into the pickup, starts it up and drives away back down the dirt trail, through the scrub brushes, over the rocks and out onto the blacktop.

"What is it, Momma?" I ask her on my way up to the house. But it's already swallowed her up.

When the door shuts behind her I read the paper the sheriff left behind.

"*Notice of eviction,*" it shouts. "*The occupants are to leave these premises in no more than thirty days. This notice serves as a warning that any more time than thirty days will be viewed as a violation to which legal action will be taken.*"

The occupants are to leave the premises?

"Momma?" I call out once my eyes adjust to the dark front room. "Where is everybody? Emma?"

In the kitchen Gammy and Aunt Lillibit are standing behind Momma, who's crumpled into a chair, holding her head in her hands.

"He should've been here for that, the son of a bitch," Aunt Lillibit says, putting her hand on Momma's shoulder. "Where is he, anyway?"

Momma shakes her head to say she doesn't know.

"Woulda, coulda, shoulda," Gammy says. "Now ain't the time to wallow. We got some work to do, packing up what all we brought." She looks at Aunt Lillibit and moves over to the sink to wash the dishes that always seem to multiply themselves.

"What're we gonna do?" Momma's voice makes its way through her hands.

"He should've thought a that when he put his hand in the till," Gammy says over her shoulder. "He should've thought a that when he went to fisticuffs at the yard. Seems to me he don't think of much 'fore he folds his knuckles up and swings."

Momma pushes up and out of her chair before I can even turn my head back to her from looking at Gammy's flowered house-coat.

"If you got something to say, Momma, say it." Momma's voice is higher than I've ever heard it. "Just say it. To my face. Not to Lillibit. To me, Momma."

Gammy turns to face her.

"Don't you take that tone with me, young lady," Gammy warns. "I'm still your mother and I deserve a little respect."

"Why can't you say what you're thinking?" I cain't tell for sure, but I don't think this is the tone Gammy was hoping for. *"Just say it."*

"All right, all right. You married yourself into this trouble. You asked for it when that man came into town holding nothing but the same two hands that bring pain everywhere they travel. You scratch your head wondering where it all went wrong . . . I'll tell you where it went wrong. You've never settled into life. You want life to be better to you but it ain't like that. Not for folks like us. Life's hard. That's the way it is. But you can't seem to settle into it and work with it like it is. You want it to be better for you? That ain't gonna happen. Y'hear me? It ain't never gonna happen. . . ."

Even though I can tell Gammy isn't finished Momma cuts her off and yells, "Get out of my house!"

"In case you didn't notice," Gammy says, moving closer to Momma, "it ain't your house no more. You were living here courtesy of the mill your own husband cursed and got throwed out of. What're you expecting? Them to tell you, 'Oh, stay as long as you please'? You got a problem with this, take it up with your husband. Don't you go raising your voice to your own momma. I come out here to see what's what. To help out best I can. All I see when I get here is tempers and tears. I see the bruisin'. I see the blood. I still got my eyesight, thank the Lord. At least *I* kept my children safe," she mutters as she turns back to the sink. I guess she's finished now.

"Get out," Momma practically spits. "Get out now. I'm going out to find Richard and when I get back I want to see an empty space where you car's settin'."

"You're throwing your own flesh and blood out?" Aunt Lillibit's eyes are open and wide like plates at suppertime.

"You heard me."

"That's fine, Lillibit," Gammy says. "We ain't gonna stay where we ain't welcome, that's for sure."

Momma shakes her hair so it all goes behind her back and then she comes out, toward where I'm standing in the front room looking in. It's like she doesn't see me, the way she walks on by, her head held up and facing out of number twenty-two.

The screen door slams. Back in the kitchen Gammy dries the plate she's just cleaned and carefully stacks it on top of the others that had their turns. The stack gets placed back in the cabinet where it almost never is 'cause we use and reuse them, never thinking to put them back.

"I'll go gather up my things," Aunt Lillibit says to no one in particular.

Gammy doesn't know I'm watching her dry her hands on her apron and settle them evenly, on either side of the lip of the sink, looking out the window into the woods that lead to the Diamond River. She stays still for what feels like hours. When she turns and faces me I see she has known I was there all along.

"Well," she says, "I s'pose we've got a lot to get going on." On her way past me she touches the top of my head and now it's me who's catching the tears in her eyes.

In the front room, Aunt Lillibit is folding her clothes and stacking them like Gammy did the plates. Gammy goes over to the sideboard and pulls her case out, settling it on the mattress. It lies there with an open mouth ready to gobble up their lives and spirit them away from here.

"Don't just stand there, go on and pull

the clothes out off the line, will you?" Aunt Lillibit calls over to me. So I do as I'm told 'cause now's not the time to give them any more reasons to be upset with the Parker family.

Shirts, pants and underthings hang like sad ghosts. One by one they snap free into my hands, hopeful, I bet, they'll be worn out in the world, away from the dark woods. I hold them up to my nose and sniff in real hard, like I do with the shag carpet that Daddy left behind, but instead of smelling like Gammy and Aunt Lillibit they smell faintly of lemons and soap.

"Don't dawdle, child," Gammy calls through the kitchen door. "We're waiting on you."

"Are you really going to go?" I ask her on my way back into the house.

"Yes we are," she says, lifting the ghosts from my arms and shaking the wrinkles out of them. "Now, come on and take the other end of this blanket so we can get it back up into the closet. I won't have your momma saying I left a mess in my wake."

I walk backward from Gammy and the blanket stretches out between us. Like dance partners we walk toward and away from each other until the blanket is in a nice neat square.

"Momma didn't mean it," Emma says from the foot of the staircase, where I guess she'd been hiding out watching them fight, just like I'd been doing.

"Hand me my hairbrush from over there, will you?" Aunt Lillibit says to Emma. "Step lightly, we got to get going."

"She didn't mean it," Emma says, handing over the brush. "Can't you just stay a bit longer?"

"I haven't got a lot," Gammy says to her and me both, "but I do have my pride. We're leaving soon as this case is full. Lillibit, where's that slip I loaned you? That's fine, you can put it in your bag, just make sure you don't leave it behind."

"What about us?" I ask her.

"You'll be all right." Gammy pats me on the head. "You just stay out of his way and you'll be all right."

The mouth closes up, full of food. Gammy snaps it locked and turns to survey the front room.

"Okay, Lillibit," she says. "Let's get this show on the road."

"I'll be right there." Aunt Lillibit goes into our one bathroom. She tries and tries but the door won't meet the wall. It never has, but that hasn't kept Aunt Lillibit from trying every single time she goes in there.

Like she thinks we're dying to walk in on her going to the bathroom. From inside I hear her sigh.

"Help me with this, will you?" Gammy hands me one of the handles of her case and we walk side by side with it between us until we get to the front door, where we turn sideways so we can fit through without having to put it down.

She sets it down by the car and turns back into the house for her purse.

"Please, Gammy." I cain't catch the tears before they start falling. "Please don't go. . . ."

But, just like Daddy always said, Gammy isn't good with tears.

Aunt Lillibit comes out with her bag, which has never fastened shut like Gammy's, and out of the side that's squeezing shut I see the arm of the white shirt I'd pulled off the line. I guess the only thing wanting to stay behind with us is the ghost.

They're in the car, Aunt Lillibit letting it warm up before pulling away.

"You be good," she says to me through the open window. "Y'hear me? Be good, Caroline."

"Come over here and give y'Gammy a kiss goodbye," Gammy says, leaning across Lillibit in the front seat, motioning me to cross over to her window. "Come on," she calls out the window to Emma.

When I get there her arm reaches out to my cheek. "Dry those tears, y'hear me? They ain't gonna do you any good. They never do."

I feel Emma at my side. She reaches her little arm through the window to Gammy. "Gammy," she cries. "Please . . ." She is sobbing so hard it takes her a second to gather enough breath for words, "take us with you. . . ."

"Go on, Lillibit" is all she says.

"Take us with you," Emma sobs. Which is an oddball thing for her to do, since she only cries when she thinks she can change something. I guess that's her being littler than me. She doesn't realize there's no changing this.

Eleven

"All right, everybody, settle down, now," Miss Ueland says, fanning her flattened hands slowly up and down, showing us it's time to quiet down.

She looks us over, her eyes resting on me a little longer than everybody else in class. I wipe at my nose 'cause she's looking at me like I have something coming out of it.

"Today we're going to talk about our *founding fathers*," she says, turning to the blackboard. "Do y'all know who I'm talking about when I say *founding fathers?*"

Orla Mae's hand shoots up, "I do! I do!"

"Yes, Orla Mae. Go ahead."

"They're the ones who were the first presidents," she says, sitting up straight against the back of her chair.

The rest of the class is a blur of questions and answers that I don't have to be a part of, thank the Lord. Soon the bell rings and I get my books together.

"Caroline? May I have a word with you,

hon?" Miss Ueland calls out over the bodies hurrying to push out the door of the class.

"Yes, ma'am?" I say to her, trying to keep my arms from shaking from the heaviness of the books. I wish I'd had something in my belly to keep from feeling like I might see stars like I do right now.

"Caroline, I'm worried about you, honey," she says, resting half her self on the edge of the desk. "How're you doing?"

"I'm fine, ma'am."

She looks at me, deep into my eyes, and for a second I want to cry. I hold it back, though.

"Tell me what's going on, honey —" her voice is practically begging me to cry "— you can talk to me."

I gulp and say, "Nothing's going on, ma'am."

"I've half a mind to come on out and talk to your parents —"

But before she can finish that thought I cut it off at the pass. "No! I mean, no thank you, ma'am. I mean, everything's fine. I fell on the rocks out back of my house and knocked my head, is all. My momma'll tan my hide if you talk to her about it. She tells me all the time I got to stop climbing rocks out in the woods. If she knows you're worried about it I'll never hear the end of it!"

I hope that'll do the trick.

She waits, looks down at her hands so prettily folded in front of her. Her wedding ring sparkling against the overhead lighting.

"I'll give it some thought," she says after a spell. "But please know you can talk to me whenever you need to, Caroline. All right?"

"Yes, ma'am."

"You understand me?"

"Yes, ma'am."

"You can go on, now."

"Thank you, ma'am."

And I'm glad she told me I could go 'cause for one quick second, about as quick as a sneeze, I thought I might tell her about Richard.

"I hear you got yourselves a problem over yonder." Mr. Wilson looks up at us from his whittling.

Now I know what Momma would say right now. She'd tell him to mind his own business. But it's Mr. Wilson. Mr. Wilson doesn't care a lick about other people's business. Seems to me he's only interested in his own usually.

To be on the safe side I don't say anything back. I'll wait till I see where he's going.

"Now, I know they're some folks in town be happy to see y'all move on outta here," he says, back to making sure his thumb doesn't get cut off along with chips of wood. "Antone, in particular. Folks over at the mill. Yep, they all hoping y'all leave and take trouble with ya. But I ain't one of them."

"What do you think?" Emma asks him from on top of the tree stump she's trying her best to balance on top of. But it's a bitty tree stump so she has to hop back on after she falls. I don't know how she can think of balancing on a tree stump at a time like this.

"I think folks got to look after one another. I think a man's got to answer for the things he done."

He sets his wood and knife aside, puts his hands on his knees and looks at both of us. Square on.

"What we gonna do about you?" he says. "Huh?"

Neither of us answer him. What would we say, anyhow?

"I about had it with a man who cain't pick on someone his own size," he says. "Got to go take it out on a child . . . I about had it wit' that, I'll tell you what."

We follow behind him out to the gun shed. "Where's he going?" Emma whispers to me.

"Shh," I hush her. "What happened to the lock?" I ask Mr. Wilson.

"Thing gave out," he says. "Did its job for two decades. Guess it knew there's no one it has to keep out. No one comes out this way anymore, anyway."

We wait outside while he opens the cabinet and pulls a different gun out. This one's small, has a shiny white handle, and instead of dark gray, it's silver. He leaves the door half open.

"In my pappy's day we'd take care of that man," he's saying to himself on his way out to the pasture where the cans sat on the fence.

"He always like this?" Emma whispers to me. I shake my head and keep my eyes on Mr. Wilson.

"Git up here, girl," he calls out to Emma. I let her learn on this gun since the shotgun's mine and this one's better suited for a little one.

"You got to learn how to defend yourself since no one else's doing it for you. Now. Take hold a'this handle. Feel how smooth it is? Don't let it fool you. This gun's a might powerful. A man could tell himself it ain't gonna do the job but I'm here to tell you, this gun shot down one of the meanest sons of bitches ever lived. Hollis Collins. Point it where you want the bullet to fly. That's right. Hollis Collins felt the licks of flames from hell nearly every day he walked on this earth. No reason for him to go making trouble for everybody, so my pappy shot him down. Y'ain't gonna be able to match up your target with cross-hairs, like a rifle, so what you do instead is move your chin over so it's nearly over the part of your arm between your shoulder and elbow. That's right. Good. Tilt it a little more so your cheek almost touches — that's right. If your arm's good 'n straight you'll hit your target, sure as manure."

"Hey!" Emma says, looking from him to me. "Our daddy used to say that!"

"Your daddy'd thank me right now for teaching y'all how to shoot," he says back. "Now, concentrate on what you're gonna hit. This can's setting in one place but most times your target's moving. So you got to be able to move your body but keep your arm straight while you do it so as soon as he stops a'moving, you can fire off a round."

"Should I shoot now?"

"Wait a second," he says. "Feel that trigger? It's gonna give pretty easy, so be ready to push back at the power once it does. Try a shot and you'll see what I'm talking about."

Pow!

Emma yelps like I did the first time Mr. Wilson fired one off. Nothing prepares you for that sound.

"That's a start," he says, once the smoke clears from the end of the gun where the bullet came out. "But see what I mean by the trigger?"

"Yeah!" she says. I can't keep from smiling 'cause I know how excited she feels.

"Now, you missed your target." He's stern like a teacher always seems to be. "You got to leave behind the notion that it's easy and concentrate on gettin' the job done. Give it over and I'll show you what I'm talkin' about. See how my arm's steady? You got to be steady 'cause the trigger'll mess with your mind, it's so loose. It'll make y'arm think it can be, too. But you got to hold steady."

Pow!

Emma runs over to the fence and holds up the can that knocked onto the ground, like it's a trophy. "You did it!"

"That's what I'm talkin' about," he says.

"My arm never moved. Let the target tire itself out moving, don't let your arm tire out doing the same. Now, try again."

Emma runs back over, takes the gun and stretches her arm out.

"Like this?"

"You got it," he says. "That's right, lock y'elbow. Now y'ready for that trigger."

Pow!

Emma runs over and sure enough, she bends down and holds the can up the same way she did before.

"That's a mighty good shot, girl," Mr. Wilson says, spitting off to the side. "A fine shot."

On the way back home Emma's skipping, she's so happy about shooting.

"You know what happens next, right?" she says, hopping up on a rock and jumping off of it like it's a ride at the carnival.

"What're you talking about?" I ask.

"We're gonna shoot Richard," she says, leaping over a tree stump. "He's gonna get shot."

I've stopped walking after her. "What?"

"Yep," she calls over to me from a mushroom she's inspecting. "We're gonna kill Richard. That's what Mr. Wilson was showing us how to do."

I'm walking again. "You're crazy. He

wasn't doing any such thing."

"He was, too," she says, skipping back over to me. "We got to kill him, Carrie."

"We just walk in one day and shoot him? Just like that?"

"Yeah, kinda," she says, falling into step alongside me, when the branches clear a bit so we can walk two by two. "And then we wouldn't get throwed out of the house 'cause the sheriff'd feel sorry for us and he'd let us stay. But even if we did have to go, with Richard dead there'd be no one for Gammy and Auntie Lillibit to hate so we could go live with them."

I started shaking my head halfway through her little solution and now I have to speak my mind.

"It's one thing to kill a can, it's another altogether to kill a man, no matter how much he needs killing," I tell her. Sometimes little sisters don't think things through, so it's up to big sisters to help them with that. That's what I think, anyway.

"Just think," she says, happily pointing to my forehead that's got a blue-brown welt on it from Richard's slapping, "that could be your last bruising."

With Gammy and Aunt Lillibit gone the

house is quiet again. Momma's stopped cleaning the clothes and I'm happy 'cause that means I don't have to help her pin them up to the line to dry. One less chore to think about. Me and Emma decide we got to have two piles of clothes in our room: one for clothes that're dirty beyond wearing, the other for reusables. Reusables are clothes that might have a stain or two, but can pass off as clean if you wear things like undergarments inside out. That's our system.

The notice of eviction stays tacked to the door and pretty soon I don't even see it when I come and go. It just blends in with everything else.

Momma comes out of her room sometimes, but I almost wish she wouldn't 'cause all she does is cry or yell. I haven't seen Richard in a couple of days, but I can tell from the empty beer bottles he's been here, probably when we're fast asleep. Maybe he's back working again.

Things could have kept on like this, I guess, but that wasn't the way it was s'posed to be.

Twelve

"One, two, three," she calls out.

"Eyes on me!" we answer her.

"Two, three, four," Miss Ueland says.

"Close the door!"

"I have some exciting news to tell you about," Miss Ueland says, walking to the front of the room. "Quiet down, everybody. I've got something I need to tell you."

Ellie Frenden whispers across to me, "I know what she's gonna say," but then clamps up and looks real pleased with herself.

"Now, class," Miss Ueland starts. "I want to tell you that I'm about to become a mother."

The class is dead quiet. All except for Ellie, who is trying to catch my eye so she can nod like the know-it-all she is. Her uncle's the town doctor so I guess that's how she knows about Miss Ueland.

"This is all very *unexpected* but very *exciting* for me," she continues, "and for Mr.

Ueland. But we are *moving* to the next county over so we can be in a bigger home that has room for a *baby*. I know babies are *small* but they do grow, you know, and soon we'll need the *larger space*."

"Does this mean you won't be our teacher anymore?" Orla Mae asks while her arm is still raised to be called on.

"Mr. Tyler will be taking over for me — don't make that face, Buddy Lee. Mr. Tyler is a fine teacher. But I'm afraid I will be leaving y'all, Orla Mae," Miss Ueland says. "And that makes me *sad*, because I've loved teaching y'all."

Her eyes rest on me when she says this last part, but I look away. Guess I won't be coming to her about Richard after all. I knew I wouldn't. I was just thinking.

I wish I could stay in my room like Momma does. Sure would be easier. I wouldn't have to think about what all we're gonna eat, how to get more food in the Frigidaire, getting homework done and then doing it all over again, day after day. Yeah, I wish I could stay in bed all day, too.

School just isn't the same without Miss Ueland and sometimes I feel like I don't even know my baby sister anymore, either.

Since learning how to shoot she's on a mission. It's like she doesn't need me anymore, really. She's taken to going off to the river on her own, working things out in her mind, I guess.

Instead of going to the river, I go with Mr. Wilson to Zebulon's a lot these days, so I guess I'm doing the same thing Emma is, just in a different way.

"Come on over here, girl," Walles calls over to me from the barrel he's setting on. "Lemme show you a lick I bet you could do real good. You hold on to the neck with yer left hand — you right-handed, right? Good. Them lefties got bats up in their heads, they so empty. So you take the neck and hold you' finger — that's right, the first finger, curl it around — on the top string and then with yer right hand you're gonna pick out a tune. Use yer first finger and yer thumb for it and hit these strings — that's right! I'll be damned. See? You got yerself a melody there. Sounds good. Sonny, play me a G, will ya? Let's lay that underneath the tune you just picked, Culver."

"My name's Parker," I have to tell him. Even though I'd rather be called Culver after my daddy.

"I thought you were a Culver."

"I was, but Momma got married after my daddy died and his last name's Parker so it's mine, too, now."

"Not Parker for that fella worked over at the mill? That the one?"

"Yes, sir."

Walles looks over at Sonny Zebulon, whose head has come up for air from the guitar he's always bent over. They look at each other for a spell.

"How'd a little girl like you end up with a —"

"Walles," Mr. Wilson says with a sharpness like if his voice was a knife Walles'd be bleeding. Walles knows it, too, 'cause he stops talking altogether. "Let's play ourselves a tune," Mr. Wilson says, placing his own guitar across his lap. "Let's git down to it. I've had 'bout enough'a this jawin'."

The music trickles over me like the water moves over and around the rocks dotting the Diamond River.

Hey, Carrie? Want to come over to my house after school? Check witch box on wether you can or cant.

Orla Mae

I look over at her to smile that I can but she's looking to the front of the room real hard, so we won't get caught passing notes.

I check yes and then fold it back up real tiny-like and drop my pencil on the floor so when I go down to pick it up I can slide it across the aisle to her desk.

Mr. Tyler's writing up on the board so he doesn't see her bend down to pick it up. She unfolds it one square at a time so it doesn't make a rustling-paper noise that tells teachers kids aren't paying attention.

After class we stack our books and wait for each other so we can walk out together.

"Wait on me a sec," I tell her out in the yard. "I got to go tell my sister to get home on her own."

"Hey, Em," my breath taking a second to catch up to my feet, finally reaching her. "You go on ahead home. I'll be there later."

Emma looks past me to Orla Mae, who's biting her nails like they're supper.

"You goin' over to Orla Mae's?" she asks, like it's against the law.

"What's it to you? Just go on home without me. I won't be late." I know she's wanting for me to invite her but I've gotten too used to being on my own lately.

She shrugs and turns away and all of a sudden I feel a pang like I wish I'd handled it all different.

"You wanna come?" I holler to her,

knowing the answer and feeling terrible about it.

The answer is no answer. Just a little sister walking away.

Orla Mae's house is not much bigger than ours, but there aren't so many trees crowding around hers, so sunlight can make its way into the rooms.

We drop our books on a table that waits just inside the door.

"Hey, Momma," Orla Mae calls out.

"Hey, honey," the voice answers from the back of the house. "How was school?"

"Fine. Carrie Parker's here."

"That's good."

"Can she stay for supper?" Orla Mae hasn't asked me if that's okay, but I reckon Momma won't even know I'm not at home.

"W'sure," Mrs. Bickett answers. "We'll eat in a bit. Why don't y'all go on and do your homework 'fore it gets too late."

Orla Mae rolls her eyes at me. "C'mon."

She motions me to follow her out a side door that's off their front room, which has pictures scattered on every flat top — pictures of babies, weddings, and sour-looking people who don't look used to standing for a photograph.

"Who's that?" I ask, pointing to a man with a tall black hat and round glasses.

"That's my grandpappy, he's my daddy's daddy. Grew up on the east shore, Outer Banks. Back before anyone even knew they were there. He was all alone there with his parents, my great-grandparents. Never had any schooling or other kids to play with. Daddy says he right near lost his mind when he got old. C'mon."

Out to the side of the house is a littler shack that looks like it's built to copy the big one. Chickens go up and down a ramp, instead of stairs, in and out of the house, pecking as they go.

"They're the stupidest things alive," Orla Mae says. "Watch. I'll feed 'em pebbles. Ha! Lookit that one — she don't even know it ain't food she's eatin'. One time I fed them a piece of scrambled eggs Momma made for breakfast, and they ate them! You know what that makes 'em? Calenbles."

"You mean cannibals," I say.

"Why you gotta always be smarter than everyone else?" She throws a wood chip to the hungry birds. "Y'always doin' that."

"No, I'm not," I say.

"Yes, y'are. In class you always get the right answer."

"*You* do. I figure you're the brainiest one there."

"Yeah." But she says it like she doesn't believe what I'm saying.

"Y'all even cracked a book open?" Mrs. Bickett calls out the upstairs window.

"We will, Momma!" Orla Mae calls over her shoulder.

"What did I tell you? Do yer homework! No supper till you finish."

"C'mon," I say. The thought of going without a bite to eat makes me weak. "Let's go on and do it."

"All right, smarty-pants."

"I am not a smarty-pants."

"Are, too."

We both sigh hard on our way back into the house.

Homework's easy on account of Mr. Tyler being fooled by Freddie Sprague, who told him we hadn't yet started our English workbook when we really had so the homework he assigns us is already done. I guess Miss Ueland left in such a hurry she forgot to fill him in on what we know and what we don't know.

It's been a long time since I heard the sound of pots and pans clanging around in a faraway room. I love knowing someone else has to figure out what we can chew on.

I wonder what Emma's gonna eat.

"We finished, Momma." Orla Mae gets up and goes to the kitchen so I follow. Past the Bickett faces staring out at me, reminding me I'm a stranger here.

"Good. Now, come put out the salt and pepper. And Carrie, will you — oh. What happened to yer hand, honey?"

I put the forks she'd been handing me back down and quickly put my hand back in my pocket, where it's been staying till it heals.

"Nothing, ma'am," I lie. "Had an accident, is all."

"Let me see that," she says.

"It's fine, ma'am. Really."

She cocks her head to the side and says, "All right then. You okay to put these forks out?"

"Yes, ma'am," I say. "I sure am."

I gulp back the spit that's been collecting in my cheeks once the smell of home cooking reached my nose.

"Now, go wash up for supper, girls. And, Carrie, take care of that hand! That cut looks like it'll loosen up real easy. Don't git it too wet."

I tried boiling the last of our eggs the other day 'cause Momma once said eggs that're old got only one use: being boiled. I tried holding the pot of boiling water real steady on my way to carrying it over to the sink for emptying but I'm not as strong as I thought I was so when it got heavy it started dropping and I had to catch hold of it on the side opposite the handle and gave myself a nasty burn. Momma always said I's clumsy.

"Orla Mae?" Mrs. Bickett says, settling into her chair at the kitchen table. "Will you say grace tonight?"

They unfold wash towels across their laps so I do the same.

"God bless this food, our friends —" she squeezes my hand across the table when she says this "— and our family," I reckon she's squeezing her momma when she says that, "and our home. Thank you for our blessings one and all. Amen."

"Amen," Mrs. Bickett says, her head still bowed.

"Amen," I mutter, just to fit in.

"Pass the butter fat, will you?" Mrs. Bickett asks Orla Mae. "My, I guess some of us are mighty hungry!" she says, looking at me. I already have a mouthful of the roast chicken that's so hot it's scalding the inside of my mouth. But I don't care. I never tasted chicken so good.

Orla Mae's still buttering her first roll

when I reach for my second, popping the whole thing into my mouth while I scoop corn onto my fork with the other hand.

I don't know why Mrs. Bickett keeps staring at me.

"How's that Mr. Tyler working out, girls?" she asks, after looking back down to her plate and delicately fixing a bite that's half the size of the ones I been taking.

"He's fine," Orla Mae answers.

"Orla Mae, do not talk with yer mouth open," her mother tells her. "You were not raised by wolves."

When she looks over to correct Orla Mae's eating, I grab a biscuit and drop it onto the towel across my lap. When I have another free second, I'll stick it into the pocket in my sweater for Emma. By the end of the meal I have three biscuits stored away. Emma's stomach's not so big as mine so three'll do her just fine. As for me, I'm stuffed fatter than a Christmas goose.

We clear away all the dishes, and when Mrs. Bickett scrapes off the plates I steal a drumstick, the only one not eaten, for Emma. It's a might greasy and will surely make my sweater not reusable, but that's okay. A big sister has to look out for a baby sister.

"Thank you for supper, ma'am," I say to

Mrs. Bickett, after Orla Mae and me finish drying the pots and pans she hands over.

"You're welcome, Carrie," she says. "You can come on back anytime you feel the urge, honey."

"Thank you, ma'am."

"Tell your mother howdy for me!" she calls after me.

"Yes, ma'am," I holler back. "Bye, Orla Mae."

"Bye, smarty-pants."

My cheeks flush red but it goes away when I look at her smiling face and realize she's not laughing at me.

The way home feels much shorter on a full belly. I even skip some, knowing how happy Emma will be with the dinner I brought her.

But there's a weird light coming from the front window. Like a candle, only not. Other times when I've come home in the dark the full window's lit up, but tonight only half is.

The closer I get, the weirder I feel.

"Momma?" I say. I don't call out too loud 'cause I don't know what's waiting for me inside.

When I open the door I cain't believe my eyes. Everything's a mess, almost like it was when we got here in the first beginning.

"Oh, my dear Lord in heaven." I say it just like Momma does when she walks into something me and Emma've done.

A chair is laying on its side. There's broken glass crunching under my shoes. And now I see why the light looked strange coming through the window — the lamp's been knocked over, its shade with it so it looks like it's taking a nap on the floor. Crossing the room to put it right, since I figure that's as good a place as any to start cleaning up, I have to step over a pillow from the couch and pieces of the china plates Gammy gave us to keep in the family.

"Momma?" I say it a littler louder this time.

The one picture we have — in a store-bought frame and every-thing — is lying facedown on the ground. It's a picture of Momma and me on the beach when I was little bitty. Daddy's the one who took it so he's not in the picture, which I guess is a good thing since if he was we'd never have it setting out like we've done. Richard wouldn't stand for it any.

I lean down to pick up the lamp and that's when I see her.

"Momma!"

The blood's spreading out from her head like a spilled coffee cup. One arm is bent like it's been pulled out of the socket. Her house-dress — the one she's worn so long the roses have faded to where they look pink, not red, like they started out — is pulled up almost to her underpants.

"Momma?" I whisper to her, bending down over her head, trying to keep my tears from falling straight into her bloody mouth.

She moves her head slightly, so the one eye that's not swollen shut can fix on me. Her lips are moving over her teeth.

"Momma?"

"Git," she says, softer than a whisper, "out." She takes in another breath but not too deep 'cause it looks like it hurts to breathe. "Now."

"I'm not leaving you, Momma," I say, trying, trying so hard, really really trying not to cry. So I shake my head no to make my point better.

"Hurry," she whispers.

The shouting hits me before my brain can figure out what the words all mean.

"Trying to provide for my *family,* such as it is," he hollers on his way into the front room. He must not have heard me come in. "Tha's whut I'm *tryin' to do.* Piece of *shit.*"

He pauses to gulp some beer and then kicks whatever's slowing him down. That's when I make my move toward the back of the room so I can slide out the kitchen door without him seeing me.

"*You* seen those prices in thar," he calls over to Momma, like she's able to carry on a conversation, "place's *beggin'* to be robbed, y'ask me! What the hell . . ."

Good thing he's drunk since it takes him a minute to figure out where the noise I made hopping over broken dishes came from. I bet he's given up looking for its source by the time I hit the woods that separate our house from Mr. Wilson's. My breaths pant in my own ears. Oh, Lord. Please let me get Momma help 'fore he kills her altogether. Please, Lord. I'll do anything. I'll never bicker with Emma again. I'll keep a good house like Momma wishes I'd do. I'll mind Richard, even. Just please, Lord, let me get to Mr. Wilson.

Pow!

The sound hits me and nearly knocks me off of my feet.

The sound I know pretty well by now. Ain't no other sound like it. A shot's been fired. *From inside our house.*

I've seen pictures of the guy in circuses who walks on a wire high up in the air —

like he's suspended. That's how I'm standing right this very minute. I don't know whether to follow the wire I'm walking on to Mr. Wilson's or to go back home to see what happened.

When I squeeze my eyes shut I see my momma lying out on the floor, the brightness of the lamp turning her whole face red with blood. There's my answer.

I'm comin', Momma.

I take the porch stairs two by two and this time I don't care who hears me come in the house.

"Momma?"

I hop over the broken glass, china and other things littered across the floor to where she's still laying.

"Momma?"

Her head turns toward me so it ain't her's been killed. I stand up and turn, looking slowly around the room. It's hard to see across the couch so I pick up the lamp and hold it like a lantern Laura Ingalls Wilder might've carried. The cord's not that long but at least I can throw some light over to the other side of the room.

And there he is. Richard.

Laid out and looking like he doesn't mind the glass and china cutting into his back. His eyes are open like he's studying the ceiling, so at first I'm afraid to go over that way . . . maybe it's a trap and he's playing dead so he can grab me when I get closer. I'm staying as far away as I can from his arms, spread out like he's making a snow angel. And that's when I see the red circle in his chest, getting wider and wider with blood.

He's not moving.

I get closer still and see his chest is still, not moving up and down, letting air in and out. Richard's the one's been shot.

And for a hair of a second, less than a hair of a second — more like a half a hair of a second — I see my daddy, laid out, bleeding onto the linoleum floor back at the old house. I don't know how that can be since Emma was the one who *really* saw him . . . I must've pictured it so many times in my brain that I've taken over her memory.

Emma.

"Emma!" I call out, hurrying over to the stairs, flying up them to our bedroom. She's not here. She's not here?

"Emma!" I shout for her but silence is the only answer I get back.

"Mr. Wilson! Help!" Like he could even hear me call him for help. Stupid me.

As fast as I ran in, I run out . . . down

the dark path to the black-top . . . down the blacktop to his pathway that seems steeper now that I'm trying my hardest to get to him. The rocks play tricks on my feet, being places I never knew they were. Just as I'm getting up from a fall I hear footsteps crunching on the gravel that's closer to his front steps. Yep. It's him, all right. I can tell by the hunched way he walks. I'm about to yell out for him when the moonlight catches hold of something shiny in his hand. A gun?

Oh. My. Lord.

The fallen pine branches breaking under my feet and my breathing're the only things making any sound in the woods; the moon, the only thing lighted up. The scrub bushes and saplings I didn't remember being here in the daylight slow me down but not by much. I don't care if I get jabbed by any of them anymore.

The Bicketts' house is absorbing all the blackness from the night, so it's hard to see where the steps end and where the door begins but I find them both and soon I'm banging on the front door.

Thirteen

"Caroline? Caroline, look at me." Momma's swollen mouth is moving but the words don't appear to be coming from that direction. She's holding a towel wet with melting ice inside, up to her forehead. The blood's all cleaned away by now.

"Caroline?"

"She's tired," another voice, a man's voice, floats overhead. "Let her rest."

"Caroline, can you hear me? What are you thinking about?"

The cottonwood tree was *made* for climbing, with fat, barky branches spaced out like a staircase, one on top of another, so you could climb almost to the top before it got scary.

"Can you see it? Can you see the house from there?" Emma called out to me from below.

"Not yet," I answered back. "Let me get up a little higher."

"Hurry up, I'm only two down from

you." She sounded annoyed 'cause I was taking so long to pull myself up. I should have let her go first, she's the faster tree climber. But I'm the oldest, so when I called it she knew I'd win.

"I can see it!" And I could. The cottonwood tree stood taller than the other trees around Hamilton's farm so there was nothing blocking our view. "Come on! Git up here."

"Okay, okay," she said, still annoyed but breathless to catch up to me. "You should've let me climb up first. Whoa, you're right. You can see it from here."

"What'd I tell you?"

Hamilton's farm was a good distance from our house, the house with the chipping shutters on Murray Mill Road. But when you're as high as a bird flies it doesn't matter so much, you can see anything from up here.

Trouble is, you can also look down and see how far you have to get back down. I tried not to look down but it was impossible: I liked to scare myself sometimes and I reckon that's what I was doing.

"How're we ever gonna get out of this tree without killing ourselves?"

"Who cares? Look! There's the Godseys'!"

I didn't think to check out what all lay on the other side of the trunk I was hugging like my life depended on it, which in that case it did. Sure enough, there was the Godsey house.

"I want to stay up here forever."

"Caroline, answer me." Momma's tired voice is getting louder even though she's not an arm's length away from me. "Y'hear? Answer me."

"What?"

"Listen to her, 'what?' Like she hadn't heard us talking at her for hours," Momma says to some invisible body that's behind me.

"Now, now, Mrs. Parker, let's go easy here," a voice says. I don't have the strength to turn around to see who the voice belongs to — I'm so tired — but it's a voice I've heard before. "It's been a long day. For everyone."

"I know it," Momma says. "I'm going 'bout as easy as I can. Caroline?" Her voice is fake soft, just for show. "Tell your momma what happened, all right? Just tell your momma."

I watch her cracked lips move along with the words coming out.

"Mrs. Parker, now, let us talk to her fo' a

while, how 'bout," the voice says. "You must be tired after all. Why don't you go git yourself a cup of coffee and we'll talk to Caroline."

"It's my husband's been killed, it's my daughter I'll be talking to," she says, her lips facing up to the man. "Now, Caroline Parker, you're gonna talk to me, y'hear? Talk to me. Tell me."

I want to reach for her. I want her to pull me onto her lap and tell me we're going home, it's all been a bad dream. I want . . .

"Caroline, if there's something you want to tell us, something you maybe need to git offa your chest, well, then," a large man I recognize as being the one who tacked the sign up to our door — the sheriff! — has moved in front of Momma. His face looks sad, his eyes locked into mine, looking for an answer to this question they keep asking me over and over again. But looking back out at him is like looking through a lace curtain on a sunny day — I see the light there but I can't quite make out the shapes. What happened, what happened, they keep saying — asking — those two words, and for the life of me I don't know what they're talking about.

I look from the sheriff to Momma and back again for a hint to the answer.

Momma doesn't let on as she knows so it's up to me to come up with the answer. I look back at the sheriff. I don't know, sir, I tell him with my eyes, since my mouth isn't following orders from my brain. Truth to tell, I don't know. The harder I think on it the less I remember.

Then, a flash of Mr. Wilson carrying something shiny. Mr. Wilson, who's been so good to me. *A man has to answer for the bad things he done.*

"How long you been firing guns off, anyhow?" Momma says, folding against the back of the chair — I guess leaning in toward me got too tiring. "A gun went and killed your own daddy . . . and you learning how to do the same from some crazy man out in the woods. No respect for her dead daddy, that's what she's got."

"Mrs. Parker, please," the sheriff says. "Let us take it from here."

She taps the pack of cigarettes so one comes out and she lights it and draws on it hard, blowing smoke up to the ceiling when it's time to breathe out.

The sheriff's voice is softer than Momma's, calmer, like it's floating across the air and petting me. "You want to tell me what happened 'fore we got there?"

I close my eyes and see a flash of

390

Richard, drinking beer at the kitchen table.

"Carrie?"

Then another flash, this one with my heartbeat loud in my ears as I run through the two rooms upstairs looking for something.

"Caroline?"

Looking for someone.

"Let's leave her be for a while," he says.

Looking for . . .

"Oh, fine," she says, from a place that might as well have been a million miles away.

Looking for . . .

"Emma" is all I can say.

"What? What'd you say, honey?" Footsteps cross the room, coming closer to me. "Say again?"

I look as surprised to hear my own voice as they do. "Emma."

He looks at Momma, who looks like all the life's been sucked out of her suddenly, her head drops down — clunk — like a rag doll's. Then it shakes slow-like from shoulder blade to shoulder blade.

"You want to tell me about Emma?"

"I was looking for Emma." I must be whispering 'cause he's leaning into me so close I can smell the tobacca on his breath.

"You were looking for Emma . . ." He

wants me to keep going but that's all I know.

"Oh, for God's sake," Momma says, her voice as tired as her head.

"Wait!" The sheriff holds up a hand to quiet her. "Go on," he says to me.

Momma, please, I'm thinking. Please help me. Make it better like Daddy always used to do. Please, Momma.

A flash again. Richard's laugh cuts into my head. My head, pounding on either side of my eyes, trying to thump, thump, thump the picture out, then back in. A door swinging open. Richard's smile turning upside down, his eyes wide. Thump, thump, thump. Heaviness in my arms, in my hands. Thump, thump, thump.

"I couldn't find Emma."

Another flash: Mr. Wilson climbing the stairs to his house. Something shiny.

The man reaches across the corner of the tabletop to rest his hand quietly on top of mine, relaxing it for a spell, its lightness surprising 'cause it's so wide and knotted.

"He was carrying a gun back in the house."

With my eyes I trace the winding veins on the back of his hand. Bumpy rivers.

"Who?" The sheriff is practically begging for the answer. "Who was carrying a gun into the house?"

I look at him and realize I have to tell him what I saw. I have to tell on my friend.

No. He couldn't have done it. No.

I can hear my own voice telling Emma, *It's one thing to kill a can, it's another altogether to kill a man, no matter how much he needs killing.*

Mr. Wilson'd never hurt a fly. But then I can hear his voice in my head, clear as day: *Back in my day a man had to answer for the things he done.* He said it himself.

Maybe he wanted Richard dead after all. And he was carrying that shiny gun, too.

"Who was carrying a gun into the house, Caroline?" the sheriff asks me again. Then again, right now I'm not even sure my name's Caroline — I'm so tired and my head keeps on a'pounding under my hair.

"Mr. Wilson."

"What?" He leans forward even closer to my face. "I didn't hear ya, honey. What did you say?"

I slowly move my face up from looking down at my dirty hands with scratches on my palms from falling on the path. I look him square in the eye, ready to say the name again. I'm sorry, Mr. Wilson.

"Mr. Wilson."

"Now, I don't appreciate your playing games with me, Caroline," the sheriff says, "but I know you've been through a lot these past twenty-four hours, so I'm gonna overlook that. Tell us who was carrying the gun into the house, honey."

"I told you. Mr. Wilson. I saw him . . ."

The sheriff looks down at his own hands and shakes his head, thinking something to himself — what, I don't rightly know.

"I'm telling you what I saw —" I start to say but he cuts me off.

"Honey, you need to start leveling with us. Your momma and I need to know what all happened back there at yer house."

"Mr. Wilson —"

"Drum Wilson is a friend of mine," he says, pointing his finger at my face, "and I happen to know for a fact that he wasn't anywhere near your house at the time the gun went off. . . ."

"But —"

"But nothing. He was with me and about half the town, down at Sonny Zebulon's celebratin' his birthday." The sheriff turns to explain to Momma. "Sonny Zebulon's the oldest living fella in town and yesterday was his ninety-fifth birthday. Man can still play like the calluses are fresh on his fingertips. . . . Anyhow, Drum Wilson was down there with the rest of us, playin' out some tunes for Zeb's ninety-fifth. Wilson even splurged and brought out the mother-o'-pearl mandolin his pappy used to play on. . . ."

While he's carrying on about the party down at Zebulon's I squinch my eyes closed, trying to picture the form of Mr. Wilson, walking up his front steps, carrying . . .

"Thing's worth more'n all of us put together . . ." the sheriff's saying.

Carrying something . . .

"It's beautiful, shell inlay, shined up nice . . ."

Something shiny! His mandolin! The moonlight only hit the thing for a second, but now I realize that's exactly what it was. It wasn't no gun after all. I *knew* he couldn't hurt a flea on Brownie's back! I *knew* it.

"Anyhow —" the sheriff turns back to me "— that's how come I know Drum Wilson ain't the one who fired the gun. So who was it, little girl?"

"Momma, where's Emma?"

Then I see something in my head. Something that almost feels like it could have been a dream.

"Git . . . out . . . now." I can still hear the way she whispered it to me while she was laying out in a bloody mess.

I remember telling her, "I'm not leaving you, Momma."

And I remember the sound of Richard

coming in from the kitchen, yelling. I can even hear him slurring the words the way he does after a few drinks.

But then something comes to me that I didn't remember until just now.

He grabbed me by the back of my shirt on my way trying to slip out the back door to Mr. Wilson's!

"Piece of *shit*," he said. But then he continued on hollering. I didn't remember that from before.

"Let me go!" I can remember squirming to get free from his grip.

"*You* seen those prices in thar," he says to me like I'd know what he was talking about. "Place's *beggin'* to be robbed, y'ask me!"

I can see myself biting the hand that's got hold of my shirt.

"What the hell . . . ?" he said.

"Where's Emma?" I remember swinging around to face him. I can even hear my voice that didn't even sound like my voice at the time, all screechy it was.

I can see the corners of Richard's mouth curl up on either side of the round bottle he's pulling beer from. He didn't answer me.

"Where is she?" I pushed past him into the kitchen.

"No need lookin'," I remember he called

out from the front room, from the ratty old chair that's the only thing settin' upright in the mess, his heel resting across his other knee. "She ain't here."

"Where is she?" I pushed back through the swinging door that separates the two rooms from each other. "Huh?"

"Don't you 'huh' me," he said, uncurling his first finger from around the bottle he was holding so he could point at me with it.

"Tell me where Emma is."

"What if I told you a little secret?" he asked, simple, like he's ordering up a cheese steak for supper. Only his mouth was in a smile. "What if I told you something I's sworn not to tell?"

"Emma!" I hollered up from the foot of the stairs. "Emma! Where you at?"

"I told you, she ain't here."

I remember looking back over at him.

"And here it is — she's dead!"

There was a rushing sound against my eardrums and I reckon it was the blood flooding my head.

"In fact, *I* kilt her," he said, swigging his beer, uncrossing his legs.

I remember taking the stairs two at a time and running into his room, then into mine. Nothing.

"No more Emma." I can still hear his

voice. And that laugh. That laugh is what told me he wasn't lying.

"He laughed." I open my eyes and tell the sheriff. "He laughed when he told me . . ." I can't say the words.

"When he told you . . ." His voice melts into the air. "When he told you . . ." He tries again. I look at him and look away, remembering what Richard told me about my sister.

"He told me . . ." I gulp. "He told me . . . he told me he kilt her." I look at him to make sure I said the words out loud instead of just plain thought them, 'cause sometimes I do that, think I say something when it's really just something batting around inside my head.

He's silent. I cain't look at Momma. In case she doesn't yet know Richard kilt her baby. I cain't look at her.

"He told you he killed Emma?"

I nod, keeping the tears inside my eyes.

The man looks over his shoulder at Momma and moves his hand up from mine. I feel Momma move in close to me.

"Mrs. Parker, hold on," he says, putting his hand into a stop sign in front of her. "Let her go on. What else do you remember, honey?"

I close my eyes and once again, scenes come back to me and I don't know whether they're real or in a dream.

Jumping over rocks. A path up from the blacktop. I remember it being dark, so dark I was relying on my feet to show me the way I'd gone so many times before. I remember seeing Mr. Wilson going in the front door. Waiting. Then . . . wait . . . I think I went around back. Did I? I think so.

I remember feeling my way along to the gun shack. Oh, Lord. I think I did. I remember waiting a spell and opening my eyes wider than they've ever been so they'd adjust to the pitch blackness of the inside of the shed.

You know what happens next, Emma said. I remember hearing her words ping-ponging from one side of my brain to the other. *We're gonna kill Richard.*

"Where's Emma?" I ask Momma and the sheriff.

"Keep going, honey," he says. "Keep trying to remember what happened next."

"Momma? Where's Emma?" But she looks away from me when she fits the cigarette into her swollen mouth and pulls smoke from it.

So I close my eyes and take myself back there.

We got to kill him, Carrie, she said. I remember it like it was five minutes ago. *We got to kill him.*

I remember picking it up and popping open the chamber to see if I had to hunt for bullets. I felt along one, two, three, four, five open holes. On the sixth my finger runs right over and I knew there was one in there. One bullet. One man in need of killing.

"He killed her," I say. Their faces look scary, unexpected. "He told me he killed her," I cry. "Momma?"

But she won't look at me. I think that's another reason why it's so easy to close my eyes. I hate seeing her turn away from me, looking the way she does.

"I got the gun," I tell them in between gulps for air. Her head snaps back to me all the sudden. "I had to get the gun." I cry harder.

"It's okay, honey." The sheriff's saying all the things Momma would if she were good with tears. "You can tell us. We'll make it all okay. Just tell us what happened next."

When I squeeze my eyes back closed

again, the lids wring out the tears like a wet dish towel after cleaning.

I remember the gun slowed me a bit but not much. The blacktop was easier to run along than the path leading down from Mr. Wilson's, but scarier, too, 'cause at any minute a car or truck could've happened along. I remember going faster. And faster still. The path up to our house was steep, the sandy, rocky ground tripping me up but never catching me altogether. I remember seeing the light in the kitchen poking through the pine trees. Catching my breath, I felt the metal of the gun handle when I wiped my hand against my forehead.

I can still see the house getting closer. Closer still. At the foot of the front steps I grabbed hold of the gun with two hands, locking my elbows like I saw him teach Emma to do. I remember counting the steps up, knowing I couldn't look down at them, my feet steadily carrying me inside on their own. I tried to breathe in and out slow through my nose like Mr. Wilson told me to before I take a shot. I think I did that for a second but then I think I panted through my mouth.

The front porch. With my elbows locked, the gun pointing down at the ground, I held the screen door open with my foot.

The porch door rested on my back and eased closed as I moved into the house. I remember the feel of it, lightening as I moved forward.

Looking at our things like it was the first time I'd seen them. I remember that. The table in the front room. The upright armchair he'd been setting in. The lamp overturned. Momma's groans from the ground beside it. I held steady. Then I pointed toward the swinging door into the kitchen.

We're gonna kill Richard, Emma said.

"I need to know where my baby sister is!" My mind's come back into the room with Momma and the sheriff. "Momma? Did they find her . . . ?" I cain't finish the sentence. Wait. Breathe. Okay, now I can go on. "Did they find her body?"

The sheriff's hands reach out for mine. Oh, Lord. They found her.

"Honey, what we need to do before we talk about Emma is hear the last part of what happened," he says. "Understand? You need to tell us. Then we can talk about Emma, all right? I know. I know. Shh. Just breathe. That's right. Breathe slow in and out. Calm down. Can you talk now? Just a little bit more. You were in the house, pointing to the kitchen door. What happened after that?"

They close again, my eyes.

I took two more steps to the swinging door. Then one more.

I can remember listening hard and finally hearing Richard's "aaah" that comes only when he's taken a bigger than usual gulp of beer. It was followed by the clear sound of the bottle setting back down on the tabletop.

I think I waited another second for it to occur to him that one gulp wasn't gonna be enough, that he needed another.

That's when I kicked the swinging door open and my purpose was revealed.

I am here to kill you, the gun said to him.

I can still see him absorbing it.

The memory of the shot firing, his face twisting from surprise to pain, shakes me in my seat in the sheriff's office.

"So you shot Richard," he says.

"He killed Emma," I say, looking straight at him. Straight into his eyes. "And he was gonna kill my momma. . . ."

The sheriff takes in a deep breath and it whistles against his teeth on its way back out of his mouth. He looks over at Momma, who inhales again off of her cigarette.

"Did you find Emma yet?"

"Caroline?" she says. Her voice sounds like it did when she tucked me into bed back when I was weensy. "Sleep tight. Don't let the bed bugs bite," she'd say. The outline of Daddy standing in the doorway, watching us.

"Caroline, look at me. I'm sick and tired of all this, you hear me? Sick and tired. It's time for it to stop. Stop."

I fix my eyes at her mouth, her eyes would be too much right now. "Emma . . ." I whisper out to her.

"That's what I'm talking about," she says, taking in a deep gulp of air and looking over to the sheriff, who's nodding his head for her to continue.

"I saw that look," I say, trying not to cry since Momma's being so nice right now and tears would surely ruin it. "You found her body. Where is she?"

"Oh, for the love of God in heaven will you *stop? There is no Emma!* You hear me? *There is no Emma!*" Momma shouts but it came out louder than I bet even she had planned.

I think the quiet in the room makes her

feel she needs to repeat it.

"There . . . is . . . no . . . Emma."

Silence.

"There *never was* an Emma." Momma's hands were always stronger than mine so when she peels my hands off my ears, the words rush in, crowding my brain. "No, no — don't turn away from me. Don't you turn away from me. *Emma never was,* girl. Y'hear me?"

"Lemme go git a tissue," the sheriff's saying. "Calm her down and I'll be right back."

"You listen to me, now," Momma's going on. "Emma never was. You started talking about a sister right after your daddy died and I just let it go on. But I never meant for it to go too far. It ain't right. It ain't right to think something's real when it ain't. You kept talking about her and talking about her — I couldn't stand it. On and on. Emma this and Emma that. *Emma doesn't like canned peas, Momma. Emma wants to ride up front with you, Momma. Emma wants to get into bed with you.* On and on and on. It ain't right, y'hear me?"

A door opens and closes.

"Here ya are." A fistful of tissues appear in front of my face. "Now breathe, Caroline. Take a deep breath. Breathe. That's it.

Now blow into the tissues, honey. Good girl."

It's hard to find air enough to breathe through my tears.

"Now, now, there," the man says. "Use them tissues like I showed you."

"On and on with Emma this and Emma that." Momma's voice moves from one side of the room to the other, footsteps along with it. "And it only got worse. Worse and worse and worse and *worse*."

"Mrs. Parker . . ."

" *'Emma doesn't know why you don't like her, Momma,'* she says to me one time . . ."

"Mrs. Parker . . ."

"Now you know why I don't like her!" Momma's bending down from standing so her face is right in front of mine, her words punching me. "I don't like her *'cause she don't exist!* There! It's out. No more stepping around you like you's breakable, like them things they sell at White's in them pretty glass bottles. I don't like her 'cause she don't exist!"

I choke on the words. "You didn't like her 'cause she looked like Daddy! 'Cause she was the only one saw Daddy die and it reminded you of that!"

"*You* saw your daddy die!" she spits. "You saw it all! It was a Saturday. I was out back hanging the wash up. That man came into the house . . ."

"Stop it." I hold my hands over my ears but it cain't block out her voice. And it cain't stop the picture in my head. A man carrying a shotgun. A sunny day. Momma pinning up the wet clothes.

"Mrs. Parker —"

"Your daddy fought 'im best he could . . ."

"Stop it!" I yell, squeezin' my eyes closed so I cain't watch her angry lips.

". . . then he shot him dead"

"Mrs. Parker!"

"He'd been warned to keep away from Selma Blake."

"Stop it!" I scream at the top of my lungs. "Stop it stop it stop it!"

"Then I had everyone up in my business, telling me to do this, do that, *go along with it,* they said." She's pacing back and forth on the other side of the table. "It wore me out. Your teachers . . ."

"Stop!"

". . . all them in town . . ."

"Mrs. Parker —"

"Everybody in that godforsaken town want to call you crazy. . . ."

"Now, that's enough, Mrs. Parker," the man says from behind, I guess. "That's enough. You come on with me and we'll let Carrie be for a while and you and me'll get a cup of coffee. We'll be right back, little one. Right back, you hear?"

A door opens and closes.

But it doesn't close all the way, I guess, 'cause their voices drift in to me in bits and pieces, like the tiny squares of carpet Daddy kept in his car.

"Her friends peeled off from her like skin on an onion, not playing with her, calling out ugly names. She thinks I didn't know, but I did. Hell, I wasn't *that* out of it I didn't know my own daughter was crazy as a loon. Her best friend wasn't allowed to come over to our house." Momma's voice snarls from outside the room. "Her momma called to tell me she could go over there where she'd be *watched carefully,* she said. Like it was *my* fault, this Emma craziness. Like if I watched my own daughter better . . . 'Course, that Phillips woman was always a little big for her britches, if you know what I mean. . . ."

No!

"Then she got herself a job unpacking boxes at White's Drugstore and I had the owner of the place calling me up telling me 'bout my own daughter, like I don't know. 'Say, Lib,' he'd start in, 'what you make of this Emma Caroline's going on and on about. I don't know if it's so healthy for us to go along with it.' Tell me somethin' I *don't* know! I never thought it *was* healthy but *no*, that uppity psychic or psychiatrist or whatever the hell she was tells us it *is* so healthy, that's what we all got to do. Play along with it, she says. . . ."

No. I remember Mr. White saying he'd be happy to have Emma help in the back room. And Miss Mary loved Emma. Played with her hair and all.

Emma was there. She was *real*. Emma was the one who pushed me out of the way when Richard called up from the bedroom. It was *Emma* he did things to.

No.

"Hey there, little one." The man's smile looks like it's trying to make up for Momma's frown coming into the room behind him. "How you doing?"

Pow! A cockroach nibbles at my brain: it's my teacher, Miss Ueland, talking to me about the bruise on my arm, the same place Emma had hers that day.

"Now that you've had some time to think on it, how things look to ya?" he asks, scraping his chair closer to me.

Emma was there. I *remember* Emma being there. I remember having to help her with the lap belt when Momma'd drive too fast on the old country road out by Hamilton's farm.

"She was real," I whisper out to them.

Another nibble at my brain: the feel of knotted hair between my fingers . . . when my fingers would run through my own hair.

No.

Emma was there. *Emma* had rats' nests in her hair. Not me.

"You got worse, not better like they said you would," Momma says through a cloud of smoke that's taking extra long to float up to the ceiling. "Town doctor came by to check on her after we got calls from school about her being beat up day in and day out, for talking to herself." Momma's back to talking to the sheriff. Not to me. "I didn't care one way or the other, but the doctor said she'd get better. 'Humor her,' he says. Like I'm a circus clown meant to keep her entertained, day in, day out. I tell you, it wore me out. Having to call both of them for dinner. Like I'm playing a fool, I was."

Her voice cracks and brings my head back into the room. Momma's gonna cry. I can tell.

"What's gonna happen to us now?

410

Huh?" she cries, pointing her shaking cigarette at me. "Didja think about that when you pulled the trigger? How we gonna get food on the table? Is *Emma* gonna take care of us now?"

"Mrs. Parker, please."

A door opens. A door closes.

Fourteen

"How much for this bowl, ma'am?" the girl asks Momma.

"Two and a quarter," Momma says, turning it upside down for some reason. "Came down from my own daddy in Rutherfordton."

The girl counts out her change and hands it over. Momma puts it in the cigar box that I used to hold Daddy's square of shag carpet that's now carefully packed in my bag, safe from the tag sale Momma's hoping will put some money in our pocket for the trip far away from here.

"This vase?" A man holds up the glass container.

"Dollar and a half," Momma says, her hand already waiting for the money he's reaching into his wallet for. "Thank you, sir." She almost smiles when she says it.

But I'm not smiling. Not one bit. I don't like the idea of our belongings ending up Lord knows where.

"Hey!" I call over to her from the table

that has everything for sale spread out on it. "We cain't sell this! It's mine."

Momma looks over to what I'm holding. "If I have to part with my stuff, you got to, too. Put it down."

But I cain't. That stamp book's mine.

"Can I see it?" a little girl still holding her mother's hand asks me.

"I s'pose," I say to her. Then I lower my voice so Momma cain't hear. "It's not for sale, though."

She lets go of her momma and takes the book in both her hands, real careful-like. Flipping through the pages, her eyes widen up. "Ooh," she says. And then she holds it up. "Momma, look!"

Her mother looks over like she's told to. "What's that?"

"It's a book of stamps from all over the world," I tell her, with more than a hint of pride. "See? There's Sweden." I point to the page she's opened it up to. "And here's my favorite — Bermuda." They're both hovering over it.

"How much you asking?" the mother asks Momma, who's come over to see what they're looking at with so much interest. Momma has a nose for money.

"A dollar," she says before I can tell them it's not for sale.

"Momma!" I holler at her. "It's mine!"

But, to my horror, the mother's reaching into the pocket on the front of her skirt.

I try to grab it back but the little girl has more strength in her hands than I bargained on. Plus Momma has a grip on my shoulder.

"It's mine," I tell the little traitor, who *knew* it wasn't for sale and went over my head to the grown-ups. "Give it over."

"Here y'are." The woman hands the crumpled dollar bill over to Momma.

"Momma, please!" I cry. "Please let me keep it."

"Hush up," she says, moving over to a family who's eyeing our mattresses.

I glare at the little girl, who's clutching the book in the hand that isn't holding back on to her mother.

"Momma." I tug at her skirt. "Momma? Why cain't I keep it?"

She whirls around and practically spits at me. "You can't hold on to things too hard, girl. Just remember that. 'Sides, look around you! Everything's gonna be gone sooner or later. We got nothing left. Nothing."

"But . . ."

She's already gone, though. Already

counting up cash handed to her by some dirty man who's trying to fit my mattress into the back of his truck, throwing string across to tie it down 'cause it's a windy day.

" 'Scuse me, ma'am," another man is calling over from down in front of the table.

I follow his finger that's pointing down to a piece of furniture, asking the price without words.

Momma stops in her tracks on the way over to him when she sees what he's pointing at. My heart stops, waiting to hear what she'll say about Richard's old tattered chair.

Over behind the man is a woman with stringy hair and a big belly that promises a new baby not long from now. Momma looks at her then back at the man.

"How much, ma'am?" he asks her, since she's not saying a word, just staring at the indent on the bottom cushion where her husband used to sit.

"Ma'am?"

"Five dollars," I say, passing Momma, straight up to the man and his wife.

"Five?" he says, looking at Momma to make sure I'm not making it up. She's stone still.

"Yes, sir," I say. "Five dollars. Not a penny less."

He turns and whispers something to his wife, who fishes the money out of her pocketbook.

"Here y'are," he says, handing me the money. "Hey, Walles! Come give me a hand with this, will ya?"

And sure enough, there's Walles from Zebulon's, striding over like a cowboy, catching my eye and winking without smiling. He picks up one side of the old drinking chair and its new owner gets the other and soon it's carried out of our lives forever, the one last piece of Richard marking our life.

"You cain't hold on to things too hard, Momma," I say to her as she watches them lift it into the flatbed truck. I sneak my hand into hers, and for the first time since I can remember, she holds on. Just for a second she holds on to me.

It's moving day again, but this time we don't need to pack boxes. Phee-you.

Momma says the price we got for everything just barely covered repair work on the car that's gonna take us away from here, away from number twenty-two, but I thought the car was fine the way it was. I s'pose Momma got tired of having to turn the key ten or twelve times 'fore it'd start up. Besides, it's got to carry us all the way to Gammy's and Momma says she doesn't want to take any chances.

"I'm gonna do one last check and then we'll hit the road," Momma tells me. "If there's anything you need to do 'fore we go, you best go on and do it."

There is one thing.

The walk down the path to the blacktop is easy now that I know where every stick is, every rock, every dip in the ground. Same with walking up to Mr. Wilson's. This time I take care to be nice to Brownie since it's the last time I'll be seeing a dog like her.

But she won't have anything to do with me. She waits till I pass and then walks a distance behind me, just in case.

"Mr. Wilson?" I call up ahead.

I don't know why I've always called up to him when he never answers back. He figures I'll find him, anyway, without him hollering all over kingdom come. And he's right.

"We're leaving," I say once I get up to his front porch.

"I figured as much," he says, without looking up from his carving.

I look around and try to memorize yet another place I'll never come back to.

"Well," I say, switching my weight from one leg to the other, "I guess I better get going now."

"Here," he says, whittling one last notch into the wood. "Take this with you."

He holds it in his hand, and until he unfolds all his fingers and passes it to me I have no earthly idea what it is. But once it's in my hand, I know.

"Hey!" I smile, looking at it. "It's you!"

"Yep." He settles back into the broken-down chair. "It's as good as I'm ever gonna git at carvin'."

I don't know what to say so my hug will have to do the talking. He looks surprised at first but then I feel his hand patting me on the back.

"You best get going while you got the sun to lead your way."

"Bye, Mr. Wilson."

"Bye, sissy-girl."

He doesn't know it but I'm smiling on my way back to the blacktop.

"You ready?" Momma asks me.

"Yes, ma'am," I answer, opening the car door.

She reaches out for the door handle and

then stops suddenly, her hand in midair. "Why you riding in the back?" I see her look that says she's wondering if I'm up to something.

"I want to be back by myself," I tell her. "Momma, where's my drawing pad I put out on the porch for the ride?"

"It's up here." And she hands it back over the headrest behind her once we're in the car. "Here y'are."

The car bumps along and Momma waits until the blacktop to fiddle with the dial, trying to find music . . . or something . . . to fill the air.

The town passes by us. Antone's. Then Zebulon's. I watch them all go by. Then I open the pad to a brand-new page.

I'm glad you can finally read and write, I scribble. *I don't rightly know how long we'll be staying with Gammy and Aunt Lillibit, but Momma says it won't be too long. After that we could go anywhere we want. Hey, Em — if you could go anywhere in the whole entire world, where would you go?*

Acknowledgments

Many people helped breathe life into this book. My deep gratitude to Anne and Taylor Pace, who shared their beloved North Carolina with me and watched patiently while it became *my* beloved North Carolina.

My thanks also to my gifted editor, Susan Pezzack, and to my tireless agent, Laura Dail, who still has no idea that her encouragement is completely intoxicating.

I am blessed to have a friend like Mary Jane Clark, who is a constant source of strength and love.

My Emily gave me Carrie's voice and helped me remember what it's like to be a little girl. My Lizzie gave me support and unknowingly saved me from myself time and time again. And my Jeffrey gave me this whole new wonderful life and with unwavering support and love made it possible for me to be a writer.

About the Author

Former print journalist Elizabeth Flock reported for *Time* and *People* magazines before becoming an on-air correspondent for CBS. Her acclaimed debut novel, *But Inside I'm Screaming*, chronicling the inner struggle of a young reporter, was released in 2003. Elizabeth lives with her husband and two stepdaughters in Chicago.

The employees of Thorndike Press hope you have enjoyed this Large Print book. All our Thorndike and Wheeler Large Print titles are designed for easy reading, and all our books are made to last. Other Thorndike Press Large Print books are available at your library, through selected bookstores, or directly from us.

For information about titles, please call:

(800) 223-1244

or visit our Web site at:

www.gale.com/thorndike
www.gale.com/wheeler

To share your comments, please write:

Publisher
Thorndike Press
295 Kennedy Memorial Drive
Waterville, ME   04901